The Fight for Life series, book two

IMPACT

KATE STERRITT

Editing and cover design by Murphy Rae at Indie Solutions
www.murphyrae.net/
Formatting by Integrity Formatting

DEDICATION

*To the Collision readers who have been so excited for
Leo and Juliette's continued story,
Impact is dedicated to you.*

We are all in the gutter,
but some of use are looking at the stars.

~ Oscar Wilde

CHAPTER 1

LEO

DARTMOOR WELLNESS CENTRE WAS NO looney bin. I'd envisaged straitjackets and padded cells, but it was more like some sort of fancy health retreat—sprawling gardens, a lake, orange trees. I wanted to see that woman suffer for what she did to Juliette, but this place felt more like a reward. The security was probably to keep people out rather than in.

"Come on." I tugged Juliette's hand gently. "Let's get this over with and then we have a lot of catching up to do." I couldn't wait to get the hell out of there and have her all to myself. I'd spent the past two months missing her with every cell in my body and had hoped she felt the same. Our passionate reunion filled me with hope, but I knew we needed to talk about what had happened before she'd left. She knew her mother had offered me money to stay away from her, and she knew I had rejected it. What she didn't know was why I had pushed her away. I would have to try to find a way to explain it to her, as I was adamant nothing was ever going to come between us again.

Beyond the orchard, two women were sitting on wooden chairs, facing the lake. As we drew nearer, both women stood. When they turned around, my flight instinct gripped my throat as the life I'd spent five years fighting for came crashing down around me. *This can't be fucking happening.*

"What's wrong?" Juliette whispered. "Who is she?"

"Darling." Isabel surged forward. "Thank you for coming."

She wrenched Juliette from me, and we locked eyes. The witch knew what she was doing bringing me here, and smug would be an understatement to describe the look on her face.

Juliette pulled out of the awkward hug. "Who's your friend, Mum?" she asked, sounding extremely uncomfortable.

I knew I had no choice. My hand had been forced, as she was about to find out regardless. Five years hadn't been kind to the virtual stranger standing in front of me. Her dark hair had greyed, and frown lines marred her gaunt face. My next two words were something I never thought I'd utter again, and nausea swirled through me on its ruthless path. I took Juliette's hand and pulled her back to me.

"Hello, Mother."

CHAPTER 2

Juliette

LEO'S MOTHER WAS DEAD. HE'D told me in no uncertain terms on more than one occasion. My heart pounded out of my chest as my mind struggled to process the situation. The fact that Leo didn't sound at all surprised spoke volumes. He'd lied to me. But why? I was face-to-face with his dead mother. His icy tone told me he wasn't at all thrilled about it, and her demeanour was hard to read. She wasn't standoffish, but this definitely wasn't a happy reunion.

"What's going on?" Given the silence, I felt the need to whisper.

Nobody said anything. My eyes darted back and forth from Leo to the woman. They were locked in a standoff.

"Juliette." My mother's cheery tone broke the uncomfortable silence. "This is Gwendolyn." She placed a hand on the woman's shoulder. "Gwendolyn, you have to meet my beautiful daughter, Juliette. Isn't she just gorgeous?"

Gwendolyn? As in the name of the farmhouse?

"Lovely to meet you, Juliette," she said, politely

extending her hand. "Please call me Gwen. Your mother has told me so much about you."

"I... um... don't know what to say." When I touched her hand, my eyes flitted to Leo. It was the same look I saw on his face the first time I laid eyes on him at fight club. The icy stare was back and my whole body shuddered, but I refused to jump to any false conclusions again. I shook her hand briefly, then took a step closer to Leo.

"Juliette." Leo took hold of my hand and pulled me closer to him. His voice was grave but demanding. "We're leaving."

"Juliette isn't going anywhere." My mother grabbed my hand and roughly pulled me away from Leo. "You just got here, and we have so much catching up to do." She looked at Leo, her expression smug. "Leave if you must." Clearly she'd set this up, and Leo's presence was no longer required. My heart dropped. After all we'd been through, she was still interfering in my life.

He glanced at me with questioning eyes. I was blindsided and confused on top of being horribly jetlagged. Why had he lied to me about his mother when he clearly knew she was alive? Misjudging my hesitation, pain flashed through his eyes. "I have to go." His voice was strained and laced with anger.

Horrified, I watched him stride purposefully away while I stood there, unable to get my head around the situation.

"I was worried that would happen," Gwendolyn whispered, snapping me from my paralysed state. I saw what I believed to be genuine sadness flash across her eyes, and my curiosity hit fever pitch.

"I'll be back in two minutes," I said, holding up two fingers.

I ran up the hill after Leo before my mother could

protest.

"Wait!" I called out. He was beyond the orchard when I caught up to him. He stopped but didn't turn around. "Look at me, Leo."

I stopped a few feet behind him and waited for him to turn. His shoulders stiffened, and he glanced upwards at the darkening clouds. His whole body was so expressive, and I realised in that moment just how much I missed him. I missed how his body felt against mine and how he made me feel. Perhaps we'd just taken a giant step back, but I wasn't going to be the one to run. I was no longer the girl who ran. I would stay and fight because he was worth fighting for.

The look of pain on his face as he turned back was crushing.

"I need to get out of here, Juliette." His gravelly voice was strained and tortured. His hands were clenching and unclenching. "I'd like to force you to come with me. I'd like to get you the hell away from that woman, but I'm about to lose my shit completely and you don't need to be around that."

I took another step forward and waited until he looked me in the eye. "Why did you lie to me about your mother?"

He blew out a long breath. "I'm sorry you had to find out like that. I'm more sorry you had to find out at all, but I told you *my* truth." He flattened the palm of his hand against his chest. "The only truth I can live with."

I shook my head, completely confused. "What does that mean?"

"That woman over there is dead to me." He pierced me with his gaze. "Do you get that? Dead. To. Me." Despite the determination in his voice, his shoulders slumped.

"Why?" I croaked. "What happened in that

goddamned house?"

"I don't talk about that." He pushed his shoulders back and stood up straighter. "I *can't* talk about it, and I don't have to justify myself to you or anyone else. No one could possibly understand, and I don't feel like explaining it. I've managed to avoid her for five years, and your mum, the Queen of Manipulation, managed to set me up. Again. But compared to my mother, yours is Mother Teresa."

I felt like he'd stabbed me in the chest. Our reunion in the reception had been so full of passion and our magnetic attraction was still irrefutable, but now I could feel him slipping through my fingers. "This is all so messed up, Leo."

"You've obviously found a way to forgive your mother for what she did." He couldn't even look me in the eye when he practically spat the words at me. "You have a forgiving heart, Jules, but you and I are not the same."

"She's your mother, Leo." I knew what my own mother had done was reprehensible, but she was still my mother. "It can't be that bad."

He just nodded, his hands firmly planted in the pockets of his shorts. "Go back to your mum. She obviously wanted us both to come but only one of us to stay." He spoke with zero emotion. "I'm leaving."

Unsure if my touch would be welcomed, I tentatively placed my hand on his arm. "Don't shut me out, Leo. Before I left to go overseas six weeks ago, you said you wanted to talk to me when I got back." I gave his arm a gentle squeeze. "Well, I'm back now."

He stared down at my hand on his arm, his brow furrowed. I had no idea what he was thinking. When he finally met my eyes, he appeared tortured. "I want to, Jules. I do. I have so much to tell you, and I wanted to hear all about your trip, but I can't right now. I can't talk about her, and I know you want to. You have to trust me when I tell you to stay away from that woman."

A sob escaped me, but I managed to win the war against the threatening tears. "I don't know if I trust you, but I know that I want to."

I had gutted him with my words, but I had opened my heart to him and he'd pushed me away at the first hurdle. I'd come home ready to fight, but he had to meet me halfway.

"I know. I fucked up with you and I thought we could get past it, but this is different, Jules." He pushed my hair behind my ears and held my face. "I have my life under control, and it hasn't always been that way." I covered his hands with mine while he continued. "It's a chapter of my life that's best left closed and in the past. No good can come from talking about it." His hands dropped from my face. "I made a choice almost five years ago to block her out of my life, and that was taken away from me today."

I swallowed the lump in my throat as the realisation hit. Leo was far more damaged than I'd ever suspected. As much as I couldn't deny I loved him deeply, I knew our happily ever after was now nowhere in sight. I closed my eyes briefly, trying not to appear defeated.

"You're asking me to trust you, but you're giving me nothing," I mumbled.

"Can you just promise me one thing?" he asked.

I met his eyes, and the desperation in them floored me. I nodded, knowing I would do just about anything to take away some of his pain.

"Don't believe anything she says. She's manipulative and she's a liar. I can't force you to come with me now, but I need this to be the end of it. Regardless of whether you want anything to do with me after this, I don't want you having anything to do with her once you leave here today."

I stared at my feet, kicking divots in the grass. "I thought this was going to be our new start."

"I'll call you in a few days. Okay?" He closed his darkened eyes briefly. My heart ached for the sadness they conveyed. "I need some time to sort things through in my head again. I'm sorry, Jules."

"Leo." His name fell from my lips. I didn't want him to leave, but I could see he couldn't stay. "Whatever happened to you, I'm sorry."

"Don't be sorry." He grazed the back of his hand across my cheekbones. "Just don't ever mention it again."

I glanced back before I made it to the first orange tree because I couldn't resist. I wished I hadn't. The crazy part of me hoped he'd still be there. Instead, I saw him jogging up the hill, clearly in a hurry to get away. What the hell had happened to make him react like this to his own mother?

A lone tear slipped down my cheek, and I brushed it away angrily. He didn't need my tears. He needed my strength, and I would give it to him because he still held every part of my heart.

CHAPTER 3

Juliette

THE ONLY SILVER LINING TO the situation I'd found myself in was that I now felt wide awake. Jetlag had taken a back seat to the adrenaline rush of seeing Leo again, and then his mother. The weird thing about jetlag was that it could play tricks on your mind. Walking back through the orchard, I had a momentary out-of-body experience. Was I asleep? I had dreamt of Leo almost every night I had been away, so it would make sense if I were. I stopped and shook my head, knowing I was being ridiculous. This was no dream. It was a waking nightmare.

"Darling," my mother cooed as she rushed forward. "Is he okay? I thought he'd be happy to see his mother. What a happy coincidence, don't you think? Can you believe—"

"Stop, Mother." I raised my hand to keep her at arm's length. "Please just stop."

I turned to Gwendolyn. "Were you part of this setup?"

"Darling—"

I glared at my mother. "I'm talking to Gwendolyn." I

returned my gaze to the pale woman who had just turned a few shades paler. "Did you know Leo and I were coming together today?"

We locked eyes, and I was immediately struck by one thing. Her eyes were the same two-toned blue as Leo's, and like his, they were a window to her soul. The shadows I saw were probably caused by the fading afternoon light, but I saw a darkness that Leo didn't possess.

Gwendolyn nodded her head and lowered her eyes.

"Why are you here?" I asked, choosing to ignore the fact that she couldn't look at me.

"Don't be so nosy, Juliette," scolded my mother. "I raised you better than to ask rude questions."

I closed my eyes and tried not to snarl as I turned back to my mother. The woman was absurd. She'd raised me to pretend to be someone I wasn't, settle for less than I deserved, and made me feel inadequate and unworthy because of it. "Really, Mother?" I taunted. "After all you've done, you're going to call me rude?"

Completely gobsmacked, my mother stumbled backward slightly. "I... I..."

"I think it's best you say nothing at this point."

She pursed her lips but said nothing.

"I knew he wouldn't want to see me, but I still hoped he might change his mind."

I turned my attention back towards Gwendolyn's soft voice. She had regained a little colour in her cheeks. "Why are you here?"

"I'm under a lot of stress, and this place is the best." She glanced at my mother before returning her gaze to me. "If Leo took any interest-"

I interrupted her. "He told me you were dead."

"The way he has shut me out for the past five years, I might as well have been dead." Her eyes glazed with tears. "Sometimes I wish I was."

The anguish written all over the features of her face was hard to witness, but Leo's plea was front and centre in my mind. *"Don't believe anything she says. She's manipulative and she's a liar."*

"How did you make the connection to my mother?" I felt like a ruthless interrogator, but I had burning questions and all this cryptic bullshit was doing nothing to douse the flames.

"I love my son, Juliette." She paused.

"I didn't ask if you loved him." Sleep deprivation did not agree with me, and I was getting snappy. "I asked how you made the connection to my mother."

She smiled, but it didn't reach her darkening eyes. "I knew my son was dating the daughter of Melbourne's society queen, Isabel Fontaine, so when she turned up here, I knew immediately who she was." She took a deep breath and let it out slowly, glancing at my mother. "Well, I couldn't help thinking it was meant to be somehow."

My mother piped up. "How about we change the subject?" She clapped her hands together. "Juliette, you have no idea what I've had to endure here."

I rolled my eyes.

"I'm leaving Dartmoor today." Gwendolyn ignored my mother, keeping her eyes fixed on mine. "Perhaps we could have lunch together sometime later in the week." She looked around. "Somewhere that isn't here?"

My mother interrupted like a petulant child knowing she was being ignored. "That sounds wonderful," she said. "We would love that."

"You don't come home until next weekend, Mother."

"So you can wait 'til then."

"This is a very private matter," Gwendolyn interjected. "I'd like to speak to Juliette alone."

"I'm sorry, Gwendolyn, but I can't." I had come home to resolve things one way or another with Leo, and despite the curve ball this whole situation had thrown our way, there was no chance I was going to jeopardise what I knew we could have on a stranger. "I'm sorry."

She nodded solemnly. "I understand and I admire your loyalty." Moving forward, she wrapped her arms around me. "Thank you for bringing my son back into my life," she whispered in my ear.

I untangled myself from her tight embrace, feeling awkward and a little creeped out. I took a step back and looked her in the eye. "I don't know what happened between the two of you, but my loyalty will always lie with Leo."

"If you change your mind, I'd love to hear from you." She handed me a small, white card with her name and a number written on it. She appeared dangerously sincere. "Goodbye, beautiful Juliette."

I stood in silence, watching the last person on earth I would've expected to meet today float gracefully towards the lake's edge.

"What a bitch," my mother stated firmly once she was out of earshot.

I swung around to face her. "Excuse me?"

"Oh, nothing, dear."

I'd heard what she'd said and was in no mood for her. "I have to go, Mother."

"Look, sweetheart." She glanced down towards the lake. "I'm not just saying this because of who her son is, but I don't trust her."

I placed my hand on my forehead, wishing I'd just stayed in bed today instead of coming here. Again, the word trust was being thrown around by someone who had broken mine.

"I'm afraid I don't give the slightest credence to your

character judgement. In fact, it makes me want to run down there," I said, pointing towards the lake, "and be her best friend." I was starting to feel delirious with frustration and fatigue. "You set Leo up. Again."

"Don't lash out at me, darling. I was right about the kind of man he is." She raised her eyebrows and appeared self-righteous. I wanted to punch her in the face. "He was hiding a pretty big secret from you."

"Oh my God, Mother." I rolled my eyes. "You have no clue what kind of man Leo really is. All you see is that he was on your staff and, therefore, beneath you."

"Well, of course he's beneath us, Juliette." She appeared genuinely affronted. "Most people are."

I clenched my teeth and started walking back up the hill. I tried to swallow past the lump in my throat, but it was impossible. My eyes brimmed with tears at the realisation that she might never change. I just had to find a way to be okay with that.

I could hear her calling after me.

I stopped and turned around. "There's nothing left to say, Mother. I'm really tired and I just want to go home."

"I don't trust her, Juliette."

"Well, I don't trust you, so we're at an impasse, aren't we?"

She sighed. "I'm fine now, I promise. We can start fresh when I come home and forget all this silliness. I have such big plans. I'm thinking we need to move. Maybe Sydney?"

I shook my head. "Dad will pick you up next weekend, okay? Take care of yourself." I closed the distance between us and kissed her on the cheek. I hadn't expected a miracle, but I'd hoped for more than this. If the definition of insanity is doing something over and over again and expecting a different result, perhaps it was me who belonged in the looney bin, too. I was done.

CHAPTER 4

I JOGGED ALL THE WAY back to my Jeep, climbed in and slammed my palms on the steering wheel repeatedly. Over and over again, I pummelled it, trying to block out my mother's face. I'd spent the last few months thinking my time in the cage was over. My future with Juliette was my priority, and I had even been in serious talks with my childhood coach, Nick, about re-entering the boxing circuit. All that had come crashing down the second I'd come face-to-face with the devil. She was pure evil, and I hadn't been able to get away from her fast enough. I wanted to beat the living shit out of someone or something, and at that moment, the steering wheel was copping it.

The fact that I'd left Juliette in there consumed me with guilt, but I couldn't go back. There was no way I could go back there ever.

My phone rang, and I answered the call in a bit of a daze.

"Is this Leo Ashlar?" a man asked with an accent I couldn't place.

"That's me," I replied, rubbing my forehead, unsure

why I had answered the call in the first place.

"Pete Sanders here. Fight promoter from Perth."

Surprised, I didn't immediately reply. Promoters rarely called a fighter directly. They would negotiate with the manager or coach. "This isn't a good time, mate."

"I want you over here for a fight next weekend. I saw footage of your fight at the Melbourne Pavilion last week, and you're exactly who I need. My fight is the weight division below, but you strike me as the kind of fighter who likes a challenge. I know—"

"That was a one-off fight." I cut him off. *Jesus Christ,* the guy didn't draw a breath. I pinched the bridge of my nose, struggling to think straight.

"I was told you wouldn't be interested, but I wanted to hear it directly from you."

"Hold up." His earlier comment suddenly hit me. "Did you say the weight division below?"

"That's right." He sounded very casual about a pretty big deal-breaker.

"Are you insane? Even if I wanted to fight, I can't lose seven or eight kilos in a week."

"There are ways, Leo." He paused. "If you really want something, you find a way."

I couldn't believe I was even considering this, but the idea of taking my mind off what had just happened with my mother and the opportunity to get the hell out of Melbourne was appealing, regardless of the potentially insurmountable issue with the weight.

"So I presume you spoke to Nick."

"The one and only Nick Matthews." He chuckled. "Told me to go to Hell."

"There are hundreds of legit fighters you could get. I don't understand why you would come after me, especially given I'm in the wrong weight division."

"My local boy needs a bigger challenge, and you're the fighter I want. I asked around my Melbourne contacts, and your name kept coming up as the next big thing. I know about your caged Muay Thai background, and that just makes you even more perfect."

I looked out the windscreen at the dark clouds and took a deep breath. "If I can get Nick on board, I'll do it."

"Call me back by tonight."

Two months ago, I'd returned to Lilydale the day after Juliette's fight and reconnected with Nick Matthews, my childhood boxing coach and mentor. I'd been inspired by Juliette's performance in the ring and asked Nick if he could line me up with a fight. Given my reputation in the cage, he had been able to secure me a high-ranked opponent at the Pavilion. I'd completely smashed him and taken victory by knockout. It had been exhilarating and a reminder of how much I loved the boxing ring. However, my first thought when I'd seen my mother was how much I wanted to be in the cage. It had become my refuge and my own personal oblivion that I didn't think I could find in the ring. Perhaps this Perth fight could serve as a good distraction though.

Needing to talk to Nick in person about it, I headed to Lilydale, leaving Dartmoor, Juliette and my past behind me.

I poked my head around Nick's office door. "Everything okay?" he asked. "Come in." He stood up and moved around his desk to shake my hand. This man had played such an important role in my life before I'd stopped boxing, and I was surprised by how much I was enjoying spending time with him again these past few months.

Led Zeppelin's "Stairway to Heaven" strummed

soulfully through the speakers. "Still listening to 70s music?" I asked, smiling.

He narrowed his eyes. "Don't go knocking the greatest era in music history." Shadow boxing, he gave me a mock warning. "I can still kick your butt, you know."

"Good luck with that, old man." I chuckled as he returned to his chair.

I sat down in the uncomfortable plastic chair and glanced around the small room. Memories of my youth flooded my mind. They had been the 'before' years, the years when my life had been simple. I had been normal and untouched by tragedy. A familiar picture caught my eye, and I squinted to focus on the image.

The sound of his voice pulled my gaze from the picture. "Remember that day?" asked Nick. "It was the day I knew you were destined for greatness."

"I remember." I was surprised by the nostalgia in his voice.

"I told you at the time you were my once-in-a-career fighter, but you'd already made up your mind." He shrugged his shoulders. "I was devastated, but I saw the magic again at the Pavilion last week."

I linked my hands behind my neck, stretching my legs out in front of me. "I remember you saying that all those years ago." I looked back at the picture of a sixteen-year-old me holding up a trophy and smiling broadly. I remembered the decision behind my easy smile. I'd won the fight no one thought I could win except Nick. I was satisfied and ready for something new. I was young, idealistic and had the world at my feet. "You were pretty pissed when I quit."

He shrugged. "So what brings you out this way? You want another fight?"

"Pete Sanders called me."

"Ugh. That snake. Trust him to do the unethical thing

and call the fighter direct." The look of disgust on his face matched his words. "Did you tell him to go to Hell just like I did?"

"Not exactly." I narrowed my eyes and waited for his reaction.

"Tell me you're not serious."

"Deadly serious." I leaned forward, resting my elbows on my knees. "Will you come with me?"

"Why the fuck would you even consider this? Besides the fact it's got 'dodgy' written all over it, you would have to practically kill yourself to make weight, and that arsehole would know it."

I hesitated. Would he understand the truth? "I need this, Nick. I need your help."

Nick groaned. "I don't know, Leo. I don't like this at all."

"Please." The more I thought about it, the more I wanted to do it, however crazy it was.

"This is insane, but it's your body, not mine, so if you really want to do it, I'll be there." He shook his head. "I know you're gonna do it either way."

Releasing the breath I'd been holding, I relaxed a little.

"Thank you. I'll text you the flight details when I have them."

When I got to his door, I turned to shake his hand. "Thanks again, mate."

"I can't believe I'm agreeing to this, Leo."

I patted him on the arm. "It's gonna be fine. A good challenge. You are always telling me to push myself to the limit and then some."

"This is definitely in the 'then some' category."

"I know."

When I got back to my car, I called Oliver, an old

school friend. If anyone knew about losing weight fast, it was Oliver.

"I have to lose a lot of weight by Friday night weigh-in," I said, skipping any small talk. "I need to know how to do it."

"Jesus, Leo," he replied. "Why would you want to do that? You have no weight to lose."

"Can you tell me or not?" I rubbed my face with my free hand a little more forcefully than necessary and, again, wondered what the fuck I was doing.

Turned out Oliver knew exactly how to lose that kind of weight in five days. He was a jockey, and a jockey's life revolved around weigh-ins. The information he shared filled me with dread and hope in equal measure. It was batshit fucking crazy, but I knew if there was any chance of making weight on Friday night, I would have to follow his regime to the letter, and the distraction was perfect.

CHAPTER 5

Juliette

WAKING UP FACE DOWN ON my bed at two in the morning was just one of the joys of jetlag. My body clock was still all over the place, and my mind was close to melting down. I sat up and wiped the drool off my cheek and the sleep from my eyes. I must've been quite the picture of loveliness. I wasn't going to get any answers lying in bed alone with my thoughts, so I decided to send Leo a text on the off-chance he was awake. It actually didn't matter to me why he hadn't told me or why he had lied about his mother. The only thing that mattered was doing whatever it took to help him deal with it.

Are you awake?

I stared at my screen for several long minutes, willing a positive reply to appear.

I'm awake.

Energised, I quickly typed back.

I need to see you.

Nothing.

I sent him another text.

> *Can I come to you?*

Eventually, he responded.

> *I don't think that's a good idea. I'm sorry.*

I didn't know whether I should push it or just leave him alone. My brain was still sleep-deprived and foggy despite my desperation, so I decided on the former.

> *I'm not giving up on us.*

I wanted him to know I was prepared to fight.

> *I'm in a bad place and you deserve more than this.*

I replied quickly, suddenly angry at his words.

> *You don't get to make that decision for me.*

Exasperated, I threw my phone down on the bed and lay back on my pillows, covering my face with my hands. What was I doing? I needed to have this conversation in person, so I shot Leo another text.

> *I'm coming anyway.*

I showered and dressed quickly. He'd told me he needed time, so I stood a very real chance of being rejected. But we were meant to be together, and nothing about his past was going to get in the way of our future. I was going to remind him of why we belonged together.

There was more traffic on the roads than I'd expected at that hour, but I still got to his apartment in far less time than I would have during the day. It was almost three in the morning, my brain was awake but foggy, this guy had some serious baggage and there I was sitting alone in my car, staring at his apartment like some kind of stalker. *Fuck it.* Before I thought about it too much more, I took some deep breaths and got out of my car.

As I walked up the path, I stopped in my tracks. Leo was standing on the front step, shirtless.

"What took you so long?" he asked. "I thought you were a race car driver?" His handsome features were made more so by his sexy smirk.

Without any conscious thought, I found myself running towards him. When I got close, he started moving, too. When he opened his arms for me, I launched myself at him, wrapping my legs around his lean waist. The moment of impact when my lips met his was exhilarating. It was like coming home, because I was his and I hoped he was my mine.

I kissed him all the way up the stairs and down the hallway, refusing to let him go. My tongue eagerly finding his, I knew I would never leave this man again. I loved him with all that I had, and regardless of his past, I was going to be his future.

"I need to put you down for a second, Jules," Leo whispered against my mouth, our foreheads still touching. "I need to unlock the door."

I slipped down his body, only too aware of the hard bulge straining the front of his navy track pants hanging deliciously low on his hips. I couldn't resist rubbing my palm over it, revelling in the groan that escaped from his mouth. Chuckling, I danced past him into his apartment.

"Not so fast," he said, grabbing my arm lightly and pulling me back to him.

I was only too happy to oblige as my body melted back into his embrace. He held either side of my face, and his expression turned serious. "Are you sure about this, Jules? I lied to you and I'm a complete fuck-up."

"Stop talking and kiss me." I smiled for a millisecond before Leo's mouth crashed down on mine again.

He swiftly lifted me into his arms and carried me to the bedroom, never once breaking our connection. I didn't know if this was going to be slow and sensual or hard and fast. I honestly didn't care either way as long as he stayed as close to me as physically possible.

"I want you so bad, Jules," Leo groaned.

"Take me. I'm yours."

Something in my words changed the air in the room. It went from lust-filled to full-blown raging inferno in that split second. It would've been disconcerting having my clothes literally ripped from my body if I hadn't been right there in the moment, ripping at his clothes with equal fervour. It was the reunion I'd dreamed about, and our desire had moved to a level impossible to describe. I felt his body move against mine. I felt his breath, hot against my neck. My back arched when his fingers grazed my bare breasts. When he thrust into me, it was fast and hard, yet measured and deliberate. Every touch breathed new life into our connection, and if I had died right there in his arms, I'd have been found with an indelible smile on my face.

I woke up a few hours later to the sound of the shower running. I glanced at the clock. It was six, and I needed to get home to get ready for my first day back at work. I knew it was going to be a punishment, but it had been worth it to be with Leo.

He walked back into the bedroom with a towel wrapped around his waist, and I drank in the sight of him.

"Good morning, beautiful."

"You're up early."

"I've been out for a run already." Closing the distance between us in a few strides, he leaned over to kiss me. I closed my eyes briefly just to enjoy the fact that Leo was right in front of me and we were together.

Leo's stomach broke our kiss with a loud grumble, and I opened my eyes. "I think it might be time for breakfast."

He scrunched up his nose and rubbed his eyes with the heels of his palms. "I can't."

"What do you mean you can't? What's going on?"

"I have to lose a bit of weight by Friday. I've signed up to do a fight in Perth on Saturday night. Weigh-in is Friday night."

"You mean a proper fight?"

He nodded. "A proper fight, but it's a lower weight division."

I was torn between the excitement of watching him in a boxing ring without the fear of the caged Muay Thai brutality and confusion as to why he would sign up for this particular fight. "Why would you sign up for a lower weight division? You can't possibly be fight-ready by starving yourself."

"I was approached by a fight promoter in Perth yesterday, and he wants me to fight his local guy, who happens to be a little lighter than me, next Saturday night."

"Shit, Leo. Why are you doing this?" I sat up in bed and placed my hand on his arm.

He stood up, dropped his towel and started to get dressed. "I just need to get away for a bit." I wasn't sure if he was still addressing me or just voicing his thoughts. "I'll be fine. My old boxing coach, Nick, is coming with me."

I got out of bed and slid my arms around his waist, hugging him from behind and resting my cheek on his back. I could feel every muscle in his body begin to relax. For now, I couldn't worry about the fight. All of my focus was on getting the answers I'd come for. "It's because of your mother, isn't it? That's the reason you signed up for this craziness."

He turned to face me. "What do you mean?"

"I'm not stupid. You told me both your parents were dead. I just want to know why."

His eyes darkened, and I could feel his body stiffen. "It's in the past where it belongs. I'm sorry I lied to you, but it's as I told you. She is dead to me, and I don't want to talk about it."

I shook my head and picked up my clothes, scattered around the room. I had to get going, and I didn't want to leave on a bad note.

"You're leaving?"

"It's my first day back at work today. I have to go home and get ready."

He bit his bottom lip but said nothing.

I got dressed in silence, feeling his gaze on me the whole time. When I was done, I met his eyes. "You're going to have to trust me at some point if this is going to work, Leo."

"I do trust you, but this is a deal-breaker for me. I don't talk about it. That is how I cope. If you can't live with that..."

"If I can't live with that, what?"

He ran his hands through his hair. "I'll call you later, okay?"

"You're a hypocrite. You know that?"

"What are you talking about?"

"You told me once that life isn't something you throw away because it gets too hard. You told me your instinct is to fight." I cocked my head to the side. "I don't see you fighting for anything. Give me a call when you're ready to fight for us."

I kissed him on the cheek and walked out.

CHAPTER 6

Juliette

FIVE MINUTES AFTER GETTING TO work, it felt as if I'd never been away. Heath welcomed me back by dumping a pile of paperwork on my desk.

"Hey, Jules." I looked up from my desk to see Nicole, one of the other desk assistants, standing there clutching a bunch of folders.

"Hey, Nicole." I smiled.

"Welcome back. I'm dying to hear about your trip."

"It was incredible. Bit tough being back, to be honest."

"I bet." She smiled.

Nicole was stunning and so incredibly lovely, it was almost unbearable. She was half Fijian, giving her an exotic look with flawless olive skin and pale blue-green eyes I couldn't help but stare at. Every straight man in the building lusted after her and was no doubt waiting for her to break up with her long-term boyfriend.

"I've taken on Sia's advisers, so my workload just doubled. I'm surprised you didn't stay over there with her."

I swivelled my chair around and crossed my legs. "I

came back for family reasons. My mum hasn't been well."

"Oh, I'm so sorry. Is she okay now?" God, she was so nice.

"She is," I lied. Nicole didn't need to know about my mother's deep-seated and possibly unfixable issues.

"Oh hey. Did you hear your ex lost his job? He was a pretty big deal over there, so the rumour mill kicked in."

"Richard?"

She scrunched up her nose. "Yep. Word is he got the sack, but they agreed to let him say he resigned if he left quietly."

I blew out a breath. I hadn't seen that arsehole in months, and running into him at work—or anywhere, for that matter—was not on my agenda. The fact that my father had no idea about all that sordid business with him and my mother weighed heavily on me, and I knew I had to find a way to tell him. Every time I spoke to him, I touched on the subject, but he quickly cut me off. It felt like he simply didn't want to know, but it wasn't right that he had been kept in the dark. "I honestly don't give a crap what he does."

She shrugged. "Do you want to grab lunch today?" she asked.

"Love to."

She smiled. "See you later, then."

I yawned regularly, and by lunchtime, I was glad to get some fresh air to wake me up a bit.

"Where do you want to go?" Nicole asked when the lifts opened on ground level.

"McQuillens on Little Bourke?" I suggested. "They make a killer tomato soup."

The second we stepped out through the revolving glass doors onto the footpath, I froze at the sound of a familiar voice calling my name. I found myself a few feet away from Leo's mother. Despite her relaxed and carefree demeanour, something about her made me uneasy.

"Can you just excuse me a second, Nic?" I raised one finger.

Nicole glanced at Gwendolyn and then me, completely oblivious to my fury. She just shrugged her shoulders, then pulled her phone out, probably to check Facebook.

"Hi, Gwendolyn," I said through gritted teeth when I got closer. "What are you doing here?"

"Oh, I was..."

"Don't tell me you were in the neighbourhood," I said sardonically.

She smiled. "I thought I would see if you'd changed your mind about lunch." She stared at her shoes as she shifted her weight from one to the other. "I was just hoping for a bit of company, really."

I bit the inside of my cheek, not wanting to make a scene in the middle of a busy footpath with my friend standing five feet away. "I told you yesterday it wasn't going to happen."

"I know." The lines in her face deepened, and she dropped her shoulders. "I'm not trying to make trouble for you, I swear."

I felt like a complete bitch, but this was out of order. "I'm sorry, but I already have lunch plans." I glanced at Nicole, who was tapping away on her phone.

"Oh. Of course." Her cheeks reddened. "Another time maybe."

"Maybe," I conceded, but there was zero chance I was going behind Leo's back on this.

"It's no wonder Leo is infatuated by you." She

chuckled. "You're a tough nut."

"I've had to be."

She nodded. "I've done nothing wrong, Juliette. Leo has no right—"

"Stop." I held up my hand. "Leo must have good reasons. This is all wrong. You need to go."

"For five years, he has refused to see me." Her eyes brimmed with tears, and I felt a strange pang of empathy towards her. "I've tried to communicate with him, but it's a one-way street. I'm his mother."

"He doesn't want anything to do with you," I whispered, unsure why this conversation was still going.

"I hoped you could help me with that." Her eyes softened. "The love he has for you has changed him, and I was selfishly hoping he might have a place for me in his life again." She looked to the sky, and when her eyes drifted back to mine, the pain on her face was evident. "I'd just like an opportunity to speak to him in person," she continued. "I don't think that's too much to ask."

Her words resonated with me, but this was Leo's life, not mine. "My loyalty is to Leo, and he's made his position very clear."

She touched my arm gently. "Please just ask him to call me."

I needed her to leave. "I'll think about it, but please don't just show up at my work again. It's not fair."

"I'm sorry." She dabbed at her eyes with a tissue. "You've given me more hope than I've had in years."

As I watched her walk away, my mind was a whir of warring thoughts. I didn't want to pressure Leo to open up before he was ready, but I hated the idea of him doing that crazy fight in Perth. I knew it had to have something to do with seeing his mother again, and I just had a really bad feeling in the pit of my stomach.

"She seemed pretty intense," Nicole said, interrupting my thoughts. "Who was she?"

"She—" I bit my bottom lip and shuddered "—is a problem."

"Well, I'm starving. You ready to get some lunch?"

I nodded. I was absolutely ready for some to-die-for tomato soup and a light chat with a lovely, sane person who knew nothing about all of this.

After work, I headed home, disappointed that Leo hadn't called but not surprised. He was stubborn, proud and damaged—a bad combination for accepting help. I didn't want him to go, or if he had to, I wanted to be there with him. I got Nick's number from Zac and called him at the fight club in Lilydale. Leo had said he was going with him to Perth, and I needed details.

"Nick Matthews," he answered after a few rings.

"Hello, Nick. It's Juliette Salinger here." I paused, feeling awkward. "I'm not sure if you remember—"

"Well, well, well. How could I forget you? You were a killer against Christina Lee."

"Oh, thanks. Kinda feels like a million years ago now."

"To what do I owe this pleasure, Ms Salinger? I'm betting it has something to do with Leo Ashlar."

"Yes, it does, actually. How did you know?" I asked, stopping on the footbridge to watch the water run silently underneath.

"I've seen a bit of Leo over the past few months, and you've come up."

"Oh." I didn't know if that was a good thing or not.

"It's all good, darlin.'" He chuckled. "I'm pretty sure you're the reason he wants to get out of the cage and back into the ring. You know, clean up his act for the love of a good woman."

"Oh." I banged my forehead with my palm. Why was

I incapable of speech?

"You wanna tell me why you're calling?" he asked, chuckling.

"Right." I lifted my gaze from the mesmerising river and focused on the point of my call. "I know Leo is fighting in Perth this weekend, and I want to know how crazy it really is."

I heard him blow out a loud breath. "Leo is special," he started. "Always was. He's the most naturally-gifted fighter I've ever known. There's no doubt going up against a champion fighter in the condition he'll be in is off-the-charts crazy, but if anyone can pull it off, it's Leo."

"Okay." I felt sick at the thought of it, despite Nick's semi-reassuring words.

"Look, Juliette. I've got his back, and if it gets out of hand, I'll take him down myself."

"I wish I could be there for him."

"He'll need to focus."

"I'm worried about him." I paused, unsure if I should go on, but this was the guy who was going to be responsible for Leo's well-being. He needed to know. "He saw his mother yesterday, and it's clearly had a big impact on him. He's taken this fight for the wrong reasons."

When he didn't reply, I looked at my screen to see if the call had dropped out. "Hello?"

"Sorry. I'm here." Another pause made me feel anxious. "Thank you for telling me."

I blew out a long, frustrated breath. "Can you keep me updated from Perth?"

"Sure, darlin.'"

I hung up and rummaged in my bag for the card Gwendolyn had given me at Dartmoor with her phone number on it, then sent her a text. I did not want to be the messenger because everyone knows the messenger is the one who gets shot.

> *I'm not getting between you and Leo. I'm*
> *sorry.*

Without giving it too much thought, I'd given her my phone number, and at some point in the future, that would turn out to be a life-threatening decision. None the wiser, I went back to staring at the river. I found it calming. I figured Leo wasn't going to call me until after the fight, and whilst that pissed me off, I knew his mind was all over the place.

My phone rang, snapping me out of my tortured thoughts. It was Dad. I knew he wanted to know how it went at Dartmoor with Mum yesterday. He had tried to talk me out of going and asked for me to wait until she came home next weekend, but Mum had sounded different on the phone. She hadn't demanded I visit. She had asked, and strangely, her simple request had filled me with false hope.

"Hi, Dad," I said quietly.

"Juliette. Why haven't you called me back?"

I sighed. "Sleep and work, I guess."

"I spoke to your mother last night, and she told me what happened with Leo."

"Yep." I was so not in the mood.

"There are things you need to know about your mother." He paused. "Things you deserve to know."

I almost laughed so I wouldn't cry. There were so many things *he* needed to know about my mother. "I don't want to know."

"Please, Juliette. I would like you to come to dinner next Sunday night, and I'll explain everything I've learned over the past few months. I think it will really help you."

I stared down at the murky, brown water of the Yarra and suddenly wished I could transport myself back to a bridge in Paris or Budapest or pretty much any of the incredible places I'd visited in Europe over the past few months. Anywhere but right there, listening to my father tell me there was more I needed to know about the woman who'd hurt me so damn much.

"Fine," I said, resigned to one more confrontation. "I'll be there."

Shit.

The next few days, I just went through the motions. *What am I doing with my life?* was on constant loop in my head. At least I had my first training session after work with Zac to look forward to since being back from my trip. I had missed my boxing training and I needed it.

CHAPTER 7

LEO

MONDAY TO THURSDAY WAS A battle of mind over body. I focused all my energy on the challenge. To cut my weight by Friday, my diet consisted of fruit and vegetables. Dousing them in spices did nothing to improve the flavour. I tried to trick myself into thinking the mushrooms were meat, but I craved a big, juicy steak and, about a thousand times a day, came very close to throwing in the towel. I had to keep exercising to accelerate the flushing of fluids from my body, but with very few calories, it was increasingly difficult. I didn't need a medical background to know how reckless it was. With very little fat to strip, the loss was muscle and fluid.

By Thursday evening, I was ready to rip someone's head off, and I was relieved Jules wasn't going to see me in this state. I would call her when I got back from Perth and could think straighter.

The run I'd just completed was one of the toughest of my life. My feet felt like they were weighed down by cement. When I finished my shower, I draped a towel around my waist, nearly slipping on the wet tile as I rushed to answer the phone ringing from the bedroom.

I hit the green button. "Leo Ashlar."

The voice that greeted me sent icy shivers down my spine, and I immediately stopped drying myself. "Leo. Hello?" I didn't respond. "Are you there?"

"This is a private number," I seethed. "How did you get it?" I asked but almost immediately knew the answer. "Forget it. Isabel gave it to you." I shook my head. I fucking hated that woman. "What do you want?" Infuriated, I pressed the phone closer to my ear while I hissed out the snarky question.

"I want to meet in person." My mother's tone was quiet, but stern.

"I have nothing to say to you and have no interest in anything you have to say."

"Leo. I'm your—"

"Stop. I have to go. Don't call me again."

"It was lovely seeing Juliette again."

"What do you mean *again?*" My blood ran cold.

I could hear her chuckling. "I showed up at her work and offered to take her to lunch earlier this week, but she's a loyal little lady, isn't she?"

"Do not," I seethed. "I repeat. Do not go near her again." When there was no answer, I looked down at my phone. She'd hung up.

I crumpled down on the edge of my bed and attempted to get my brain to assess my options, but I couldn't think straight. I called Juliette, but it went to voicemail. I left her a message asking her to come into the bar tonight and told her we needed to talk.

I finished getting ready as quickly as my fatigued muscles would allow. I jumped in the Jeep and headed into the city. I was glad I didn't ride the bike. Just looking at the parking spot reminded me of Juliette and the way she'd sat on the bike with her legs wrapped around me, kissing me as if she had no choice. This was all just so fucked up.

My boss, Adriana, greeted me as I walked into the bar. "Hey, Leo." Her dark hair fell over her shoulder as she cocked her head to the side. "You okay?"

"All good," I lied. "You?"

"Freaking awesome."

I was slightly taken aback by her enthusiastic reply. There was usually sadness that followed her like a shadow. She'd never really recovered from being jilted at the altar a few years earlier. Last she had heard, her fiancé had been mixing it with a biker gang.

"Freaking awesome, huh?" I asked as I walked into the staff room after her.

"I met with the new bank manager today, and I got the pre-approved loan to buy the cottage."

"That's awesome, Adri." I knew she had her heart set on a cottage at Aireys Inlet on the Great Ocean Road. "I'm really happy for you."

"He might be coming in for a drink later." Her cheeks flushed.

"The banker?"

She grinned sheepishly. "Yep."

I winked. "Go for it, Adri. You tell him I'll take him down and have his balls if he hurts you."

"Hate to say this, Leo, but you look like shit." She stepped closer. "You don't look like you could *take* anyone. Are you okay? Have you lost weight?"

"Maybe a bit." I waved her off. "I'm okay."

"If it's quiet later, take off early. Okay?" she suggested. "You might be coming down with something."

"Thanks, my friend." Wallowing in self-pity was appealing, but I was also determined to win the war raging in my mind. A body's survival instincts are strong, and when pushed to the limit, you find out just how all-consuming. My plan had been to solely dwell on my body's most primal need, but my mother's phone call had put an end to that.

Yawning, I dragged my arse back to the bar. The fatigue was hard to fight, but it was just one more mind game I was up against. It was busy enough to make time pass fairly quickly, but I was constantly watching the door for Juliette or checking my phone whenever I had a chance. I knew I wasn't working at the pace my fellow bartenders were accustomed to, but I was doing my best to keep up with the demanding patrons.

A man wearing an expensive-looking suit sidled up to the bar.

"What can I get you?" I asked.

"Canadian Club and dry."

"Coming right up."

"Is Adriana here?" he asked, looking up and down the bar.

Figuring this guy was her banker, I motioned with an upward nod. "She's out the back. I'll call her out in a second."

"Thanks. Appreciate it." He appeared slightly nervous, but he didn't look like a creeper, which was a relief. He reminded me of the actor who had played Superman in that *Man of Steel* movie, but I couldn't remember his name. I would be keeping an eye on him. Adri was my friend, and I looked out for my friends.

When I'd given Superman his drink, I wandered out to the staff room. My feet felt like dead weights and the room spun if I moved my head too quickly. I felt like shit.

I poked my head around the door. "You have a visitor, Adri."

"Thanks, Leo." She grinned like a schoolgirl. "I'll be

right out."

I turned to leave.

"You'll be scaring off the customers in your state," Adri called out. She chuckled as she studied her reflection in a small compact mirror. "You're meant to be the eye candy."

"Thanks." My body was screaming at me, and I just wanted to sleep.

I got back to my job and plastered a smile on my face. When I thought I heard Juliette's name, I glanced down the other end of the bar and locked on to her talking and laughing with a group of people I didn't know. She looked incredible. Her long hair hung loosely around her shoulders, and her fresh face was makeup free. No woman had ever looked more beautiful than she did in that moment with her own special brand of sexy confidence. She was talking to a muscled-up dude, and my blood instantly boiled when he put his arm around her shoulders and pulled her into his side. She didn't look particularly annoyed, but she was batting his arm away. *What the fuck?* I stalked towards them. "Get your fucking hands off her." I had almost no energy, but I was ready to tear limbs from his body if he didn't remove them from Juliette in the next two seconds.

The guy threw his arms up in the air as if he were under arrest. "Cool it, mate." He chuckled, which just made me want to punch him in the face. "You two know each other?" he asked.

Juliette's eyes burned into me, and I couldn't look at her again. I knew I was on the edge of losing it completely. "I'm more interested in how *you* know her."

"I'm standing right here, Leo." Juliette sounded angry, and I recoiled. "Westie and I race cars together."

My poor brain was in no shape to deal with this connection. "Right." I broke eye contact and shifted on my feet.

"You look like hell," the Westie fucker goaded.

I ignored him and focused on Juliette. "I need to speak to you. I left you a message hours ago."

"I had boxing training with Zac," she said, clearly confused by my tone. "I got your message, so I went home and got changed rather than coming here in my sweaty gym gear."

We locked eyes, and I felt a primal urge to protect her. She'd just come from a boxing class, for god's sake, and I'd seen her fight. She was far from helpless, but emotional scars cut far deeper and I would not have her anywhere near another manipulative woman. She'd suffered a lifetime of emotional abuse from her own mother. She didn't need to deal with mine, who was on a whole other level completely.

Westie cleared his throat. "Is anyone gonna get me a beer?" he asked.

I pulled a beer bottle out from the fridge below the bar, clipped off the top and handed it to him without losing eye contact with Juliette. Westie disappeared, shaking his head.

"How are you doing?" she asked softly when I didn't say anything.

"Been better." I placed my hands on the bar.

Juliette's face was unreadable. "You said in your message you wanted to talk."

"Hey, Leo," Adri interrupted. She turned to Juliette. "You must be the girl that's got my boy here all tied up in knots. It's nice to meet you."

"Leo speaks highly of you," Juliette said, shaking her hand.

"Can you take him home please?" she asked. "He's gonna scare away my customers."

"Thanks, boss," I said, grateful for the reprieve. I turned to Jules. "Can you wait a sec. I'll grab my things."

When I returned, I took hold of her elbow and guided her towards the exit. The cool night air was a welcome relief. I was so glad to be out of there.

"I didn't think you would call until after the weekend." Jules moved away from me, leaning against the brick wall, her arms crossed over her chest. Her tone wasn't angry though.

"I wasn't going to," I admitted. "But the plan's changed."

"What plan?" she asked. "The one where you shut me out and bolt in the opposite direction, you mean?" Okay. So maybe she was a little pissed.

I needed to cut to the chase. I desperately wanted to reach out and touch her but thought better of it. She wanted me to talk. "I want you to come to Perth with me this weekend." I blurted it with no conscious thought. I had planned on asking her to go stay with her dad or one of her friends while I was away, but my desire to keep her close was overwhelming.

"Nick thinks it's a terrible idea."

"Why do you say that?" I asked, blindsided.

"I called him earlier in the week to ask him how crazy this fight was. He confirmed what I already knew, that you're out of your mind, but he also said you'd need to focus and it was good I wouldn't be there."

"I don't give a shit what Nick said."

She narrowed her eyes sceptically. "Why do you want me to come with you?"

I bit the inside of my cheek. I didn't want to lie to her, but I wasn't yet prepared to tell her the truth. "Please, Jules," I implored. "I need you there."

She placed her hands on her hips and let out a long

breath. "Okay. Fine. I'll come, but you'd better tell Nick this was your idea and you better start thinking seriously about telling me what the hell is going on."

"Thank you." I exhaled. "I'll get you on our flight. We leave tomorrow morning, so I'll take you home to pack a bag. I want you to stay at mine tonight."

She nodded, placing her hand on the side of my face. "Seriously, Leo. You look terrible."

"I didn't want you to see me like this, but I need you with me." I took a step closer to her.

Her eyes softened. "Are you ready to fight for us?"

Her question hit me hard. When my first and only instinct was to run, she was giving me a reason to stay. I took her angelic face in my hands, pushing my body against hers. "You deserve more."

"That's true." She reached up and kissed me lightly on the lips. "I do deserve better than this. I deserve a whole lot better than this, you selfish bastard," she whispered. "And you're going to give it to me."

I didn't waste another second. My lips crashed down on hers, and we both groaned as our tongues reunited in a frenzy of lust. She wrapped her arms around my neck, and for a long time, neither of us came up for air.

Eventually, she pulled back and scrunched her nose slightly. "Um... Leo. Your breath isn't great."

Mortified, I covered my mouth with my hand. It was the last thing I had been expecting, but it wasn't surprising. My body was suffering a horrendous detox, and kissing me wouldn't have been a picnic.

I took a step back, but she grabbed my arm. "I'm sorry, Jules."

"It's the diet, isn't it?"

I nodded. "One of the side effects, I'm afraid."

She punched me in the chest lightly. "You're an idiot."

Resting her cheek on my chest, she hugged my waist. Her voice was more of a whispered plea than a demand, and I shut my eyes, enjoying the feel of her against me, safe in my arms.

When she looked up at me, I ran my thumb across her bottom lip. "I know. Trust me, Jules. I know."

"I want to understand you," she whispered.

Her words rattled me, but I loved her conviction. "It's gonna get ugly," I told her.

"Stop trying to protect me from the ugly. I can handle ugly. In case you've forgotten, I like a little ugly action." She smiled in a way that didn't work. The conversation was just too serious for an injection of humour. "What I can't handle is being blocked from your life when the going gets tough. I don't need you to fully open up to me tonight or tomorrow or even the next day. Let's just get through this weekend together and see what happens." The hope in her eyes was contagious. I was more when I was with her. I wanted to be more for her.

CHAPTER 8

Juliette

I WOKE EARLY AND SLIPPED out of bed. Grabbing my phone, I headed for the kitchen. I had received several texts from Gwendolyn since I'd messaged her, insisting that she means no harm and is just trying to reconnect. Another few had come in overnight. The woman was incorrigible. I deleted them all. Leo was going to extreme lengths for a stupid fight on the other side of the country, and my heart broke for him. There was no way I would be telling him his mother kept trying to speak to me. I would wait 'til we got back from Perth. One hurdle at a time.

I made myself a coffee and a green herbal tea that smelled like dirty dish water for poor Leo. He would be weighing in tonight, so the end was in sight. It was killing me to see his beautiful body being so mistreated. When I returned to his bedroom, he was sitting up in bed, scrubbing his hands with the heels of his palms. He looked completely drained. I sat down on the bed next to him and offered him the tea.

"Thanks, Jules." He took it and winced as the fumes

hit his nostrils. "Fucking hate this green crap."

"It helps flush you out. Drink up, you big baby."

He looked at me with a mixture of love and indecision in his eyes. "Thank you... thank you for being here." He took a small sip of the tea without looking away.

"Let's just get through this. Okay?"

He set his cup down on the bedside table and eased himself up. "I'm going to go for a quick run."

"Are you sure you're up for it?" He looked like he could barely stand up.

"Not really, but I'll take it easy. I'm actually feeling a bit better today. I think my body might be getting used to this abuse."

"Better not be. The second you've weighed in, I'm taking you to the closest burger joint."

"I won't be arguing with you."

I smirked, raising my eyebrows. "That'll make a nice change."

Before I knew it, I was pulled against his hard body. He held my head firmly to his chest so I could feel his heart beating. "Thank you," he whispered.

"You're welcome."

"As much as I'd like to kiss you now, I am disgusting."

Nick reluctantly swapped seats with me so Leo and I could sit next to each other on the plane. Leo held my hand the whole way, even during the lunch service. I knew he needed my unconditional support to get through this crazy fight, and I was going to give it to him. I'd done some research and found out the local guy he'd be fighting was an intimidating brute. Under normal circumstances, Leo would annihilate him, but I was so worried about him in this weakened state. He was going to have to draw on every physical reserve and every ounce of mental stamina he had left.

"Have I told you how beautiful you are?" he asked.

"Not today," I replied, giving him a coy smile.

"You are the most beautiful woman I've ever seen, and I can't believe you're here."

The conversation got intense suddenly, and my heart rate picked up. "I wasn't sure you still wanted me."

"Please don't ever doubt that, Jules. It kills me that I can't give you everything you deserve."

I angled my body towards him. "Please stop with the martyr crap, Leo. I'm tired of it. Do you remember what you said to me when you took me on our first date?"

"My feeble attempt at a romantic date, you mean?"

"Yes. And it wasn't feeble. It was perfect." The memories of Leo rowing a boat down the river came in blissful waves. "You said that I'm yours and you're mine. Fait accompli."

Leo smiled. "It was."

"It was then and it is now. Stop trying to protect me. *Please.*"

"Let's get through this weekend, then talk about where we go from here when my brain isn't trying to eat itself."

"I have something I really need to talk to you about then, too."

Leo's face darkened. "With the exception of one subject, I'll talk to you about anything."

My stomach flipped. How was I going to broach the subject of his mother if the subject was a no-go zone?

"As you said, let's get through this weekend."

We arrived in Perth at two o'clock and were met by a driver waving a placard with Leo's name on it. With the weigh-in only hours away, I could feel the tension building. Nick made a few calls to double check that Leo would have exclusive use of the hotel sauna for the afternoon. Leo's shoulders were tense, and he gnawed ruthlessly on his bottom lip. I had to place my hand on his knee to stop the incessant tapping. There was little doubt he'd lost weight, but the number that flashed up would either mean he was eligible to fight or the trip had been a complete waste of time. Neither were great outcomes, in my opinion.

We were taken to a flash hotel near Claremont. Leo and I waited with the bags while Nick checked us in. When he returned, he held up the room card. "I have a meeting with Pete and the other manager in an hour. I'll be back later on to check on how the weight's going. The sauna is all yours."

"Thanks, Nick." Leo took the card and turned to me. "Hope you don't mind sharing with a sweaty, cranky man?"

"As long as you're the sweaty, cranky man, I think I'll cope." He took my hand and we walked to the lift, leaving the bags with the concierge.

When we got to our room, Leo lay down on the bed and closed his eyes. It was startling to see him so weak and vulnerable. The idea of him in a boxing ring tomorrow night filled me with dread. I had stepped into the role of protector for a change and knew I would do anything to see him get through the next twenty-four hours and home safely.

A knock at the door startled me. I left Leo dozing on the bed and went to answer it, checking the peephole first before opening the door.

"Can I have a word in private for a second?" Nick asked.

I stepped out into the hallway, leaving the door slightly ajar. "Sure. What's up?"

Instead of answering me immediately, he ran his

hands through his hair. "Look. I know you have some understanding of this game. I saw you fight yourself. I just wanted to make sure you're not a distraction for him."

I was actually really touched by his concern and glad he was in Leo's corner. "I get it, Nick. I do. I'm sick with worry for him and really wish he wasn't doing it, but he's determined and I want to help him, not make it harder."

Nick dropped his shoulders, and his tense features relaxed slightly. "I care about him. I always have. He's not the same person he was at sixteen, and I worry the change isn't for the better."

"What do you mean?"

"The death of a parent changes a person, and he can't seem to move past it."

"I have no idea what happened. It's a closed subject."

"The past is the past, Jules. He has a big future ahead of him if he can just let all that go, and we should be focused on that." Nick looked at his watch. "I have to run now. Remember, Jules. Eye on the prize."

"I got this, Nick."

I walked back into the room and sat down on the bed next to Leo. I nudged him gently.

He sat up and let out a loud huff. "Guess I can't put this off any longer." He looked at me. "You really don't have to come with me. Maybe you'd like to do some sightseeing?"

"I won't be leaving your side. In your current state, I reckon I could take you, so don't go pissing me off."

He chuckled. "You're a stubborn woman, Juliette Salinger."

"And don't you forget it." I leant over and kissed him on the cheek. "Tell me what we need to do."

"Can you get the tub of Vaseline from my bag, please?

It's time to hit the sauna."

"This sounds bad already."

Leo headed into the bathroom, returning a few moments later wearing a hotel robe. "Let's go."

As we stepped into the elevator, I quizzed him about the Vaseline. "So what's this for?" I asked, waving the jar at him.

"It's a tip a jockey gave me for losing fluids quickly. Nick booked the sauna for the afternoon, so we shouldn't be disturbed."

"I really don't like the sound of this, Leo."

"I'm not exactly looking forward to it, but I've come this far and I'm still over. There is no other way I can make weight by tonight."

The sauna was located in a deserted change room. Leo stripped the robe, and I couldn't help ogling his still-magnificent body. He was the ripped Adonis I'd always known, and he was an impressive sight. His naked form made me go weak at the knees, even if the circumstance was about as far from sexy as I could imagine.

Leo stood on the scales and nodded. "This better work." He said it more to himself than to me.

"Okay. So what now?"

He looked at me and sighed. "I really wish you didn't have to witness this, Jules."

"Shut up and tell me what to do."

"I need you to smear my whole body in Vaseline before I go into the sauna." He grimaced. "I need my pores to be blocked so I can't sweat while I'm in there."

"This is crazy." I shook my head and chewed on my lip. "You know that, right?"

"I've had a lot of crazy in my adult life. This is just another fucked up thing to add to the list." His resigned tone made my heart ache. This man was carrying around some heavy baggage, and I had a feeling I'd barely scratched the surface. Why would anyone in their right mind put themselves through this? He wasn't money driven, so it had to be some kind of masochistic punishment.

"This is the last time you're doing this if I have anything to say about it."

Leo shook his head. "I run my own race, Jules."

His words cut me deeper than they should've, but I didn't let on. Instead, I scooped a dollop of Vaseline and slapped it on his chest. He jumped back in shock from the cold jelly-like substance he hadn't been prepared for. "Sorry." My smirk let him know I wasn't.

"Maybe a little warning?"

"That *was* your warning." I tried to hold back my laughter, but a chuckle slipped out.

"You're a pain in my arse. You know that?"

"Stand still and let me finish the job."

It wasn't exactly a chore smearing Vaseline over his body. Each stroke of my hand made him flinch slightly, and he appeared to be holding his breath most of the time. It was a strangely erotic experience in that poorly-lit change room miles and miles from home.

"Having fun?" The sly question was redundant. He knew exactly how much I was enjoying it.

"I am, actually. Thanks for asking."

"I think you're done, Jules."

I stepped back and admired my handiwork. He looked completely ridiculous.

"Okay. Okay." He waved me off. "Show's over." He tipped his head towards the sauna. "Would you like to join me?"

"God, no. I hate saunas." I'd been in one before and absolutely detested the feeling of being overheated. I couldn't imagine how horrible it was going to be for Leo when his body was unable to sweat. "Don't stay in too long, or I'll come and drag you out."

Reaching for a towel to dry my hands, I watched him disappear behind the heavy, wooden door. I sat down on one of the benches, leaned back to rest my head on the wall and waited.

About a half hour later, the sauna door opened.

"Jules?" Much to my horror, Leo stumbled out looking like he was on fire. His face was red, and his whole body glistened from what was left of the melted Vaseline.

"God, Leo." I leapt off the bench. "Are you okay?" A wave of sheer panic washed over me at the sight of him.

He looked dreadful, and even more alarmingly, he spoke in a jumbled slur that I could barely understand. Pushing down my fears, I placed my hand on his elbow and ushered him towards the bench. "Come here and sit down."

"I hate saunas," he slurred. "My nostrils are burning."

"It's okay, babe." I reassured him. "I've got you. Tell me what you need."

"Towel," he mumbled, looking at the stack next to me.

I used a few towels to wipe his body clean of the wet substance, and what happened next turned my stomach. Sweat pulsated out of his body at such a rate, I just stood back in shock. I'd never seen anything like it, and I knew it had to be a horrifying experience for Leo. His face was contorted, his eyes were shut, and his muscles twitched violently.

"I'll be back in a sec." I called over my shoulder as I rushed from the room to get some ice. "Try to relax."

I returned within minutes to Leo, who was hunched over with his head in his hands and elbows resting on his knees. The sweat was still pouring out, but the rate had decreased.

"Suck on this."

I placed another cube on the back of his neck, and he groaned with pleasure. After a few minutes, he staggered over the scales to weigh himself and I followed, praying he'd done enough.

He groaned. "So close."

I was horrified but had to just stand back and let it happen.

Despite his slurred voice, the determination in his tone was unmistakable.

"Only a few minutes," I pleaded in barely a whisper. "I don't think you can take much more."

He came out every few minutes and headed to the scales.

After the fourth time, I was ready to put my foot down. Enough was enough. Helping him to the scales, I released him only when he was standing safely on them.

"No more." He exhaled, stumbling backward into my arms. "I've made weight."

"Thank God." I shook my head, giddy with relief.

After giving him a proper dry-off, I somehow managed to help him back to the room. He just let me take charge like an obedient child. As much as he would've liked a shower to get rid of the pungent smell of salty sweat, Leo refused. He mumbled something about the pores absorbing the water, which would counteract his achievement in the sauna, and I was beyond arguing by that point. Exhausted, he sat down on the edge of the bed and slumped forward, resting his face in his hands.

"Lie down, Leo. We have two hours before we have to be at weigh-in, so you should just rest. I'll switch on the TV."

"Don't let me go to sleep." His voice was strained and barely audible.

"Why can't you sleep?" I questioned, confused. Surely sleep would've been sweet relief for him after what he'd just put his body through.

"I'm dehydrated. If I go to sleep, I'll wake up with an unbearable headache."

I gave him another ice cube to suck on. My beautiful, strong man looked gaunt and broken in the soft afternoon light.

I'll never let this happen again, I thought to myself.

CHAPTER 9

AT SIX THIRTY, NICK KNOCKED on our door. It was time. The weigh-in was going to be in our hotel rather than at the stadium, and I was glad. I was spent and wanted the whole ordeal over and done with.

"You ready?" Nick asked as we walked towards the lift.

"Ready." I silently prayed the torturous week had been worth it, and I could put on a good show. I had my suspicions that this fight was never meant to be fair. Pete knew I'd have to starve to make weight and would be weak because of it. I was a scalp, and I was okay with that because I had an ace up my sleeve. I could channel rage through my body, and that's what made me unbeatable. I might look and feel like shit, but I was not going to go down easily. *This Perth prick better be ready for me.*

Juliette squeezed my hand as we travelled down to the conference rooms on the ground floor. When the doors opened, I was surprised to see TV cameras and journalists setting up. Clearly, this was a bigger deal than I had anticipated.

I whispered to Nick from the corner of my mouth.

"Did you know about this?

He shook his head. "Nope. Pete's a snake in the grass. I don't trust him."

Jules gripped my arm. "I've got a bad feeling about this." Her voice was laced with panic.

"I'll be fine." I kissed her on the cheek, then jogged forward into the throng of people waiting to see me fail.

A few flashes went off as I stopped in the middle of the room.

"Over here, Leo." I glanced over and saw Pete standing at the officials' table with a fancy-looking weigh-in scale.

Unwilling to show my weakness, I walked confidently towards them. Nick appeared at my side, and I didn't try to see where Juliette was. I needed to focus on the task at hand.

"You made it." Pete held out his hand and shook mine firmly. "Leo. This is Lucas Albright."

Lucas and I nodded at each other before he went back to jogging on the spot and shadow boxing. He was a showman, and that filled me with hope. Show ponies were my easiest competition.

"Okay, Lucas. You're up first."

Lucas easily made weight, and fist punched the air like a tosser. "Are you sure you're up for this, Ashlar?" he asked, making a beeline for me. "You don't look so flash."

I was going to enjoy putting the cocky little fucker in his place tomorrow night.

"You just worry about yourself, mate."

"I was told you were the ultimate fighter, but you look like you'd be better off in the women's comp."

"My girlfriend could send you to the canvas in seconds flat, so be careful what you say about women in front of her."

Lucas glanced at Juliette, and I immediately regretted drawing attention to her. "The gorgeous blonde is a fighter?"

"Yeah, so keep your dirty mitts to yourself." I'd all but forgotten my starvation when I saw him watching her with hungry eyes.

"Can I have your attention, ladies and gentlemen?" Pete's booming voice cut through the crowd. "Next up we have the official weigh-in for Melbourne fighter, Leo Ashlar."

More flashes went off and a few people clapped. I tried to block everything out as I stared at the scales. Suddenly it felt like a test of my will to survive. I was outside my comfort zone, and I'd need to fight like hell.

Nick patted me on the back. "Good luck."

The numbers on the scale seemed to flash forever. Underweight, overweight, underweight, overweight. When the final numbers locked in, my nerves were shot.

Underweight by the skin of my teeth.

I did it. I fucking did it.

Juliette's voice erupted before anyone else's. "Yes!" she cheered.

I turned and smiled, immediately catching her eye. She blew me a kiss, and for that moment, I was on top of the world.

"Well done, mate." Nick's relief mirrored my own as he ushered me away from the scales and into a chair, handing me a bottle of Gatorade. I casually sank down into the plastic chair and downed the hydrating fluid in one long guzzle.

"Leo Ashlar's official weight has been recorded, and we have a fight." Pete's announcement sent a rush of satisfaction coursing right through me. I had achieved the impossible. The first hurdle had been overcome.

I managed to get away with only doing one interview for the West Australian Newspaper. They asked a few questions about my fitness and general health. I couldn't hide the fact I'd barely eaten all week. I was fading fast, and I was grateful when Nick told me it was time to go. I glanced around the testosterone-charged room. Hungry and thirsty fighters were eagerly awaiting their turn on the scales to decide their fight readiness.

I was incredibly relieved to get the hell out of there. Desperate for food, we caught a taxi to what turned out to be a pretty decent restaurant. I didn't speak once my food arrived. I quickly realised my eyes were far bigger than my stomach. I could only eat half my burger, but no burger had ever tasted better in the history of burgers. Nick had also ordered me a jug of lemonade, which I picked up and drank without bothering with a cup. I had no idea what damage I'd done to my body over the past week, but I'd made weight and that was what mattered.

"So from what I could work out from the hushed conversations I overheard, Pete never intended for you to stand a chance in this fight. He knows you're a dangerous fighter, but you're definitely the scalp."

Juliette put down her fork and wiped her mouth. "What an arsehole."

"There's worse than him out there," Nick said. "I still can't believe you agreed to this fight."

Juliette piped up. "Me neither."

"Can you two leave me alone, please?" I didn't need to justify my decision to anyone. I was a free agent.

"Let's focus on the job at hand, shall we?" Nick waved his fork at us. "You'll need to do exactly as I say from here on in. Okay?"

Nick talked all through dinner, barely pausing for food. His insight was invaluable. To compensate for my weakened state, I was going to have to change the way I fought.

"I need to go," I said, wiping my mouth with my napkin. "I'm beat."

"Get some sleep and take it easy tomorrow morning," Nick said as we shuffled out of the booth. "We'll have a light training session after lunch tomorrow and go over some strategies."

We returned to the hotel and said goodbye to Nick in the lobby. He said he wanted to make a few phone calls and was meeting one of his mates in the hotel bar.

Juliette and I rode the lift in silence. My hand found hers, and she melted into my side.

"I'm so glad you're here," I whispered, kissing the top of her head.

She looked up at me and smiled. "No place I'd rather be."

As soon as we got back to our room, I headed straight for a much-needed shower. Juliette followed, stripping off her clothes on the way. As soon as I stepped in, I pulled her to me and my mouth found hers. The gentle touch of her hands on my body felt like therapy, massaging my aching muscles. I felt completely weighed down by total exhaustion.

"God, you're beautiful," I whispered against her lips before feathering kisses down her throat and neck.

While the water washed away the horrors of the day, her delicate fingers traced lines on my back that drove me completely insane with desire. Her breath hitched when I claimed one of her breasts with my greedy mouth. Without enough conscious thought, I grabbed her backside, intent on burying myself deep inside her. She placed her palms on my chest and gently pushed me back. "You can't be serious, Leo."

"Fuck." I dropped my head back under the water and

rubbed my face with my palms. "I actually feel like shit and can barely hold myself up." I hadn't been thinking clearly, and I might've actually dropped her if I'd followed through with my lust-fuelled plan.

She chuckled, kissing my chest. "Let's get you to bed, then."

The crisp sheets felt cool against my naked skin. "Come here," I said, opening my arms for her.

She nuzzled into my side and laid her cheek over my heart. I stroked her silky hair and knew I had to find a way to be enough for this girl.

"I nearly went out of my mind without you." My words were muffled by a yawn.

"Never again, babe," she whispered back. "Get some sleep."

As I drifted towards sleep, I felt her kiss my chest again, right above my heart. Despite the fact I was too weak to make love to her, the woman my heart would always choose was safe in my arms.

CHAPTER 10

I WOKE THE NEXT MORNING with Juliette's warm body tangled around mine. She met my gaze and smiled. Her incredible navy eyes and silky blonde hair were captivating, but it wasn't what held me. The beauty from within is what stole my soul. Hers was the kind of beauty that could make men lose their minds.

"Good morning, beautiful." My voice sounded scratchy, and I had to clear my throat. "How did you sleep?"

She edged closer to me. "Really well," she cooed. "You?"

"With you next to me, how could I not?" I kissed her, wrapping her in my arms.

"I ordered breakfast about half an hour ago so you can fuel up this body again." She ran her fingers down my chest and abs, causing blood to rush south.

"I want you," I whispered against her mouth.

"You need to conserve your energy." A knock at the door had her jumping out of bed and jogging to answer it in tiny shorts and a white tank top.

I launched myself out of bed before I realised I really

didn't have the energy to do it. She made it halfway across the room before I managed to throw a robe around her. "You are far too sexy to be answering the door dressed like that."

"Are you going all caveman on me, Mr Ashlar?" she asked, reluctantly tying the robe.

"This body is for my eyes only." I kissed her neck, feeling her shiver when my lips touched her skin. I wanted to affect her always and looked forward to the post-fight celebration, which only included her being naked beneath me.

Juliette had ordered almost everything on the menu, and I managed to fuel up my body as much as I dared.

"So I was thinking we could do something together today," I said, leaning back in my chair.

"What did you have in mind?"

"Something to keep my mind off tonight. I've done some Googling."

"Oh god." She laughed, putting her hands over her face. "Most romantic date in Perth by any chance?"

"Where to take a sassy princess, actually."

She narrowed her eyes but smiled. "You did not."

"Do you want to know what we're doing or not?"

"Tell me, Casanova."

"Cottesloe Beach." I glanced at my watch. "We don't have a whole lot of time, as I have to be back for my training session, but we've got a few hours to relax."

She stood up, walked around the table, and climbed into my lap. Wrapping her arms around my neck, she kissed me lightly. "Sounds perfect. Thank God it's not swimming weather, because I'm a little scared of sharks."

"Juliette Salinger—adrenaline junkie. I thought swimming with sharks would be right up your alley."

"Nope." She shuddered. "We don't belong in their territory. We deserve to be eaten."

I laughed. "I'd rather not be anyone's dinner, but no fear of that today. Google recommended Il Gelato for the best ice cream along the beachfront, so that might make it worth your while?"

"Now you're talking my language."

"I remember you practically inhaling the ice cream at the St Kilda pier on our first date."

She smiled, but it didn't reach her eyes.

"What's wrong?"

"I was just thinking about how quickly things deteriorated between us when everything seemed so perfect. It scares me." She bit her bottom lip and couldn't look me in the eye. "I'm scared of losing you again."

I lifted her chin. "So you're scared of sharks and losing me, huh?"

"Mostly the second."

"How about this? When we do go swimming together at the beach in the summer, if a shark tries to get you, I'll offer myself up as a tasty alternative."

"That doesn't work out too well for my bigger fear, does it?" Her soft giggle was music to my ears.

I met her eyes and spoke directly from my heart. "You don't have to be scared about losing me." I brushed her cheek with the back of my hand. "I'm not going anywhere."

"Let's go to the beach."

Cottesloe Beach was less than a ten-minute drive from our hotel. As promised, I bought her a gelato and we walked along the beach hand in hand, stopping briefly to admire the impressive Indiana Teahouse.

We walked in comfortable silence for several minutes.

"Does this feel like the calm before the storm to you?" she asked. "It's just so incredibly beautiful here, and it feels like we could just be a regular couple on holiday."

"We've never really been a regular couple though, have we?"

The sad look on her face made me regret asking the question.

"I guess not."

"Do you want regular?" I asked.

"Sometimes." Even after taking a moment to think it through, her admission gutted me. "Sometimes I yearn for a simpler life."

"What do you mean?"

She didn't speak immediately. She appeared deep in thought, and my jaw clenched. "I spent some time in a rural village in France." She paused. "All the villagers were so welcoming and kind. There was a real community spirit, and I felt so incredibly welcome." She stopped and stared out at the Indian Ocean, breathing in the salty air. "I felt peaceful. I felt a contentment I don't think I'd ever felt before."

"Are you planning on upping and moving to France on me?"

She shook her head. "Australia is my home." She paused briefly. "My life just feels too complicated sometimes, and I wonder if I'm doing it all wrong."

"It'll work out, Jules." I stared at the ocean. I wished we could've stayed to watch the sun set. "We just need to keep moving forward."

She squeezed my hand and moved closer to my side. "I went back to work this week."

"Oh, right. Of course." The change of subject threw me for a second. "Was it good to be back?"

"It was okay, I guess. Sia's staying in England with a

guy she met over there." She scrunched up her nose. "I miss her."

"Did you consider staying over there with her?"

She looked at me and smiled. "I did really love it, and I hope to do a lot more travelling, but no." I could see her shoulders rise with tension. "It felt like running away, and I didn't want to be the girl who ran."

She must've seen the disappointment on my face as she placed her hands on either side of it. "My heart never left you, Leo."

With no further thought, I kissed her, holding her close to my body where she belonged. When I pulled back, I looked her in the eye. "You are strong and beautiful with the world at your feet." For a long time, we stood side by side, holding hands and staring out to sea. "I believe in you, Jules."

"I believe in me, too, and I believe in us."

"Come on." I took her hand, and we continued along the beachfront.

"Can I tell you something random?" she asked.

I chuckled. "Of course you can."

"So, I was in London. Sia was spending the day with the guy she met, so I thought I'd do some touristy things."

"No shortage of touristy things in London."

"That's for sure. Anyway, I came out of the Oxford Circus tube station and was confronted by the busy intersection." She waved her hand around. "Cars and people going in every direction. Horns blaring, kids crying, buskers at every corner."

"Sounds... noisy."

"It was. I'll get to my point." She stopped and turned to face me. "I stood at that intersection for ages, not having a clue which road to take. I mean, it didn't really matter. I had nowhere I had to be, but it made me stop and think about my life back here."

"A busy intersection made you think about your life? Did you come to any conclusions?" I asked.

"Do you ever feel like you're at a crossroads somehow and you don't know which direction to go in?"

I tilted her chin up. "Every decision we ever make has other options, other consequences and other possibilities." I broke eye contact and stared out at the blue ocean. "I don't think there are right and wrong choices. There's just ways of dealing with the road you take."

She leaned against my arm. "That's pretty much the conclusion I came to, surrounded by strangers twelve thousand miles from home." She wrapped her arms around my waist. "I came home to fight for the life I'd already chosen the day our lives collided."

"It was torture being away from you for so long," I admitted. "I just told myself you'd come home to me, and when you did, I'd never let you go again.

"Didn't anticipate the Dartmoor bomb though, did you?"

I stared at the ground. "Nope."

"I haven't had a chance to apologise on behalf of my mother about that. I'm really sorry she set you up like that."

I nodded. "Me too, Jules. Me too." I put my arm around her shoulders, and we started walking again. "Tell me more about your travels." I was eager to hear all about it and keen to change the subject. "Did you meet anyone other than the welcoming French villagers on your travels?" She paused, and when I looked at her, she was biting her bottom lip. *Oh God.* "Jules?"

"We made a few friends." She was really struggling with whether to tell me this story or not, and I wasn't sure I wanted to hear it. "Sia took a real shine to one of them, and she stayed in London with him."

"Okay," I said slowly. "And what about you?" I was a masochist.

Her beautiful navy eyes demanded my attention. "As I told you, my heart never left yours."

I got the feeling there was more to that story, but it wasn't the right time to dig any further. I needed to relax and then focus.

Before heading back to the hotel, we grabbed a light lunch of fish and chips and sat at one of the tables on the grassy area beside the beach. Whatever storm was brewing, we got to enjoy that lunch together in one of the most beautiful locations in the world.

When we got back to the hotel, Nick was in the lobby on the phone. I swear he had that thing permanently attached to his ear. When he saw us, he ended his call.

"How are you feeling?" Nick asked.

"Fighting fit," I responded immediately.

"Good to hear." Nick was all business now. "Meet me in the gym in ten minutes."

Whether it was true or not about how I felt, I knew I had to get in the right mindset.

"I think I'll head into the city if you don't need me for anything?" Juliette said casually.

"Will you be okay on your own?" I asked before I realised how condescending I sounded.

She gave me a look that said *really?* Smiling, she stood on her tiptoes and kissed me. I didn't want her to go, but Nick's loud throat clearing forced us apart.

"Don't forget," she said. "Cowards never start, the weak never finish and winners never quit." She walked backward a few steps, maintaining our intense connection before turning and heading back out the front doors. I couldn't take my eyes off her until she disappeared out of view.

"Gym. Ten minutes," Nick repeated when I hadn't moved from my spot a few moments later.

"Got it." I headed back to the room and got ready for my last-ditch attempt to prepare for whatever tonight would bring.

Jules was still out when I returned to the room a few hours later. Nick had put me through my paces but kept it a lot lighter than he would've under normal circumstances. It was more about him testing my limits and assessing my capabilities than anything else.

"I missed you." I sat up in bed as she walked through the door a short while later.

She sat down next to me and let me kiss her passionately. "I missed you, too." She smiled against my lips. "How was your training? Are you ready?"

"Not really. I'm nowhere near where I should be, but I'm not one to back down from a challenge." I was trying desperately to stay positive. "How was your afternoon in the city?"

"Pretty fabulous, actually. I think we should come back to Western Australia sometime for a holiday."

"You don't think this is a holiday?" I asked, smirking.

"Watching you kill yourself for a dumb fight?" She cocked her head. "Worst holiday ever." She punched me lightly on the arm.

CHAPTER 11

LEO

AS THE TIME TO LEAVE for the stadium approached, Juliette became increasingly nervous and jittery. To stop her pacing, I took her in my arms, holding her head against my chest. "I've got this, Jules. I've even got my lucky socks on. Don't worry about me."

She looked up at me. "I do worry. I can't help it."

I took her face in my hands. "I need this, Jules. I know you don't understand, but I can't explain it any better."

She swallowed hard, doing her best to give me a reassuring smile. "Okay."

"Okay," I repeated. "Pete has organised for you to sit in the VIP section, and I'll meet you straight after the fight."

I kissed her hard and felt her body melt into mine. Imagining the male-dominated crowd ogling her, I felt a territorial pang spike through me. I saw the way men looked at her like she was a menu item. It pissed me off and made me want to smash their faces in, but Juliette coming to Perth hadn't been a mistake. I'd never been the jealous type until I met her, probably because I'd never cared about anyone before—including myself.

When I was with her, I wanted to be more, fight harder, love her with every fibre of my being and kill anyone who got in my way of achieving all those things. Juliette was my Achilles' heel, and I would gladly die for her. I was also glad to have a bloody big desert between her and my mother.

∿∿∿∿

Nick and I parted ways with Jules at the stadium. Pete met us in the foyer and escorted her to her seat. The impact of what I was about to do was crippling. The decision to fight had been made on a whim at a time when I hadn't been thinking clearly. I was nowhere near ready for this fight, and every inch of my tortured body was screaming in protest as I geared up for the fight of my life.

"Where did you just go? Focus, Leo." Nick's exasperated voice snapped me out of my pathetic musings. "You're a dead man walking if you keep this shit up."

"I'm good." I shook my head and arms in a feeble attempt to refocus. "Sorry, Coach."

"Remember what I told you about Lucas. He's quick and strong, but he's interested in pleasing his hometown crowd." He slapped his hands down on my shoulders. "That's your only real advantage, I'm afraid."

"Thanks."

"I'm serious, Leo. You're all over the place. Mistreating your body doesn't just affect your fighting strength; it affects your ability to focus. Your edge has always been your ability to outsmart your opponent." He tapped the side of his head. "Use that oversized brain of yours and dig deeper than ever before."

"Show ponies make it too easy for me. I'm good, Nick."

"This isn't the cage. Remember our fight plan."

"I told you, I've got this."

I was wearing black satin shorts with a matching hooded robe. The music noise level dropped, and the MC announced me. "Let's give a big welcome to 'Lethal' Leo Ashlar."

Rock music blared through the speakers as I jogged down the aisle to a mixture of applause and light abuse. Compared to the illegal fight clubs, this place was a kindergarten. They had no idea who I was, what I was capable of or the rage I could tap into just below the surface. I was no scalp and I was about to prove it.

The crowd went completely mental for the local hero. I'd been brought over as a spectacle, but Lucas's smug demeanour as he climbed into the ring made me more determined than ever to ruin that plan. I enjoyed winning, but fighting had a very specific enticement for me, and it wasn't just about the end result. I relished the mind game and the sweet sensation of blindsiding my opponent. Fighting in any arena was as intricate as a chess game. Every move was calculated—a hook, uppercut, block or jab—all designed to take another piece from my opponent. In the end, only one will reign supreme—and little did the Perth crowd know, I was the king.

"Eight rounds is going to be a marathon in your condition, so make sure you stick to our plan, okay?" demanded Nick. "Wait for him to attack, counter strike, and then move off." Nick pushed my mouthguard in. "Listen to my instructions and don't get carried away. You are not anywhere near your full strength, and you need to be smart. You need to listen to me. We both know you shouldn't be here. Don't be a hero out there."

I nodded before turning to face my pawn.

Adrenaline kicked in. The hairs on my arms stood up,

and my feet felt lighter. This was my moment, and all other thoughts left my head. This was what I craved. This was my oblivion.

Lucas bounced around his side, and I felt his eyes studying me. That always indicated a smart fighter, and my eyes narrowed. I would give him nothing predictable. He would've gleaned little from meeting me at the weigh-in, and he only had my one recent fight to go by. I might have been weaker than I would've liked, but I was formidable when I was in the zone.

Lucas threw the first punch: an obvious right hook I had no problem dodging. I was only vaguely aware of the crowd erupting before they fell away. I waited for the split second his weight was on his back foot to slam my gloved fist into the side of his head before moving off quickly. As expected, he toppled backward, caught off balance. He righted himself and closed the distance quickly. I knew he was about to go for a combination. He was rattled. I'd taken his knight, and I was about to take his castle.

Nick and I had agreed on a strategy whereby he would make the defensive and offensive calls as the fight played out. I would be too close to my opponent and wouldn't have the same perspective as Nick in the corner. In my current physical state, I had to concede my ability to make instinctual decisions was compromised.

Lucas attacked, and I countered and then moved off. I was holding my own and preserving some of the precious energy I had to work with. The first four rounds were fairly uneventful, and the crowd no doubt felt a little ripped off. I had to force myself to remain present a lot of the time as my mind drifted away. *Get your shit together,* I mentally chastised myself.

"You're doing okay, Leo," Nick said as he pulled out my mouthguard and towelled me off at the end of the fourth. "Your hits were cleaner, but you are tiring."

I nodded, wincing when he dabbed at a small cut above my eyebrow.

When the bell rang, I moved back into the ring. I was feeling the heavy toll on my body, and doubt started to infiltrate my psyche. I pushed it away, angry at myself, but the next couple of rounds, I couldn't deny he was starting to dominate. His body appeared to blur, and I had to narrow my eyes to focus. I wasn't anticipating his moves, and much to my horror, he was anticipating mine.

"Are you still sure about the plan, Nick?" I asked, as he towelled me off. "I need the knockout."

"I'll call offensive when I see fit. You're holding up, but I'm not sure you have the reserves for it."

"I can do it. I can take down this little fucker."

He waited 'til I looked him in the eye. "You have to trust me, Leo."

I nodded but couldn't make eye contact. I barely trusted myself at that point, but I ran my own race and made my own decisions.

The bell rang for the second-to-last round. I blocked out everyone and everything other than the other player in my game. He was about to go down, and I relished the shot of adrenaline that would take away the pain.

The knockout was all about the timing. I needed to focus everything I had on one powerful, he-can't-come-back-from-this blow. I let him do his little dance a while longer. Then I drew him towards me by lowering my gloves for a split second. He would see it as a sign of fatigue and get himself ready for the kill. He was pumped up on ego, and I was about to capitalise.

The next ten seconds happened in slow motion. With adrenaline coursing through my veins, I recoiled my arm, sending every cell of my body into high alert. I slammed my fist into him with all the force I could muster, then closed my eyes briefly from pure exhaustion, relieved this nightmare was over.

Regaining my composure, I looked out into the crowd. *Get ready for disappointment,* I thought to myself. My eyes found Juliette's and her expression wasn't what I was expecting. She looked nervous and had her hands over her face.

I felt the impact, my knees hit the canvas and then my world went black for a split second. I was on all fours, and the referee had started the countdown. *Fuck!* I pushed off my gloves and struggled to my feet.

Suddenly, I could hear Nick's angry voice above the crowd's roar, and I made a quick sweep of the ring in complete disbelief. My arrogance had definitely cost me the round. If Lucas's hit had been cleaner, he could've knocked *me* out. I glanced at Nick and he gave me the death stare that said, *Pull your head in, you fucking idiot.*

"What the fuck was that?" Nick seethed as he removed my mouthguard at the end of the round.

"I needed to take him down." My nonchalant reply enraged him, and his face went from flushed to beetroot in seconds.

"A blind man could see you didn't have the strength to take him out, you arrogant son of a bitch."

"Interesting choice of words," I snapped.

Nick just shook his head as I took a seat on the stool in the corner, a towel wrapped around my neck.

"I've got this."

"Don't be so sure. You are not the clear winner, and there are two local judges to one interstate."

Lucas was bouncing on the spot with his gloves in front of his face, clearly enjoying the moment in the sun. Rage coursed through me, and I wanted to flatten him.

"Stay back." Nick's instruction was said with such blatant venom, I reigned myself in.

Lucas tried to get more blows in, and I managed to hold him off and get a few in of my own. I was fighting for my life, and I could still win. One setback would hand the win to Lucas. I dug deeper than ever before and gave that little fucker the very best of me.

When the final bell rang, the crowd went wild. Granted, it wasn't clear cut, but I was confident I'd still done enough to take the win.

Much to my horror, Lucas was declared the winner on a split decision two points to one.

Check mate.

When we returned to the change rooms, I paced in front of my locker. "Pete's a fucking snake."

Nick stood in the middle of the room with his arms crossed over his chest. "Pull your head in. It was close, and yes, you probably should've won, but the result wasn't unfair. If you'd listened to me, I could've gotten you the knockout at the right time. Lucas was tiring quickly. He was getting sloppy, but he was still okay when you went rogue."

I felt the ugly pang of shame.

"You scared me, Leo." Juliette pushed her palms against my chest when she was let into my private change room. "You told me not to worry, then you go and nearly get knocked out." She was trying so hard to be nice to me, and it just pissed me off. Reality started to inject itself back into my brain as I tried to process. I had been in a fight I was supposed to win. But I hadn't won. I'd lost. I'd fucking lost. *Fuck!*

I sat down on the bench. "I'm sorry." My voice sounded cold and harsh. I'd deserved to lose. I would've deserved for my face to meet the canvas with a powerful thud. It was dumb luck that Lucas hadn't knocked me out.

"What are you apologising for?" She sounded confused and edgy.

I shook my head, breaking eye contact with her. "Nothing. I'd just like to be alone for a bit."

She didn't say anything, and eventually I looked up from my hands that I was unwrapping. We looked at each other and neither of us spoke. Her expression was unreadable, and I felt like a dead-end fuck-up. I certainly wasn't proving her mother wrong. In fact, if she could see me now, I think she'd probably be thrilled.

Juliette couldn't belong to me any more than I could belong to her. I wasn't worthy and she was worth too much.

"Stop." I snapped my head up to Juliette holding her hands up in a firm demand. "What are you doing, Leo?"

I didn't answer because I didn't have an answer. I had no idea what I was doing.

She squatted down in front of me and placed her hands over mine. "You freaked out seeing your mum, you agreed to a fight you shouldn't have and you lost. Get over it."

"Get over it?"

"Yes. Shit happens. Get over it."

"Shit happens?"

"Are you going to repeat everything I say?"

I pulled my hands from hers and stood up, walking over to my locker. Rage overtook me, and I slammed my hand against the metal door five times in quick succession. "Shit doesn't just happen, Juliette. People *make* shit happen."

"Why won't you tell me what is really going on?"

I turned around, expecting to see fear in her eyes from my sudden outburst, but instead she was standing tall, her shoulders back and her eyes intense.

"Do you really want to know?" I asked, stalking back to her. "Do you really want to know why I'm a complete fuck-up?"

She closed the distance I had put between us. "You're not a fuck-up, Leo. I don't know why you'd think that. One loss in a stupid, unfair fight doesn't make you a fuck-up." Her voice softened and her eyes filled with tears. "You're the best person I know. Please don't push me away now."

"I'm not good for you," I whispered.

"Says who? Certainly not me, and the only other opinion that matters is yours, and I don't think you believe that. I think you're scared to trust me because you don't fully trust anyone, including yourself. And I'm pretty sure it has a whole lot to do with your mother."

My body stiffened. "I can't do this now." I sat down in front of my locker and buried my face in my hands. I looked up to see her shaking her head. "Go back to the hotel, Jules."

She closed her eyes and exhaled before opening them. "Fine. Have your little pity party. I'm sick of your cryptic bullshit. I know you want to love me. You have to trust me to look after your heart, or we have no chance."

I stared at the space where she was standing long after she had disappeared from the room, trying to process her words. *I know you want to love me* was on constant loop in my head.

CHAPTER 12

Juliette

WATCHING LEO IN THE BOXING ring had been impressive, but... well, it had been disappointing. I knew he could have ended Lucas Albright in a New York minute had he been at full strength. As it was, he appeared lethargic. In the cage, his movements had appeared effortless and instinctual, but tonight, it was almost too hard to watch. To his credit, he still put up a good fight, and if Lucas hadn't had the hometown advantage, Leo actually could've claimed victory. Leo had needed to be the clear winner, and he clearly hadn't been. I was devastated for him, but it had been pretty fucked up thinking he could beat a local champion in his state. His behaviour after the fight had made me think he knew it, too.

Leo had pissed me off, and I was relieved to have a quiet taxi ride back to the hotel. Rather than heading straight to the room, I ducked into the hotel bar and ordered a gin and tonic. Gin wasn't necessarily the best idea, but it was exactly what I felt like.

"Rough night?" the bartender asked as he placed my

drink down in front of me.

I smiled. "You could say that."

"Did you know bartenders are some of the best listeners in the world?" I didn't get the feeling he was flirting with me. With the bar almost empty, I think he might've just been bored.

"Not all bartenders," I mumbled.

"Do you want to tell me about your night?" He leaned his hip against the bar as he dried the glasses.

I scrunched up my nose. "Well, let's see." I let out a long breath and thought back over not just tonight's fight, but the last year. I drew in another breath, then started to ramble out my exhale. "My mother just got out of a looney bin. My ex-boyfriend's a gold-digging douche bag and had an affair with my mother. My current boyfriend just lost his first fight ever tonight and is having a big sook, and surprise, surprise..." I threw my hands in the air. "He doesn't want to talk to me about it." My bartender friend's eyes were wide as saucers, and he was no longer wiping the glasses.

Wow, he mouthed.

"Oh, it doesn't end there." I downed the rest of my drink in one go and watched as it was refilled without me asking.

"On the house."

"Thanks." I picked up the glass and took a quick sip.

"So there's more?"

"My boyfriend told me his mum was dead but turns out she's not, and it's sent him into some kind of tailspin and I feel like I'm standing on quicksand."

"Quicksand, huh?"

"Yep." I took another swig of my drink, then looked up to see my new friend looking over my shoulder with raised eyebrows.

I swung round to see a very intimidating Leo standing right behind me. His eyes were dark, and I could see the blood pulsing through the vein in his forehead.

Rather than continue to face him, I swung back to the bar. My friend appeared casual and unfazed by the sight of a beaten and bruised Leo. I guess he'd probably seen it all from that side of the bar.

I felt Leo move up next to me at the bar, and I shivered when his forearm touched mine. He took my hand in his. "Come with me."

His grip was firm, but his touch was gentle and I could never resist his touch. I slid off my barstool and allowed Leo to lead me over to one of the comfortable-looking lounges in the far corner of the bar.

"I got back to our room and you weren't there."

"Hope you're not looking for an apology," I replied indignantly.

He ran his hands through his hair and clenched his jaw. "I'm not. I came to give you one." Picking up my hand, he ran his thumb over my knuckles. "The second you left, I knew I'd done the one thing you asked me not to do, and I'm sorry."

"It pissed me off, Leo."

"I know." He shook his head. "I fucked up in the ring, too. I managed to piss off you and Nick all in one night."

"What happened out there?"

He looked me in the eye. "I was wrong." He shook his head, breaking our eye contact. "Simple as that."

I took both his hands in mine and waited for him to look at me again. "Do you trust me?"

"I trust you more than anyone else."

"When we get back to Melbourne, I'm going to need you to tell me what happened five years ago."

"Why?" His eyes were more pleading than

demanding. "Why do you want me to dredge up the past when we're trying to move forward with our lives?"

"Because your past that you've tried so hard to keep hidden turned up alive and well at the looney bin, and your knee-jerk reaction was to nearly kill yourself." I raised my eyebrows. "In a nutshell."

Leo closed his eyes briefly, and several minutes passed in silence. I could almost see the cogs of his brain spinning out of control. Eventually he met my gaze. "I've never talked to anyone about it before."

It had been a really long and emotional day, and I was ready to go back to our room. "Come on, 'Lethal' Leo Ashlar, let's go." I stood up and held out my hand for him.

I knew I was breaking through to him one small step at a time, and I'd keep fighting until I broke through completely. He was worth it and so was I.

When he opened the door to our room and held it open for me, I felt the electricity crackling between us. He had to be exhausted from the fight and his physically demanding week, but something told me we wouldn't be going to sleep anytime soon. As if reading my mind, he slammed me up against the wall and kissed me hard. There was nothing sweet or tender about that kiss, but it was one of the greatest kisses of my life to date. I felt consumed, hungered for and wrapped up warmly in the promises he intended to keep. Our kisses felt like the glue that bound us together, and every single one was another beautiful moment in the story of us. We were drifting souls finding an anchor in each other. Lies and hidden truths were our stormy seas, and I sensed calm waters ahead, just beyond the horizon.

Leo's hands were everywhere, touching me urgently. "I want you so bad." He groaned the words against my lips.

"I'm already yours," I panted.

My words were barely out when I was scooped off the floor and rushed across the room, past the bed and into the bathroom. He lowered me to the floor slowly to let me feel his hardness against my body. I was already high on lust and expectation, and that just about pushed me over the edge.

"Get naked," he demanded as he turned the shower on. "We're gonna try this again." It was not a polite request. It was an absolute demand said by a man who was going to take what was his. I loved the tender and vulnerable side of Leo, but the demanding alpha Leo was so damn sexy, and my clothes melted off my body of their own volition.

I knew this was in no way about getting clean. In fact, I was hoping we were about to get dirty. He raked his eyes up and down my body shamelessly, while the ultimate proof of his lust strained against his taut stomach. Every part of him called my name, from his muscular arms to his tight arse just asking to be grabbed, but I couldn't focus on anything for long when he stepped into the shower and beckoned me to follow.

His hand made its way behind my neck, and I was pulled to him. His lips crashed down over mine, claiming what was already his. I opened my mouth, and his tongue instantly found mine.

We were two souls reconnecting. Two souls remembering. Two souls belonging.

He pushed me backward under the warm spray, and I tilted my head back to enjoy its therapy. Leo's lips immediately found my neck while his hands roamed my back, always pulling me closer.

His magic hands found my breasts and kneaded them with the expertise of a man who knew exactly what turned me on. I leaned back against the cold, tiled wall of the expansive shower cubicle and was granted the luxury of Leo's mouth where his hands had just been. I lifted my left leg and wrapped it around him, willing his erection to grind me harder.

"You are so fucking gorgeous, Jules."

I gasped. "I need you to fuck me."

His hands smoothed their way down my back and cupped my backside, lifting me easily, the way he'd intended the night before. When he looked me in the eye, he would've no doubt seen my absolute desperation for him. I would never want any man the way I wanted Leo Ashlar.

"My pleasure." With those two words, he thrust into me in one fluid motion. We were together in every sense of the word, and I revelled in the fireworks that exploded around us. The outside world had no business in that bathroom, in that hotel or in our lives. The feeling of having him deep inside me, holding me as if I were the only other person on the planet, was the single most intense and liberating feeling I could imagine.

"I love..." He paused. "I love fucking you."

The mounting pressure circulated my body in escalating waves. "Harder, Leo. Fuck me harder." I could barely grunt out the words as he pounded me faster, gaining more depth. I was probably going to have bruises down my back from being slammed into the wall, but I didn't care. The water cascaded over our joined bodies, and I was soaring closer and closer to the cliff's edge. I wanted to jump off more than I wanted to breathe.

The slow burn was intoxicating, and I was addicted.

"Come for me, baby." Leo groaned the words out, then sucked my nipple into his mouth, shooting desire right through my quivering body.

"Leo," I screamed as the peak emerged, and I threw

myself into the darkness without a second's thought. "Leo." I repeated his name as I soared through my own personal ecstasy, flying on the wings of love and exceeded expectations. I was owned by one man and one man alone. There was this and there was everything else. I wanted this.

Leo gripped me tighter as he grunted out his own long release into my neck. "I need you." The words were muffled by the water but clear enough for me to absorb their weight.

We stayed there, joined together in the aftermath of incredible sex until the water started to cool.

"That was incredible," Leo whispered into my ear as he took his time drying me.

"It was." I smiled at him when our eyes met. "Incredible."

"Let's go to bed." He took my hand and led me back into the bedroom.

"You must be completely shattered." I caught him yawning as we pulled back the covers.

We climbed into bed and entwined ourselves around each other. With our faces an inch apart, I gazed into his beautiful blue eyes. "You scared me today, Leo."

"I'm sorry." He placed his hand gently on my face. "I never want that. Ever."

I watched his eyes close and his body relax. He was asleep in seconds, succumbed to the exhaustion I knew must've been right there waiting for the moment to claim him.

I kissed him three times, finding it hard to stop reminding his body of my touch. I wanted to make an indelible print on him so he knew we were forever.

CHAPTER 13

"SIT DOWN," NICK SAID, SKIPPING any pleasantries.

He'd asked for a private word before we flew home, so I'd agreed to meet him in the hotel restaurant for coffee the next morning. Juliette told me she'd order room service and pack our bags while I was gone.

I sat down opposite him and leaned back in my chair. Perhaps I was subconsciously maximising the distance between myself and the inevitable rant. When he didn't say anything, I decided I should start by apologising.

"Sorry for wasting your time, Nick. I don't—"

He held up his hand. "Stop. I'm not here to give you a bollocking. I'm sure you've done a good enough job of that yourself."

"Then what did you want to talk to me about?"

"I want your commitment."

"Okay." I was completely confused.

"If you're interested, I want to help you take it all the way, but I need your commitment." He sat forward and rested his elbows on the table. "The apartment above the fight club is empty, and it's all yours if you want it. I could give you a job training the young boxers, too, in exchange for rent if that's something you think you might be interested in."

"What?" I sat forward, blindsided by his offer. "Are you serious?"

"Deadly."

"But I fucked up last night. I don't get why you would want to train me again or offer me a job."

"You're a better fighter now in a lot of ways. Your Muay Thai training has made you a fighting machine. Pete Sanders might be an arsehole, but he knew he'd get a helluva fight from you, even though the weight loss would make it almost impossible for you to win."

I shook my head. "I wanted to prove him wrong so bad."

He tapped the side of his head. "Your mind was all over the place. Even though I was pissed you didn't listen to me, it was an unbelievable feat what you did out there."

Silence hung between us for a few moments.

"Can I think about it?"

"Juliette told me you saw your mother."

My eyes snapped up to meet his. I gritted my teeth but couldn't say anything.

"Are you going to reconnect with her?" He appeared hesitant, as if he knew he was leaning over the edge of the cliff and I might just push him off.

"Nope."

He nodded. "Okay."

I cracked my knuckles under the table. "You got a problem with that?"

"Nope."

"Good talk."

"Look, mate. I think you can go all the way, but you need to make sure you leave the past in the past."

"Have you really thought through having me back in Lilydale more often? Your wife was friends with my mother," I said. "Most of them hate me for cutting her off."

Nick scrunched up his nose. "I guess I didn't tell you about that."

"What?" I asked.

"Karen and I are divorced."

"Oh god. Sorry, man. When?"

"A while now. Said I was married to the club and my fighters."

I took a sip of my coffee and smirked. "You are kind of intense."

"Only way to be. My fighters get one hundred percent from me because I coach, manage and promote. It's not an easy job to do everything, but it's best for my fighters and that's my priority." He appeared genuinely content with his choices, but I couldn't imagine ever being happy about Juliette being out of my life. I wanted more from my life, but it wouldn't mean much without her in it.

Nick glanced at his watch. "Come on. It's time to check out and head to the airport. Is Jules coming down?"

"She might be out there already. Let's go."

As we walked out, Nick patted me on the back. "Think about my offer. I really think it's time."

CHAPTER 14

Juliette

WHEN THEY EMERGED FROM THE restaurant into the lobby, Nick headed for the front desk and Leo headed towards me. Good god, he was handsome. I wasn't sure I'd ever get used to the way my body reacted to his overwhelming presence. His grey t-shirt clung to broad shoulders and bulging biceps while his navy board shorts hung perfectly on his lean waist. I tried not to be too obvious in my ogling, but I failed dismally given the smirk on Leo's face when I raised my eyes to his.

"Hey," I said when he got closer.

Leo wrapped his arms around me, squeezing the air out of my lungs in a move I was unprepared for. "Hey, beautiful," he whispered in my ear.

"Leo," I croaked. "Struggling to breathe here."

He released me immediately. "Sorry."

"Everything okay?" I asked. I was worried Nick was going to tear him to shreds.

"Everything will be okay, Jules." He bit his bottom lip and glanced at Nick, who was approaching us. "Let's go home."

We checked out and were returned to the airport by the same driver who'd picked us up. I gave up trying to lighten the mood. Both Leo and Nick appeared to be deep in thought, so I put my earbuds in when we found our seats on the plane and selected Rob Thomas' solo album *Something to Be* as my in-flight entertainment. With "Street Corner Symphony" playing in my ears, I even managed to drift off to sleep. It was Sunday afternoon by the time we landed in Melbourne, and we'd parted ways with Nick. Words I couldn't hear were exchanged before they shook hands and Nick headed to the carpark. He'd offered to drive us home, but we'd insisted we'd get a cab.

Leo held my hand during our half-hour cab ride into the city, but he seemed a million miles away. It had been drizzling when we landed, but the rain was falling harder now, blurring the view and fogging the windows.

"So Nick wasn't too pissed about the fight?" I asked as we crossed the Yarra River. We were almost back to my apartment, and I didn't have a clue where his head was at.

Leo shook his head, appearing to shake out the thoughts. "Oh... he wasn't happy with me, but I didn't get the bollocking I was expecting."

"Well, it's over now. We can just get on with our lives." I squeezed his hand.

He leaned over and whispered in my ear. "I can't wait to get you naked."

His words shot desire straight between my legs, and I smiled at the visuals bombarding my mind.

A text message from my father interrupted our plan.

See you at seven-fifteen for dinner.

"Ugh. I totally forgot." I cringed. "I agreed to have dinner at my parents' place tonight." I looked at him sheepishly. "Don't suppose you want to come?"

"Seriously?" He cocked his head.

I nodded. "Sorry. Of course you don't. Why would you?"

The cab pulled up outside my apartment, and Leo asked the driver to wait. We both got out, and I dashed for cover from the rain while Leo retrieved my bags.

"I'm sorry, Jules," he said when he joined me under the awning. "I know she's your mum, but I'm not ready to forgive her for what she did to me, but more importantly to you."

I hated what my mother had done and completely understood Leo's stance, but I'd agreed to hear Dad out and then I'd get the hell out of there. I'd made the commitment and I'd stand by it. "I understand. I honestly do." I placed my hand on his face and looked him in the eye. "My family is no picnic, but at least I'm facing it head-on."

"You have a forgiving heart, Juliette Salinger. I'm grateful for that because you forgave me for how badly I handled everything before you went away. How could I stand by and judge you for forgiving your mum when I've benefited from your forgiveness, too?"

"Your mother showed up at my work last week," I blurted it out. I didn't know why exactly I'd chosen that moment to tell him, but it was weighing on me.

Leo tensed. "I know."

I took a step back. "You do?"

He nodded. "She told me."

"So that's why you wanted me to go to Perth?" I asked, annoyed. "You were afraid I'd go against your wishes to stay away from her? She has texted me constantly since then, and I've deleted every message. I'm waiting for you to tell me. I don't want to hear it from her."

"Fuck, Juliette. I don't want you having anything to do with her. Why didn't you tell me she's been harassing you?"

I flew to my own defence. "When exactly? You bolted out of Dartmoor like it was on fire, then you refused to talk to me until I was railroaded into the crazy Perth trip. I didn't want to bring it up over there while you were already in a shitty place and didn't need the distraction. After the fight, you flipped out at me and then were too exhausted to talk. So really, Leo." I had my hands on my hips now. "Tell me when I should've brought it up?"

He shuddered and I felt bad for my rant, but it was true. There'd been no good opportunity to raise the subject without causing more damage.

He couldn't look me in the eye, and I was pretty sure he was grinding his teeth like a madman. "You're right." He pulled his cap off and ran his hand through his hair. "I'm wrecked, Jules. I'm gonna get going, but please tell me if she makes contact again."

"I won't be late tonight." I felt sick about his reaction to my confession. "I'll call you when I'm done, okay?"

"Sure." He met my eyes. "I'll talk to you later." He kissed me on the cheek, then returned to the waiting cab. I was wracked with indecision as I watched him retreat. Had we left on bad terms? Was it always going to be like this? The questions swirled around in my head, and he'd gone before I could decide on any answers. Perhaps I'd never know all the answers.

When I walked into to my apartment, it felt like I'd been gone a lot longer than a couple of days. I thought about the rollercoaster I'd been on since returning from Europe and was thankful for the quiet reliability of George, my trusty coffee machine. Even though it was late afternoon and I didn't usually drink coffee after midday, I felt tired and needed a boost before heading to my parents.'

When I flicked the power button, I smiled hearing the melody of happy beeps.

Revived by the instant effects of caffeine, I went through the motions of unpacking, showering and getting dressed.

Going to my parents' house for dinner was the last thing on earth I felt like doing, but I had made the commitment. I'd considered pulling out, but I was curious about what Dad had to say.

My phone rang on the hands-free as I pulled out of my apartment building around seven, silencing the radio.

"Juliette. Hi. How are you? It's Gwendolyn."

My desire to hang up on her was great. This woman either had balls of steel, no ability to take a hint or was driven by desperation. Possibly a combination of the three, but she had to stop contacting me. "I can't talk to you behind Leo's back, Gwendolyn. I've told you this already."

"I... um... I was just wondering how—"

I could hear a desperation in her voice that tugged at my heart strings, but Leo was my priority.

"I'm sorry."

"Juliette. Listen to me. I—"

"I have to go." I cut her off. "I have dinner with my own crazy mother." I cringed. "I didn't mean you're crazy, too. I just meant... shit. I don't know what I meant."

"Be careful with your mother." Her tone changed, and it sent shivers down my spine. "She's unstable."

"Yeah, I kinda got that, but thanks for your diagnosis." I knew I sounded sarcastic, but I was ready for this conversation to be over. "I really have to go now."

"Please just tell him I need to meet with him?"

"Don't call me again." I ended the call and felt emotionally drained. I simply didn't know what the right thing was to do. Should I be trying to get them to talk and maybe resolve their differences? If I'd learned one thing from my experiences with my own mother, it was that interfering was a one-way ticket to nowhere.

I sat at the red light and peered through the windscreen at the people shuffling along the sidewalk, holding umbrellas. The windscreen wipers made them appear blurry, but they were just normal people getting on with their lives. I had no doubt they had their own issues. Everyone was dealing with something, and I never presumed anyone had it any worse than anyone else, but I was beginning to feel the walls closing in again. A horn beeping snapped me out of my daydream to see the light had changed to green. Glancing in my rear-view mirror, I saw a red Honda changing lanes to move out from behind me. I sat up straighter and pushed my shoulders back. The old Juliette would've craved an escape. But no more. I would face my life head-on, whatever it threw my way.

CHAPTER 15

LEO

I KNEW I SHOULDN'T HAVE just walked away from Juliette standing outside her apartment like that, but I needed to go before I said anything I might regret. She had done nothing wrong, and of course she'd be curious about my mother. Unfortunately, curiosity in this instance was dangerous. I needed to try to explain to her exactly what had happened when my world had completely imploded. I'd speak to her later, after she'd had dinner with her parents. I just needed to clear my head a little.

The trouble with living in a small apartment was feeling stir-crazy. Within ten minutes of being home, I couldn't escape my own thoughts. Coming face-to-face with my mother, the feelings of rage, reuniting with Juliette, losing my first fight after nearly killing myself through starvation and dehydration, Nick's job offer and knowing Jules was with her witch of a mother was all just too much.

I scrubbed my face with my hands and paced my living room. I needed to get out of there, and rather than clearing my mind, I was suddenly desperate to cloud it. I called the one person I knew would be up for a drink any night of the week.

I grabbed my wallet and keys and jogged down to meet Adam in the part of St Kilda tourists didn't regularly frequent. This was the bar I had practically lived in after my father died. I got a job there as a bouncer but quit when I couldn't control my urge to take out my grief on drunken idiots. It had felt way too good. Adam, aka Ginger Ninja, had approached me one night and told me about the illegal cage-fighting scene he was a part of. I had been like a moth to the flame.

Time seemed to stand still in that place, and it made no difference what night of the week it was, the customers and atmosphere were exactly the same— seedy and rough. I could still remember losing myself easily in the booze and bleary-eyed bodies. I had far too much on my mind and, like I had five years before, I made a beeline for the bar to rectify the situation as soon as possible.

I jostled amongst the bodies and elbowed my way to the bar. Maeve had been bartending at The Tavern for a while now, and she smiled when I caught her eye.

"What can I get you, Leo?"

"Tequila. Straight up."

She nodded her head and reached for the bottle and a shot glass.

"Tough night?"

"You could say that." I shuddered, attempting to push all thoughts from my mind and have a few hours off from my life. I picked up the shot glass and downed it quickly. I held up two fingers. "Thanks, sweetheart."

"Maeve," the guy I recognised as the bar manager called out across the bar. "We have other customers, you know."

She rolled her eyes and smiled at me. She was flirting and my body barely reacted. It felt wrong, but the tequila was relaxing my senses and I couldn't be bothered to walk away.

"It's good to see you, Leo." She batted her eyelashes. "It's been a while."

I downed my next two shots, then leaned forward on my elbows. Her breath hitched. "I've been busy."

"I'll have what he's having." I felt a strong hand slap me on the back, and I looked up to see the Ginger Ninja plonking himself down on the stool next to me. "You started without me?"

"Sorry, mate." I laughed. It was great to see him. "Was the wife okay with you ditching her on a Sunday night?"

"She has the girls over watching some reality TV shit." He groaned. "You did me a favour."

"Good to see you, Adam." I slapped him on the back and downed another shot.

"What's been going on, mate? We don't hear from you for the last few months. What's that about?"

I thought back to the last fight night I had attended when Jules had been attacked. "I've been thinking about going back to the regular ring."

"Really? Is it 'cause of the shit that went down when you took out Reaper?"

"Partly." I flinched as an image of the hooded fucker roughing up Jules on the other side of the cage flashed through my mind. "I don't want my girl there. I can't focus when I'm watching out for her in the crowd."

"You know there was some dickhead sniffing around here asking about you after that fight. I didn't give him shit, but I got a bad feeling. Tall, blonde, skinny fucker."

"He found me." The bastard had pointed a gun at me and threatened Jules.

I remembered seeing missed calls from Adam, but I'd checked out from that scene for a few months and wasn't sure I'd be going back.

"I'm taking a break now if you want to join me?" Maeve leaned over the bar, whispering seductively. "Meet me by the bathrooms."

"Sorry, darlin.'" I sat back. "I have a girlfriend."

I knew I'd flirted a little with her out of habit, but even in my increasingly-drunken state, I knew I was playing with fire and had no interest in her. She had warmed my bed many times, but there was no chance I was going anywhere with any girl other than Juliette.

"Well, I'll be damned." She shook her head and laughed as she refilled our shot glasses. "The untouchable Leo Ashlar has been tamed." When she finished pouring, she looked me in the eye. "Tequila will mess with your head, you know?"

"I'm banking on it." I held up my glass and downed it quickly, enjoying the burn as it washed down my throat.

When she walked away, Adam let out a long whistle. "If I wasn't married..."

CHAPTER 16

Juliette

WHEN I PULLED UP OUTSIDE my parents' home, I cleared my mind.

Walk in, be civil, brace for impact. Without the mask I'd always hidden behind, I had no clue how to tolerate my parents anymore. What I did know was that they'd taken too much from me, and this dinner was my final concession.

I glanced at the digital clock on the dash and saw it was seven twenty-three, eight minutes later than the time I was expected to arrive. I hadn't planned on being late, but I didn't mind in the slightest knowing I was.

"Nice of you to join us," my mother hissed when she opened the front door.

"Fashionably late." I grinned, knowing I was just antagonising the woman.

"There's nothing fashionable about it, Juliette, especially wearing that hideous bohemian top. Where on earth did you purchase that monstrosity?"

"Good to see you, too, Mother." I walked past her, determined to let her criticisms wash over me. I was stronger now and disinterested in her approval that I now knew was impossible to achieve anyway. "Where's Dad?"

"Your father is in the lounge room on his third drink, thanks to your tardiness."

I turned back, irritated. "I'm eight minutes late, Mother, and to be honest, I didn't want to come at all. Get a grip."

Without waiting for her response, I strode down the hallway to the lounge, knowing my mother was hot on my heels.

Dad was standing by the window, staring out at god knows what. There was nothing but the side fence as a view.

"Hey, Dad." When he didn't turn around, I cleared my throat and repeated myself. He snapped his head around and shook it as if he were coming out of a trance.

"Juliette." He crossed the room and gave me an uncharacteristically warm hug. "Thank you for coming."

I could smell the alcohol on his breath. "Sorry I'm late."

He waved me off, and I had to stop myself from chuckling. My dad was tipsy, something I'd never seen before.

"John." Mum's voice boomed with authority. "That's enough."

Dad glared at her and I felt incredibly awkward. I knew this had been a bad idea. Something was different. "Maybe we should have some dinner." I turned to Dad. "Maybe switch to water for a bit and eat something?"

He rolled his eyes. "I'm fine." He sauntered past both of us towards the kitchen.

"Mum. What's up with Dad?"

"He's behaving like a silly child." She raised her

eyebrows. "You might look more like me, but you definitely take after your father."

The old me would've felt belittled by that comment, but now I just took solace in the fact I didn't take after her.

Their housekeeper, Jean, had left a casserole in the oven for us, so it was easy enough to just dish out onto three plates and carry through to the dining room. Dad was sitting at his usual place, sipping mineral water.

"So, why am I here?" I asked when we were seated.

"I'm really relying on both of you to keep my stress levels to a minimum." Mum gave both my father and me equal serves of her condescending gaze. "Can I trust you with that small task?"

"Juliette." My father ignored her question and looked directly at me. "Before I get into why I called you here tonight, I wanted to tell you I have a new client I'm meeting with tomorrow, thanks to you. A very lucrative client."

"Really?" I had absolutely no idea who he could be talking about.

"Charlie Quinn? He said you met in Dublin and travelled extensively around Europe together."

"What?" I coughed and patted my chest, choking on a piece of meat.

"Son of Charles and Grier Quinn, one of Sydney's wealthiest families?" my mother asked, and I swore she licked her lips. She turned to me, her attention piqued. "Why didn't you tell me you met Charlie Quinn?"

"Mainly because what I do and who I meet are none of your business." I tried to keep my horror from my tone. I turned to Dad. "I had no idea he was here."

"The Quinn family would be an incredible coup for my firm."

I glanced at my mother, who looked like she might combust with excitement. "Will you be catching up with him, darling?"

"Oh my God, Mother." I shook my head in disgust. "Can you be any more obvious?"

"I'm just showing some interest in your friends, darling." She appeared affronted. "You don't have to be so rude."

"Oh, I know all about you showing 'interest' in my friends." I used air quotes to place emphasis on 'interest.' I wouldn't take comments like that lying down.

Bizarrely, my father tapped his fork on his empty wine glass and stood up. "Okay, ladies. I have a few things to say to the both of you." He looked at me. "Firstly, thank you for coming, Juliette. I know it's not where you want to be right now, so I want you to know I appreciate it."

I didn't disagree with him. I just nodded.

"What's all this about, John?" my mother asked.

He pushed his chair back, and his glasses slipped down his nose a little. He pushed them back up, then ran his hand through his thinning hair. "I want you both to know things are going to be different around here from now on." He glanced between my mother and me. "I know about Richard. I know about the blackmail. I know everything."

I dropped my knife and fork. The sound of clanging cutlery hitting my plate was deafening, even over the blood rushing past my ears.

I looked to Mum, and she appeared strangely composed. "I have no idea what you're talking about, John."

"Please, Isabel." He started circling the table. I suddenly felt like Mum and I were on trial. By all accounts, he was formidable in the courtroom and I was starting to see why. "Shhh." He held his finger up to his mouth and shook his head. "You don't get to speak now."

Mum huffed and puffed but didn't speak. Keeping the secret from my father had haunted me, and as it turned out, he already knew.

Dad stopped behind Mum's chair. "I ignored so many red flags for too long, and that's on me." He met my gaze and held up one finger. "The state your mother was in when you turned up here a few months back with Richard. She was meant to be out with a friend. Red flag." He held up another finger. "Leo showed up a few nights later telling me he'd been blackmailed at gunpoint. He'd just beaten the shit out of Richard, who he'd assumed was the blackmailer. Turned out, it wasn't Richard. It was your mother."

"It wasn't me," Mum sobbed. "It wasn't my—"

"Isabel." Dad cut her off, again putting his finger against his lips. "Shh."

I was shocked. It must've been the night we'd gotten home from the farm after our picnic. We'd gone to bed professing our love, and I'd woken up to him doing a complete one-eighty. "I had no idea he was threatened at gunpoint." I choked back a sob. "He broke up with me the next day."

"It alerted me to the gravity of the situation. I have to say, I was impressed by Leo. He was only concerned with ensuring your safety. We were both worried, Juliette. I asked him to give me a few days to sort it all out."

I shook my head. He had been trying to protect me, and when he'd tried to explain, I had refused to listen.

My dad turned to my mum and spoke in his lawyer voice, calm and sure. "I've given you far too much rope, Isabel, and you nearly managed to hang yourself with it. You tried to string up your own daughter, too, but fortunately we have a strong girl here and she's weathered it all." He turned to me. "I turned a blind eye for too long, but not anymore."

"Lies." My mother's voice was barely a whisper. She looked at me. "All lies."

My mother pushed her chair back so hard it toppled backward when she stood up. "I've just been stressed, and I'm sure I have diabetes, but everything is absolutely fine now."

"Sit down, Isabel. Everything is *not* fine, and you *don't* have diabetes. You've been tested four times, and you need to stop trying to deflect attention from the real issue." He moved around the table and stopped opposite me, leaning forward and placing both hands on the dark wood. "Your mother has been diagnosed with Borderline Personality Disorder."

"Nothing borderline about her," I blurted out but immediately felt guilty for my insensitive quip.

"It's ridiculous," Mum mumbled. "Bunch of quacks. I have low blood sugar levels."

Ignoring both of us, he continued. "She had a clinical assessment done at Dartmoor, and we had lengthy discussions with a psychiatrist."

"So what is it, exactly?" I asked, realising that I felt relieved to have a name to put to her behaviour.

"Well, as the name suggests, it's a personality disorder." He let out a long sigh. "One of the most marked symptoms is the acute fear of rejection and abandonment."

I glanced at my mother, but she was just staring at her food, so I looked back to Dad for further information.

"She presented a frightening number of the criteria for the diagnosis." He held up his thumb. "Unexpected actions without considering the consequences." He added his pointer finger for the second point. "An unstable and capricious mood." He raised another finger. "Going to excessive lengths to avoid abandonment." His eyes softened when he met my stunned gaze. "I think we all know who copped the brunt of that symptom." I thought back to the way my mother had broken down at the mere mention of me travelling and had insisted I be at her events with such intense determination despite telling me I was a disappointment most of the time. I hadn't ever truly understood why. "And the most concerning of all is the recurrent threats of self-harm or suicide." Dad hung his head, appearing shameful.

"You told me the way she behaved was because she'd lost the baby and she'd never fully recovered."

"I'm afraid that's what I always thought and just kept thinking time would heal, but I was wrong and I should've acted far sooner than I did to take control of the situation."

"Does it explain her..." I felt awkward about what I was going to ask but felt it needed to be aired. I dropped my eyes to my plate. "Does it explain her affair with Richard?" When he didn't answer immediately, I dragged my gaze up to meet his.

My mother slammed her hand down on the table. "This is preposterous. I'm right here."

Ignoring her outburst, my father began speaking. "Since you asked, I will tell you what I've learned. It's not clear-cut, but it has been theorised that sufferers of this disorder have reckless sex lives because they feel emotional emptiness and are constantly looking for fulfilment." He tugged at his collar as if it was restricting his breathing. Understandably, he was struggling with this subject. "It is a way of validating their own self-worth."

I glanced at my mother, who was rolling her eyes dramatically, then returned to ask the one question I would also need to ask myself. "Can you forgive her?"

He gave me a tortured smile. "I'm working on it, sweetheart. I love your mother, and I haven't been the husband she needed for a long time. I also haven't been the father you needed either, and I hope to make amends if you'll let me."

I nodded. When I stared at my mother, I felt so many things, but the overwhelming emotion was pity.

I pushed back my chair and stood up. "I just need to use the bathroom." I really just needed a breather from the suffocating bombardment of information and some space to process. "I'll be back in a minute."

I walked briskly from the room and grabbed my bag from the hall table before heading to the downstairs bathroom at the back of the house. I locked the door behind me and reached for my phone. I hit Leo's number and held it to my ear, waiting to hear the only voice that could bring me any comfort right about now. When I got his voicemail, I waited a few minutes before trying again, but still no answer. We hadn't parted on great terms, but I didn't think it warranted ignoring me. I felt frustrated and irritated as I stuffed my phone back in my bag.

I stood at the marble vanity and stared at my reflection. My lifelong struggle to cope with my mother's behaviour towards me was over. Her struggle, however, might never be over, and that's something I would have to come to terms with over time. I knew my compliance over the years could've been viewed as spineless and that I should've stood up to her long ago, but I knew deep in my gut she wouldn't have coped and I knew I could. My naïve mistake had been thinking my actions would help her when, in actual fact, I'd simply been an enabler. I had never let it conquer me though, and it wouldn't define my future. I was strong, I'd always been strong and I'd come out the other side knowing everything I'd done had stemmed from a natural desire a child has to be loved by their mother.

Mum and Dad both looked at me when I re-entered the dining room and sat back down.

"Okay. So..." I placed my hands on the table and looked from one to the other. "I'm sorry I didn't tell you about Richard, Dad, but he had threatened to leak incriminating photos if he lost the Fontaine account." I stared at my plate. "I should've told you."

"It's taken care of. Leo retrieved the hard drive full of photos and video clips, as well as the physical copies."

My mother placed both her hands over her face. "They were photoshopped. I didn't do those things with him," she stated indignantly.

I cringed, not even wanting to think about what was on that hard drive.

"Socialite Isabel Fontaine, wife to legal royalty John Salinger, caught in sordid affair with daughter's boyfriend," Dad stated. "Do you think it'll matter if they're photoshopped or not?" He shook his head. "None of us wants to deal with that kind of scandal."

"It doesn't matter anyway," Mum hissed. "Juliette's tramping around with a bartending cage fighter. She's been more than willing to drag us through the mud."

"Are you serious?" I was outraged she had the audacity to turn this on me still. "I've done everything I can to help you, and you throw it in my face at every turn."

"Enough." My father's voice boomed. "Richard has been removed from the Fontaine account. He has no leverage to hurt us anymore, so that's the end of that." He fixed his gaze on my mother, who appeared unmoved by all of this. "You are on notice, Isabel. Do you understand? You leave Leo and Juliette alone." He turned to me. "We are going to start seeing a therapist this week. We're going to try to manage it and move on."

I glanced at my watch, and it was much later than I had anticipated. I stood up. I was physically and mentally exhausted, and I just wanted to go home. "You've both taken your toll on me over the years." I glanced from my mother to my father. "I need to leave, and I won't be back for a while." My eyes were filling with tears.

My father moved around the table to me. "You're not going to break, sweetheart. You're the strongest person I know, and we love you."

I said goodbye and left the house. My mind was spinning, but my heart felt lighter. My dad was right—I was strong.

CHAPTER 17

LEO

"I'M GONNA BAIL." ADAM HALF-stepped, half-stumbled off his stool. Chuckling, he punched me in the arm. "Don't be a stranger, Leo the lion."

"Leo the lion?" I smirked.

He nodded, a goofy grin on his face. "That's what the wives call you. They all think you're dreamy." He rolled his eyes, gagging.

"Oh god. Really?"

"Yep. I'll tell them you have a girlfriend now to put them all out of their misery."

I tried to stand up and shake his hand but nearly fell off the stool. "Good one, mate. Hey, thanks for coming out to keep me company. Appreciate it."

Maeve chuckled as she poured me another shot, shaking her head as she placed it in front of me, and then moved away to another customer. Great company coupled with tequila shots, and oblivion was in sight. I had enough brain cells left to return Jules's phone call before I succumbed to the drug now flowing freely through my bloodstream.

I tapped my phone, and after a few clumsy attempts,

I managed to call her.

"I thought you must've been asleep." She sounded tired.

"I'm out. I'm sorry about earlier, Jules." I may have slurred a little. Just the sound of her voice made me instantly remorseful and extremely horny.

"Are you drunk?"

"I am," I stated firmly, nodding my head. "I just needed to clock off for a few hours."

"What does that mean? Clock off from me?"

Fuck. I shouldn't be speaking to her on the phone.

"No. I want to see you. Can I come to yours?"

"I'll pick you up. Where are you?"

I glanced around the seedy bar and cringed. "I'll get a cab."

"Just tell me where you are, Leo."

"St Kilda Tavern. You shouldn't come here. It's not safe."

"Oh my God. Seriously? Everyone knows that's a sleazy pickup joint."

I ran my hand through my hair, sobering me slightly from her angry words. "There's no one but you, Jules." I shook my head, wishing like hell I'd just stayed home. "I promise you."

"Be out the front in ten minutes."

She hung up, and I really wished I hadn't had those last few shots.

"Everything okay?" Maeve purred.

I looked up and cringed, knowing I hadn't made myself clear enough. "That was my girlfriend on the phone. I'm sorry if I gave you the wrong idea." The tequila was definitely making me slur my words.

She threw her head back and laughed. "And here I was convinced we were about to start a committed relationship." She continued to laugh and I just stared at her. When she stopped, she leaned over the bar. "We've only ever been about a good time, not a long time." She cocked her head to the side and winked. "That works for me. I'm heading out now, so if you change your mind, meet me in the side alley in five minutes."

I shook my head, knowing that was exactly what I used to look for. I wasn't that person anymore, even if tonight I was behaving like it.

"Don't sell yourself short, okay? You can do better than this." Her expression changed in an instant as the colour drained from her face. It was as if I'd struck a nerve, and no one had ever said anything like that to her before. "I'm outta here."

I stood up and headed for the exit, swaying more than I had expected. The alcohol had worked its magic dulling my senses, and I hoped I could get the hell out of that bar without falling over. When I got outside, I breathed in the night air, hoping to sober up a little before Jules got there.

My ears pricked up when I heard shouting coming from the side alley, and when I rounded the corner to check it out, I could see Maeve being pushed roughly up against the wall by a much larger man.

"Hey," I called out to get their attention, jogging down the alley, cursing my drunken state. No man should treat a girl that way under any circumstances.

The large man turned towards me, holding Maeve against the wall with his right hand around her neck.

"Get your hands off her," I demanded.

The arsehole let her go and puffed his chest out.

"Calm down, Stuart." Maeve's voice was quiet and resigned. I suspected this wasn't the first time she'd found herself in this situation. She put a hand on the man's arm. "We broke up, remember? You have a wife."

"Shut up, you little whore." He glanced over his shoulder to me. "I saw you flirting with him."

I glanced between Maeve and the man who was about to get a lesson in how to treat a woman. Unfortunately, the tequila I'd been drinking like water was going to make for a sketchy lesson at best.

"Calm down, mate." I closed the distance between us. "We were just talking. Maeve and I are old friends."

"Don't tell me to calm down, arsewipe." He gave me a decisive push in the chest with the palm of his hand. "I'll put you to the ground faster than you can say you're a grass-cutting snake."

"I'd watch yourself, mate." My voice was calm.

"I'm not your fucking mate. I train in Krav Maga, Aikido, Karate and Muay Thai and could show those Israeli commandos a thing or two with my interpretations." He then assumed a stance I could only describe as a flamingo with constipation. "I take bits and pieces of all of them and have created my own style." He waved his arms around comically before resuming his flamingo stance.

I laughed. I couldn't help it. It might have been the tequila causing me to react in a way I knew would be highly antagonistic, but this guy was a first-class fuckwit. I was aware I was no fighting machine in my current state, but I knew one thing for sure. This guy could be shut down with one punch.

"Pull your head in, Stuart." Maeve moved between us and stood directly in front of him. "No one cares about your stupid moves except you and your equally stupid mates. Where is King Dick, by the way, anyway?"

"What's going on, Stuart?"

I turned around to see another guy walking towards us. *Fuck.*

"None of your damn business," Stuart said. "I've got

this covered."

"Go home to your wife, mate."

"Excuse me?"

"You heard me."

I was now desperately wishing I were sober. I could see the rage pulsating through the throbbing vein in Stuart's neck, yet my body was sluggish and groggy. There were a whole lot of dots floating around in front of my eyes. I just couldn't quite join them.

"How dare you try to tell me what to do," Stuart spat.

I really didn't need to be in that alley, but I wouldn't leave Maeve alone with these two fuckwits. I tried to get her attention and beckon her over to me, but she was focused on Stuart, whose face was now on fire, and I could see his fists clenching.

"He's right." Maeve stepped forward and put her hand on his arm again, trying in vain to calm him down.

I saw what was about to happen too late. In what felt like slow motion, Stuart's arm swept up and slammed into her shocked face. Horrified, I rushed to help her.

"What the fuck?" I stumbled forward to get to Maeve. I hunched over and gently prised back her hands covering her bloodied face. "You'll be okay, darlin.' I've got you."

Stuart hadn't done any serious damage to Maeve, but she needed to be cleaned up and I was about to help her up when I heard Jules's voice. Horrified, I glanced up just in time to see Stuart circling her. The second guy was nowhere in sight, and I felt immediately sober.

Maeve was sobbing against my chest, but I had to prise her from me and prop her against the brick wall. "Stay here. Okay?" I whispered to Maeve, who nodded her head, choking back further sobs. I jumped up and started running.

"Well, well, well. Aren't you a pretty thing?" Stuart said, and I saw red.

I was going to kill him.

When he made his move, I panicked, knowing I was too late to stop him from touching her, but she expertly sidestepped, pulled her arm back and punched him in the face. Grabbing him by the upper arms, she then slammed her knee into his balls. He hit the ground, writhing in pain, and Juliette stood over him, cradling her fist.

"Are you okay?" I pulled her away, turned her to face me and held her face. "Are you okay, Jules?"

She nodded, smiling.

"Greedy, aren't we?" Stuart's snide laugh made us both turn to face him sitting up on the ground, cradling his bloodied nose.

I grabbed Juliette and pulled her behind me. "I told you. Maeve and I are friends, you son of a bitch, and you were hurting her. This is my girlfriend, and if you touch her, I'll kill you."

"Let me go, Leo." Juliette struggled to release herself from my grip and move around me. "I can handle myself." She was so strong, and I was unable to hold her behind my back in my drunken state.

"What is going on out here?" The manager of the bar appeared next to us with Maeve, holding an ice pack against her cheek.

"Stuart was hurting me, and these two helped me out." Maeve pointed at Stuart, still a groaning heap on the ground.

"This guy is always in here causing trouble," the bar manager said. "I'll sort this out." He was clearly used to this kind of mess. "You two get out of here." He pointed at Jules and me. "Thanks for coming to Maeve's rescue."

"Can you grab me an ice pack and some bandages,

please?" I asked the bar manager.

Hesitating only briefly, he disappeared back into the bar and returned a minute later holding what I'd asked for.

"Thanks, mate."

I turned to Jules and gently picked up her right hand. She'd been cradling it, so I knew it hurt. I placed the ice pack over her knuckles and kissed her forehead when she let out a small yip.

"It's fine," she said, scrunching up her nose.

"You just decked a guy with your bare hands, Jules," I waited until she looked me in the eye. "Let me take care of you."

She nodded and allowed me to wrap her hand in the bandage.

After saying goodbye to Maeve, I gently encouraged Jules to walk back up the alley, my arm firmly around her shoulders. "We'll grab a cab, and I'll come and get your car in the morning. Neither of us should be driving."

CHAPTER 18

Juliette

WE SAT IN THE BACK seat of the cab in silence. I was on such an incredible high, I was past the point of speaking. I was ready to jump Leo right there in the back seat if the next set of lights was red. He probably thought I was on the brink of some kind of internal meltdown after what had just happened, but I couldn't summon the energy to tell him otherwise. I would show him soon enough. We just had to get to my goddamn apartment.

When we finally arrived, I got out, not waiting for Leo before heading for the lift. I was a woman on a mission.

Hurry up. I mentally willed the lift doors to open. I could feel Leo's eyes on me, and I looked to my left. When I locked eyes with the hottest man on the planet leaning against one of the columns, my mind went completely blank. Besides, there were no words that could adequately express how my body reacted to Leo.

"Hey." He was a few feet from me, but I could feel the electricity that always crackled between us. His eyes were dark, and I wanted to take away the evident pain.

I gave him my most seductive smile and beckoned

him with my pointer finger. His eyes went from dark to lust-filled as he took one long stride, closing the distance between us and pulled me to him. His lips crashed against mine and my arms flew around his neck, frantically pulling at him to get him closer.

My whole body was on fire as the desperation fed our frenzy of lust. Groans of pleasure escaped both of us.

I bunched the front of his shirt and dragged him through the opening doors. We practically fell into the empty lift, and I reluctantly had to deal with my security pass to make the lift ascend. Leo took the opportunity to kiss my neck and caress my whole body, and I thought I might die of sexual need. "You are the sexiest woman in the world."

As the lift made its way north, I was slammed up against the wall, my arms raised above my head and held in place with one of his strong hands, while the other ventured under my t-shirt. When he cupped my breast, I groaned loudly, but the sound was quickly muffled by his mouth and tongue. I lifted my leg and hooked it around his. He grabbed my thigh and pulled it higher, thrusting his hips into me exactly where I needed him. The lift doors opened on my level. Leo picked me up so I was straddling his waist, and he strode purposefully for my door.

I had my key ready and managed to get the door open without skipping a beat, our mouths locked together, refusing to be parted. The fireworks exploding behind my closed eyes were breathtaking as he carried me directly to my bedroom, falling on top of me as we landed heavily on my bed.

Pinning my hands to the bed on either side of my head, he propped himself on his elbows. "I need you now." He growled, making my own need for him explode.

"Hurry up, then." I was desperate to feel reconnected to him in the most intimate way possible, and he was wasting time verbalising his need that was currently stabbing me in the thigh.

The next thirty seconds were a blur of clothes as we both yanked and pulled each other's clothes from our writhing bodies. Punching that arsehole in the face and watching Leo take care of his friend had been more than enough foreplay. He thrust into me, and our simultaneous groan was that of relief and pent-up sexual need.

When I had expected him to start pounding into me furiously, he slowed down and caressed my face. The gentleness of his touch contrasted his massive, cut physique. It was one of the things I loved most about him. The love he was capable of showing with the simplest of gestures was just as powerful as the physical blows he could throw in the cage or the ring.

"I want you so damn much." He scrunched his face up, as if in pain. "I always want you so damn much."

He started moving slowly, still refusing to break eye contact. As his speed increased, I closed my eyes, unable to withstand his gaze any longer. I felt his mouth against my neck, feathering a light kiss in time with every hard thrust of his hips. His mouth made its way to my chest and up the swell of my right breast. I could barely stand the sweet agony, and my back arched of its own accord, pushing into his caressing lips. His answer was to suck my hard nipple, flicking it with his expert tongue. Without any shame, I cried out his name, knowing I was so close to what my body was screaming for.

"I want you on top." His demand was coupled with my body being flipped, and I quickly found myself straddling his rock-hard body. He was sitting up and had his arms wrapped around me, his mouth immediately finding my neglected left breast as I found my own rhythm to drive us completely insane.

"God, Leo. I love having you inside me," I panted out as the white light took hold of my vision.

I felt his grip around me tighten, and his lips found mine and we both surged to climax.

"That was..." Leo couldn't finish his sentence when I climbed off him and lay down on my back, my arm over my face, exhausted.

"Mind-blowing." I finished his sentence with the only words I could summon.

"Mind-blowing," he confirmed.

When we'd regained our composure and our breathing had returned to normal, we both turned to face each other. Leo ran his finger down my arm, then across the dip of my waist and over my hip. He was tracing the line of my body, leaving goosebumps in his wake.

"You are so fucking beautiful, Jules."

I blushed. However many times he complimented me, it still made me blush. They were never throw-away comments. He spoke with such intensity and emotion, and he spoke directly to my soul.

"I'm so sorry about tonight, Jules." He stroked my face, then kissed the palm of my hand. "I should never have been at that bar. I can't seem to pull my shit together since I saw her again." He closed his eyes briefly. "I put you in danger again."

"I'm so used to crazy, I don't even know what normal would feel like. Maybe crazy is our normal?" I lay on my back and covered my face with my hands, trying not to laugh.

"What?" Leo poked me in the side. "What the hell are you laughing at?" He pulled my hands away from my face and held them down.

I bit my bottom lip. "I really liked punching that guy."

Leo flopped down on his back next to me. "Oh God, Jules." He laughed a little. "What am I going to do with you?"

"Stay with me." The words tumbled out of my mouth before I gave them any conscious thought.

"Always," Leo whispered.

We were both quiet for a few minutes.

"How did it go at your parents'?" Leo asked, yawning and clearly struggling to keep his eyes open. "The normal kind of crazy?"

"Dad told me about the night you confronted Dick."

He glanced at me with a concerned expression. "I didn't want to worry you, and I took care of it."

"You should've told me, you know."

"There's a lot of things I should've done differently, but that's all in the past now, so—"

I cut him off. "You told me you loved me. Then the next morning you broke my heart." My eyes filled with tears. "I know I jumped to conclusions and I have to own that, but you should've told me what happened."

He was lying on his back, rubbing his eyes with the heel of his palms. "It was a fucking mess." He removed his hands and turned on his side to face me. "My only goal was to keep you safe, so I won't apologise for that. I had to give your dad a few days to ensure your mother's threats were empty."

"Information you could've shared, Leo."

"Jules." He sat up and rested his back on the headboard. "I had just had a gun in my face, thanks to your mother, with a message to stay away from you or you'd be hurt or worse." He winced. "Forgive me for not thinking clearly."

"No more secrets. Okay? My mother might've been

the villain in all of this, but you broke us. I trusted you and you took that away, too."

"I know, baby. It kills me to think you left feeling that way. It killed me that you left at all, but I did what I thought was right at the time, and protecting you will always be my number one priority."

It wasn't lost on me that neither one of us had said 'I love you' since I'd been back. There was no doubt our connection was still there, and I did love him. I was confident he loved me, too, but a part of me didn't want to hear those words again for a while. That part of me was still a little broken.

I could barely keep my eyes open. It was after midnight, and it had been a marathon weekend. We had a lot to talk about, but sleep soon dragged us both into its clutches.

CHAPTER 19

Juliette

"DO YOU HAVE TO GO?" Leo asked after we'd made love the next morning. "Aren't you tired?"

"I'm fine." I yawned, giving away my lie. "I've only been back a week. It's poor form if I take a day off so soon, don't you think?"

Leo pulled me to him. "I just want to keep you all to myself."

"So what are you going to do today?" I asked as I buttoned up a sleeveless cream blouse and tucked it into a black pencil skirt.

I sat down on the bed next to him to put on my favourite Bally heels.

"I'm going out to Lilydale to talk to Nick," he replied. "He wants to train me again, and he's offered me a job."

I dropped my second shoe to the floor, a little shocked, mildly unnerved, but mostly excited for him. "Really? Are you considering it?" I asked.

He nodded. "I think I am. I might do some work at the farm today, too, but I'll be back this evening."

"Well I think that sounds amazing. I can't wait to hear all about it after work." I kissed him goodbye and left for work with a strange feeling in the pit of my stomach. Was I worried he was going to leave me behind this time?

As I walked across the footbridge, I couldn't help reminiscing about the love locks that used to hang there by the thousand. My body visibly shuddered as I remembered my ex- boyfriend, Richard, presenting me with one, engraved with our initials. I'd known at the time our love hadn't just been breakable; it had been a complete farce. Council workers had done me a favour when they'd taken to the padlocks with bolt cutters a short time later. My mother had taken metaphorical bolt cutters to my relationship with Leo, but ultimately they were rendered useless. I just hoped we could move forward now, and no one else was going to get in our way.

When I got to work, I shuffled through the endless paperwork piled up on my desk. Since I'd returned from my travels, I found myself questioning more and more what I was doing there.

Heath walked past my desk on his way back from the morning meeting with his phone to his ear, not even acknowledging me with a smile or a wave. I was invisible. I was also replaceable. The temp who had filled in for me while I had been away had left things a little more disorganised than I'd kept them, but life had gone on. Heath was certainly happy I was back, but only because he knew I made his life easier than he deserved. I was in no way key to his success, and he wouldn't blink if I resigned. It was depressing. I slumped over my desk, resting my head on my crossed arms but was jolted upright almost immediately by the phone ringing.

"Juliette Salinger. How can I help you?" I answered robotically.

"Jules."

I closed my eyes when I heard Charlie's voice. "Charlie."

"It's so good to hear your voice."

"Yours too," I said honestly.

"Do you have lunch plans?" he asked.

"I... um..."

"Come on, Jules."

I bit the inside of my cheek and glanced around the office, not really knowing why.

"Are you there?"

"Why didn't you warn me you were coming to Melbourne?"

"It was a spontaneous business trip, and I thought I'd surprise you."

I felt immediately remorseful for arrogantly assuming he'd come all the way to Melbourne to chase me. "Right. Okay."

"So will you have lunch with me?"

I exhaled. "Yes. I'll have lunch with you, Charlie."

꩜

I agreed to meet him at my favourite café, McQuillens, and as I turned the corner, I could see him standing outside waiting for me. He was looking sharp in a perfectly-tailored charcoal suit, white shirt and dark silver tie. I'd only ever seen him in casual attire on our travels, so I was a little taken aback by the corporate Charlie. He looked damn good, I had to admit to myself. As I got closer, he turned and our eyes met. His shoulders dropped with what looked like relief, and he closed the distance between us in a few quick strides, enveloping me in a hug so full of emotion it made me want to cry. It brought back the wonderful memories I'd made with him but also the guilt and heartache I'd felt whenever I'd thought about Leo.

Two months earlier

Standing in line outside The Book of Kells on Dublin's Trinity College campus, I felt my whole body relax. I closed my eyes and revelled in the fact I was about to be in the presence of books dating back thousands of years. I enjoyed the feeling of infinite insignificance. My dramas were a blip in the overall scheme of things.

"I really don't think I can face going in." Sia sounded sheepish. "It's just a crap load of old books."

I laughed. "No one's holding a gun to your head, my friend."

"You don't mind?"

"Course not." She kept glancing over my shoulder, which I found disconcerting. I glanced over my shoulder to the line of people behind me. "What are you looking at?"

"Not what. Who." Her wide eyes were trying to tell me something. "There are two guys further back in the line, and they are hot with a capital H." She scrunched up her face. "Let's go introduce ourselves."

"No way." I glanced back and locked eyes with a man who made me catch my breath. When he smiled, I turned back quickly. Sia was waving to him and dragging me out of the line.

"I know you from somewhere," Sia stated unashamedly to the men who looked like they'd stepped off the pages of a glossy magazine. They both had a rugged charm most women would find very appealing.

Both guys stared at Sia then looked at each other, shrugging their shoulders. "Well, you're clearly Australian, so I'm thinking that has something to do with it," he said in an Australian accent, holding out his hand. "I'm Charlie and this is my brother, Matt."

"Sia," Sia mumbled, shaking Charlie's hand but looking at Matt. I was left standing there feeling a little awkward.

"And you are?" Charlie asked, looking directly at me, a warm smile lighting up his handsome face.

"Juliette." I took his outstretched hand and shook it, feeling he held on to my hand a few seconds too long.

"That's a beautiful name for a beautiful girl."

I cringed. Was he flirting with me? Did I like him flirting with me? "Thank you?" It came out more like a question, thanks to my internal debate on how I felt about the situation.

He smiled again. It was a really cute smile. Charlie wasn't nearly as muscular as Leo, but not many guys were, and he was still in great shape. His hair was longer and lighter brown, but he had similar clear blue eyes and a strong jawline that would turn the heads of most women. I needed to stop comparing every single detail of his appearance to Leo, but he reminded me so much of the man who'd broken my heart, and it scared the shit out of me.

He was motioning over my shoulder and I looked at him questioningly, unsure what the problem was.

"We're up," he said, gesturing to the big gap that had opened up ahead of us.

"Oh. Right." I shuffled forward quickly.

"You from Sydney?" Charlie asked in a broad Australian accent.

It was surprising to me how obvious the Australian accent is when you're out of Australia. When you're at home, it's just how everyone sounds. "Melbourne, actually."

"Ahh. A Mexican."

I had no idea what he meant by that, and my

expression must've told him so.

"Victoria. South of the border."

"Well, I do love Mexican food."

Charlie laughed, and I couldn't help smiling. He was so laid back, and I needed a good dose of that. I couldn't help but notice he was in great shape. His loose, white t-shirt still gripped his defined biceps. Flashes of Leo caused me to close my eyes briefly from the pain. I opened them again quickly, determined to push those to the back of my mind.

"So are you travelling or working over here?" *I asked. Small talk wouldn't kill me.*

"Matt and I work half the year in London and half in Sydney."

We were almost at the door. "So, Sia. Have you changed your mind?" *I could see as clear as day that she had taken a shine to Matt, so I thought I'd have some fun with her.* "Weren't you just telling me it's just a crap load of all books?"

Sia gave me a mock glare. "I might've said that."

"Well, thank God." *Matt laughed, looking directly at Sia, who he was clearly interested in, too.* "Guinness factory tour?"

"Totally." *Sia bounced on the spot, delighted. She turned to Charlie and me.* "You two bookworms okay together?" *Then she stepped forward and whispered in my ear.* "Rule Number One: Have some fun."

"Go away." *I pushed her lightly on the shoulder and shook my head, chuckling.* "I'll see you later."

"Oliver St. John Gogarty. Three o'clock?" *Matt suggested.*

"Done."

Matt and Sia disappeared in what seemed like a puff of smoke, leaving me standing there with a virtual stranger. An extremely good-looking stranger.

Throats being cleared alerted us to the fact that it was my turn to pay. I dashed forward to buy my ticket.

Clutching the brochures, I glanced over to my new friend, who was still busy paying. I felt awkward waiting but rude walking away without at least a wave. Charlie glanced up just as I was about to look away and held up one finger, indicating I should wait. What harm would it do to make a new friend? He seemed harmless enough.

I shifted from one foot to the other and stared down at my white Converse, which had seen better days.

"Mind if I join you?"

"Of course not. I mean. Sure. Why not?" I bit my lip, wondering why I felt so nervous around him. "Is this your first time?"

"Nope. I come here every time I visit my grandparents. This is my fifth."

"Wow."

"I'm guessing you're a virgin."

An instant blush heated my cheeks. "Excuse me?"

"A Book of Kells virgin." He smirked and started walking towards the first room.

"Oh, right. Yes. I knew what you meant," I called after him but didn't hurry to keep up.

We walked into a dark room with various display cabinets around the edges and one large display case in the centre. I made my way to the first cabinet, where a video was playing. I was fixated immediately. It was showing the early method of binding books. I felt almost teary watching the craftsmanship that went into it and was horrified that my brain immediately went back to Leo's farmhouse and the time and care that had gone into its construction. There was *something about traditional methods that created art rather than just function.*

"Pretty impressive, huh?" Charlie sidled up to me to watch the screen with what seemed like equal admiration. "I've watched it so many times but am blown away every single time."

I looked up at his side profile and wished I could be excited to meet someone gorgeous with similar interests to mine. I just felt like I was cheating, which was completely crazy. Regardless of the circumstances, Leo had pushed me away and I needed this opportunity to spread my wings.

When we'd seen all the cabinets, Charlie led me to the centre display case to see the main event: The Book of Kells.

"So is seeing this a bucket list item for you?" he asked.

"It is." Tears pricked my eyes as I stared at the Book containing, amongst other things, four gospels in Latin based on Vulgate text completed in 384AD and written on prepared calfskin. (I read that on the plaque. I wasn't that much of a book nerd.) It was overwhelming to see it in person. "My dad loves books. I guess I inherited that from him." I attempted to casually wipe my eyes to ensure no tears escaped. I'd only just met this guy, and he didn't need to know my big sob story. "He has an incredible collection of books at his house and has visited many of the world's finest libraries. He told me about The Book of Kells *when I was quite young. I guess deep down I always hoped I would see it, but this is the first time I've left Australia."*

"Really? That's incredible. Most Aussies head to Europe the second they finish high school."

"Not me," I mumbled as I walked away. I didn't want to talk to him anymore.

"I'm sorry." Charlie whispered when he fell into step

beside me just as I was about to take the stairs. "I didn't mean to upset you."

I attempted a laugh. "You didn't. It's totally fine. I had something in my eye. That's all."

We walked up the stairs in silence.

"So, is it Jules or Julie for short, or are you always Juliette?"

Hearing him say Jules was painful. He had the same deep, gravelly voice as Leo. "Jules." I almost said Juliette, but it sounded so formal and I was on holiday. "Jules is fine."

"Okay then, Jules. Let's go see some books."

We ascended the last flight of stairs and walked out into a cavernous area that literally stopped me in my tracks. My jaw dropped as I struggled to process what I was seeing. It was the most stunning, awe-inspiring, incredible room I'd ever seen, and I knew the image would stay with me forever.

A chuckle snapped me out of my stupor. "Your face just spoke a thousand words. It was a beautiful sight." Our eyes locked, and I felt the air crackle around us. "You are really beautiful, Jules."

This was not good. "I... um... I think I might go on by myself if you don't mind, Charlie?" I took a step back and broke our eye contact.

I saw what I thought to be hurt flash across his eyes. "Did I say something wrong?" he asked tentatively. "I have a bad habit of saying exactly what I think."

I swallowed the lump in my throat. "No. It's not you. It's—"

"It's not you, it's me? Seriously?"

"I'm sorry. You're lovely and I've really enjoyed meeting you, but I..." I really didn't feel like explaining to a stranger that no one would ever stand a chance with me, as Leo had ruined me for other men forever.

"I'll back off. I promise. I didn't mean to scare you off." He held his hands up. "I come in peace."

"I hope you don't think I'm arrogant assuming you are flirting with me, but I don't want to lead you on."

Charlie chuckled. "How about we pretend I find you really unattractive and just enjoy your company as friends?"

I laughed. "OK. I guess I could also pretend you are offensively ugly, too."

"Right. Then that's settled, then. We're just two ugly mugs hanging out in Dublin. Deal?"

I smiled at the ridiculous deal. He was the reason Aussie men had a reputation for being gorgeous. He could've been another Hemsworth brother, and I was to pretend he was ugly. No problem at all.

We wandered through the library, gazing at the floor-to-ceiling bookshelves cordoned off from tourists. We read the giant banners telling stories of Norse myths and legends, and we chatted easily. He had put flirtation on the back burner, and we managed to enjoy each other's company without me fearing where it was leading. He knew the score, so I could relax. It actually really helped to keep my mind off home, and more specifically, Leo. If I were honest, I'd thought of little else since we'd left. Even though Sia had banned any talk of him, the thoughts were always there. What was he doing? Was he thinking about me? Was he going to the fights? Was he okay? I had driven myself crazy.

"Did you want to buy any souvenirs?" Charlie asked as we moved through the gift shop towards the exit.

"I'll just grab a few postcards."

He was waiting for me outside when I ventured out into the sunshine.

"We're due to meet Matt and Sia. Will you let me buy

you a Guinness?"

I scrunched up my nose. "I've always wondered if it's like drinking tar."

"You can't come to Ireland and not at least try Guinness."

We had walked past a few bars on the way to Trinity University campus, and I had heard Irish bars were a must. "Okay. One pint of Guinness."

He grabbed my hand, then quickly dropped it, realising he probably shouldn't have. I was horrified to realise I liked the feel of his touch and balled my hand he'd just dropped into a fist. I wasn't supposed to like the touch of another man.

"Sorry," he said as he scrunched his nose, his voice barely a whisper. His apology appeared reluctant.

"It's okay," I reassured him but wished he hadn't done it. Now I knew his touch.

We jostled along the busy streets to the cobbled Temple bar area near the river. Bars lined both sides of the street, and buskers created a fun and lively atmosphere. A man dressed as a leprechaun standing over a pot of gold insisted we have our photographs taken with him. Of course we threw in a few coins for whatever charity he was collecting for.

"Come on. This is my favourite bar in Dublin."

Charlie opened the door and ushered me in, careful not to touch me again. It was only three in the afternoon, but it was packed to the rafters with singing and dancing patrons. I couldn't help laughing.

"You still keen to try Guinness?" Charlie shouted in my ear.

"Sure. Why not?" I shouted back, lifting my shoulders.

"That's the spirit." Charlie smiled, then elbowed his

way to the bar while I sang along to Neil Diamond's "Sweet Caroline."

A group of guys in fancy dress, or at least I hoped they were in fancy dress, gestured for me to join them on the dancefloor in front of the live band. I shook my head and mouthed, Not a chance.

One of them jogged over to me and shouted in a posh English accent, "I'm getting married next weekend." I felt immediately drunk from the beer fumes, but he had a friendly face. "Let me have one more dance with the prettiest girl in the room before then?"

"Come on!" chanted a chorus of voices who had to be his bucks.

I rolled my eyes, then thought, Fuck it!

I accepted his outstretched hand and allowed him to drag me onto the dance floor where I was spun, dipped and swirled until I was laughing so hard my sides ached. When the song finished, we were met with a loud applause. I glanced around the room and saw all eyes were on us. I looked at the groom-to-be, and we both cracked up again and bowed to our appreciative audience.

"Thank you." He lifted my hand to his lips and kissed it before bowing dramatically.

"You're welcome and congratulations." I laughed and curtsied.

He kissed my cheek and then pulled me in for a hug, whispering in my ear in a thick Irish accent something along the lines of, "Not sure your boyfriend was too happy about our dance. Hope I didn't get you in any trouble."

Before I had a chance to correct his mistake, he was singing along to the next song and was surrounded by his drunken mates.

I glanced around and found Charlie staring at me.

When he realised I was looking at him, he immediately shook off his dark look and smiled brightly, holding up two pints of dark liquid. I was in such a good mood from the music and dancing, I ignored the fact this very gorgeous guy clearly wasn't going to do the friends thing easily.

Thank you, I mouthed, taking the glass and tentatively bringing it to my lips.

I was surprised to find it was far more pleasant than I'd been expecting. I wouldn't be rushing back for another, but it was another experience and I was really enjoying everything about Dublin so far.

"Let's go outside where we can hear ourselves think."

I followed him outside a little reluctantly. I was really enjoying the atmosphere inside but was happy to grab some fresh air. We found a free bar table outside, and Charlie placed his beer down. "You're a good dancer."

I laughed as I was about to take another sip, and the froth on top sprayed out over the glass. "Thanks. Bit out of character for me dancing with strangers, but hey. You only live once."

He raised his glass and chinked it with mine. "Carpe diem."

I smiled at how much those two words, meaning seize the day, really meant something to me. Until recently, I'd done the exact opposite of seizing the day by moulding myself into something I wasn't for my mother's and father's sakes. I'd channelled my frustrations into the quest for my beloved adrenaline sports but had kept them a secret. I had been living my life on someone else's terms, and when I'd stopped, the repercussions could've been fatal.

Before I knew it, I was sculling my beer with my eyes shut tight. When I opened them, Charlie was looking at me quizzically. "Would you like another?"

I wiped the froth from my mouth with the back of my arm and welcomed the warmth spreading through my body. "Sia." I spotted her down the street.

Sia launched herself at me and whispered in my ear, "Two hot brothers. Jackpot."

I pushed her back but laughed at her exuberance.

"Let's get shitfaced," Matt proposed boldly. "We're young and free. Let's celebrate that."

He and Sia had clearly had a few already, and it was easy to forget it was only mid-afternoon surrounded by happy, drunk people.

"So what's the plan from here?" Charlie asked. "Are you just here on holiday?"

"We have no real set plan. We're just going to backpack around Europe. We both have six weeks' leave from work." Sia motioned between us. "We work together at a stockbroking firm back home."

"There are loads of stockbrokers in London," Matt chimed in. "You could get a job over there."

"What do you guys do?" I asked to change the subject.

"We run our family's office. We make and oversee all the investments and typically spend half the year here in Europe and half back in Australia. Our parents live in Sydney."

"Wow. That's very cool," Sia said.

Charlie slapped his hand down on the table. "Right, ladies. No more talk of work. Another round?"

Many, many hours later, I stood up on shaky legs. "I think I'm done." I glanced at my watch and was surprised to see it was after ten. "I need to use the ladies' before I head back to the hotel." I stood up and swayed a little. "Back in a sec."

When I came out of the bathroom, Charlie was leaning against the wall, one leg bent with his foot resting on the wall behind him. "You're not going, are you?" He tried to sound casual, but I sensed the desperation in his voice. "I'd really like to see you again." He pushed off the wall and held his hands up. "As friends, of course."

I paused. "I don't know you, Charlie, and you don't know me." I thought of the one person I was trying so desperately to push out of my thoughts. Leo. My heart ached for him.

"I'd like to fix that, but I can't if you do a runner."

I snapped back to the present at the sound of Charlie's voice.

"Thank you for coming, Jules," he whispered into my ear. "I've missed you."

"Of course." I pulled back so I could study his face. "Good to see you, Charlie."

His eyes were tired, but his smile reached them. "It's so good to see you." He held me at arm's length and studied me. "You look as stunning as always."

He made me feel warm all over. There was no doubt he was a good-looking guy, and we got along famously. Perhaps if I'd never met Leo, things could have been different between us. But I had met Leo, and I had fallen so far in love with him, there was no coming back. I could definitely be Charlie's friend though, especially if things worked out with Sia and his brother.

"You hungry?" He put his arm around my shoulder and kissed the top of my head. My body tensed. I tried to fight the instinct, but it felt too intimate. "I'm starving."

"I'm happy to see you, too, Charlie, but you know nothing has changed, right?" I stopped walking to make sure he looked at me. He dropped his arm, and I didn't like his reaction.

"So you sorted things out with Leo, then?" He was definitely trying to sound casual.

"I'd rather not talk about Leo with you." I scrunched up my nose.

"Let's go inside." I felt his hand on my lower back as he held the door open for me with the other. He was always the gentleman.

We ordered at the counter, then found a free table at the back. I loved this café. It offered wall space to local artists to sell their work. I'd bought a number of them for gifts and for myself. This month, the wall was covered in framed photos, drawings and paintings of frogs. Small bronze frog sculptures were displayed on the counter next to a small sign stating 'Frogs For Sale.' There was no way I was going to be able to resist buying a few. All the other walls were bookshelves full of second-hand books and various forms of book art.

"Books always remind me of you."

I nodded, smiling. "You make me sound like a book nerd."

Charlie laughed. "Don't worry. Skydiving and canyoning also remind me of you."

"Phew." I chuckled. Charlie and Matt had met us every weekend wherever we were in Europe. Fortunately, Matt and Sia always wanted to do the same thing, which usually involved bars, dancing and public displays of affection, while Charlie and I shared a love for adrenaline.

"Do you think about our adventures a lot?" he asked.

"Of course I do."

"If you'd stayed, that could've been our life."

"I was on holiday, Charlie. That wasn't real life." I pointed my finger down on the table. "This is my real life, right here in Melbourne with my crazy family and complicated love life." I bit my lip, wishing I hadn't said that last bit.

"Why is it complicated?"

"Nothing. I shouldn't have said that."

The café owner arrived with my coffee and Charlie's Pepsi Max. "Here you go. I'll be back with your tomato soup in a minute, Jules."

"Thank you, Sammie." I smiled, grateful for the interruption. "Hey. I love the froggy art."

She laughed. "Me too. The artist is obsessed by the little buggers." She glanced at the wall covered in frogs and shook her head. "They're getting a pretty good reaction."

"It ain't easy being green, you know."

"Thanks, Kermit." She was still chuckling as she returned to the counter.

She left us to it, and I turned back to Charlie who was smiling broadly.

"What?"

"Nothing." He continued smiling. "I'm just happy to be sitting here with you."

Sammie placed a bowl of steaming tomato soup with a crusty roll in front of me and a steak sandwich in front of Charlie. It smelled delicious.

"How did your meeting with my father go?" I asked, changing the subject. I lifted a spoonful of the soup to my mouth and blew on it gently.

"Good. We're looking at some property investments here in Melbourne, and his firm is the best to take care of the legal side of things."

"Why didn't you tell me?"

He broke eye contact briefly before returning my questioning gaze. "I was worried you'd be angry." He rubbed his forehead with the palm of his hand. "I couldn't just let you go, Jules. I had the most incredible time with you, and then you just leave as if it was the easiest thing in the world."

"I loved the time we had together, but you knew it was never going to be more than friendship and that I was coming home to the man I was in love with. I was honest with you."

He ran his hands through his hair and let out a long breath.

"You showing up here and hiring my father," I continued. "It all felt a bit manipulative, to be honest."

Just then my phone rang and I looked down to see Dad's name on the screen. I gave Charlie an apologetic look.

"Hi, Dad."

"Juliette. How are you?"

"Fine, thanks. What's up?"

"Charlie's not answering his phone, and I need him to come back briefly. I have something he needs to sign."

"How did you know I'd be having lunch with him?"

"He told me. Don't be so paranoid, Juliette."

I glanced at Charlie, who was looking at me curiously.

"Fine. Is that all?"

"I know last night was a lot to take on, but I think things are going to get better now. Your mother is trying really hard. She's worried she's lost you."

I put my hand over my phone and turned to Charlie. "Sorry about this."

He shook his head and waved me off.

"Is she okay at home alone?"

"Jean's there. She's fine."

She could no longer control my life, but I would always be concerned for her well-being. She was damaged, and I would continue to support her.

I said goodbye to Dad and hung up. "Dad needs your

signature on something."

"Are you okay? You looked troubled by that conversation."

"It's my mother."

"Is she doing better?" I had mentioned her as being one of the major reasons I had left Melbourne when the four of us were travelling through France. I just hadn't given any details.

"Sort of." I sighed. "It's a long story."

"Well, I'm all ears if you want to unload." He reached across the table and placed his hand over mine. "I want to be here for you, Jules."

"That's not necessary, Charlie."

"I hate that you seem so nervous around me now."

"I told you from the start we could only be friends. My heart belongs to someone else."

"You can't deny this." He waved his hand between us. "I've never felt anything like it before, and I'm not giving up without proving I'm all in if you'll have me. I can give you everything, and I can take you away from the drama that seems to surround you here."

"The drama is temporary, and it's going to get better."

"Don't you ever think sometimes that when something is too hard, it isn't meant to be?"

"Don't you ever think the best things in life are worth fighting for?" I quipped.

"You just seemed so different in Europe."

"Different how?"

"Lighter, maybe. You are still the most beautiful girl I've ever seen in my life, but you appear to have the weight of the world on your shoulders here. In Europe, away from your family and your life here, you were so carefree."

"I was on holiday, Charlie. Of course I was lighter, but

holidays aren't real life. I have responsibilities here. My mother still needs me, and I'm in love with someone else."

He looked at the ceiling, and when he faced me again, he appeared angry. "On one of our last nights together before you left, you told me about how you were done being at your parents' beck and call and were going to get on with your own life as an independent woman."

"I am," I spat back with more venom than I meant. "I am trying to get on with my life, but I still love my parents." I felt tears welling in my eyes. "They are still my parents."

I was done with this conversation. I needed to get out of there. Leaving enough cash to cover both our meals on the table, I waved to Sammie, then walked out the door.

Charlie followed me out onto the footpath and immediately pulled me into a hug. Despite wanting to push him away, I enjoyed being in his arms, but it felt wrong. I pushed him away.

"I'm sorry, Jules. I didn't mean to upset you." He held my face in his hands and kissed my cheek. "I hate seeing you sad. I'm just trying to find a way to make you happy."

"No. You're trying to find a way to make me choose you." I shuffled out of his hold and crossed my arms over my chest.

"Jules." His soft tone made my heart skip a beat. "I actually had a proposition for you, but you never gave me a chance to tell you about it."

I raised my eyebrows. "You asking me to marry you?" I smirked, but when his expression remained serious, I froze. He appeared offended by my joke. "What is it, Charlie?" I half-smiled.

He exhaled and ran his hands through his hair. "I'm not asking you to marry me, Jules, although I don't find the idea quite as funny as you obviously do."

If I hadn't already known he wanted more than friendship, I knew right then. It was written all over his face from the hurt eyes to the furrowed brow.

"I have a job offer for you."

Taken aback, I must've looked like a deer in headlights. "What? Where? Why? What?" I stuttered.

"Can we go for a walk? All I ask is that you keep an open mind before you shoot me down with all the reasons you can't possibly leave Melbourne." He waited 'til I faced him. "Okay?"

Reluctantly, I nodded my head, but my brain was already in firing-squad mode—I was locked and loaded. He was obviously nervous about what he was about to propose, and I couldn't help feeling flattered that this incredible guy thought so highly of me. This beautiful, normal, stable guy.

"So you know I run the family office, right? Matt and I manage the Quinn family wealth, overseeing the global investments and trusts."

"Yes. I know what a family office is, Charlie. My boss's best client runs the family office for one of Melbourne's wealthiest families."

"Right. Of course. Well, we'd like you to join us as the Sydney office manager."

I was flattered and knew it would be a big step up from what I was currently doing, but there was no way I'd be accepting it. *Firing squad at the ready.* "Thank you so much for the offer, Charlie, but—"

He cut me off. "I think you'd be perfect. There'll be plenty of travel involved, and it would really help us out to not have to go through the hiring process."

"I'm not leaving, Charlie."

"If you are happy in your job and your life here, just

tell me you're not interested."

I glanced at him quickly to catch his smug look. "I'm not leaving."

Charlie moved into my personal space, and for a moment, I thought he was going to kiss me. Instead, he brushed the loose strands of my hair off my face and looked in my eyes. "I think about you all the time. I've thought of little else since you left." His hands were moving up and down my arms, and I cursed my traitorous body.

I stepped back so his arms dropped to his sides.

"I have to go back to work now, Charlie. Thank you for the offer, but the life I want is here."

"I don't believe you," he said.

I shrugged. "You don't have to."

"I think we were meant to meet in Dublin, and there is more than friendship here."

"I'm sorry. It's been a really big year, and the last thing I need is a friend who isn't really a friend."

"What are you running from, Juliette?" Charlie's whispered voice was soothing and heartbreaking.

I squeezed my eyes shut even tighter and shook my head. Taking a deep breath, I relaxed my face and opened my eyes. I was met with a concerned yet warm expression. "I'm not running." The corners of my mouth twitched, unsure whether to smile or frown. "When I met you, I was running. I came home to fight for the life I want."

He moved in front of me and held my face with both his hands. "You don't have to fight for me, Jules. I can make you happy."

My eyes widened as he moved his face towards mine in slow motion. When I felt his lips on mine, I was startled by his audacity. It was intimate. It was wrong, and I pushed him hard against his chest.

"I'm with Leo." Tears welled in my eyes. "I'm in love with Leo."

He ran his hands through his hair. "I know." He shook his head. "But where was he when you spent months overseas, and where is he now?"

"You shouldn't have kissed me." I didn't want to consider that I had kissed him back even for a split second or that his lips had felt nice against mine. He was safe, and a part of me wanted safe. But the bigger part of me wanted Leo.

"I'm not sure I should be telling you this."

"Then don't," I whispered, pleading him with words and my eyes to stop.

"I don't think I took in a single thing at The Book of Kells other than the fact that you twirl a lock of your hair when you seem nervous, you have a freckle right at the edge of your lip that I wanted to touch, your navy eyes sparkle when you see something you are excited about and your nose twitches ever so slightly when you are thinking carefully about something." He barely drew breath as he continued. "For those following six weeks, I could barely stand to be apart from you. I moved meetings, rescheduled trips and pretty much threw my whole life into chaos to get any snippet of time you were willing to offer me." His eyes seared me with their intensity. "Tell me you didn't feel it, too."

When he stopped speaking, I exhaled. I'd been holding my breath for too long and was light-headed. "I think you should go."

"That's all you have to say?"

I chewed my lip, unsure how I actually felt about his speech. "I'm in love with someone else." I hated witnessing the pain in his eyes, but his feelings were unrequited. "I'm so sorry, Charlie."

"That someone let you go. If you were mine, I would never let you go."

"I left *him* to go overseas. He let me go because I gave him no choice." I looked into his pain-filled eyes. "We are friends, Charlie. There will never be anything more. If I'd met you before I met the love of my life, maybe I could have had a future with you. But it's too late. My heart is taken, and even if it doesn't work out with Leo, my heart will always belong to him."

"So I imagined it all?"

"I didn't lead you on. I was upfront from the beginning."

I kissed him on the cheek, said goodbye to one of the best guys I'd ever known and walked away.

I half-walked, half-jogged away with my arms still wrapped around myself. It occurred to me that whilst I had fought against my mother's tight hold on my life, it had given me some kind of anchor, even if I had constantly been pulling away from it, and part of me had relied on its security. I would never go back to that, but it was unreasonable to think I could transition smoothly away from her stronghold. I had to learn to do what was right for me.

When I got back to the office, I collapsed into my chair and sighed, a loud exhale that came from the pit of my stomach.

Heath waltzed out of his office and stood at my desk. "Oh good. You're back."

"Yep," I confirmed, slumping farther into my chair. "I'm back." I couldn't hide the complete disillusionment I was feeling.

He dropped a piece of paper on my desk. "I need you to fill in five account opening forms in these entities." No please and no thank you. He wasn't necessarily rude. He just didn't waste time with pleasantries when he was focused and busy. Come to think of it, he was rude. *Arsehole,* I thought to myself, scowling. "Mr Voss called while you were out and is in the city." He was already halfway back to his office. "He's going to come up to sign the forms. Oh, and can you arrange for some afternoon tea in one of the meeting rooms?"

I groaned when he disappeared into his office. I was done.

I turned to my computer and opened a blank Word document, ready to compose my resignation letter. I didn't want Charlie's job, but I didn't want this one either.

CHAPTER 20

Leo

I HEADED HOME TO CHANGE, then rode my bike out to Lilydale to see Nick. If I'd taken anything from the past week and particularly the weekend in Perth, it was that I needed to get my shit together. Coming face-to-face with my mother had sent me into a tailspin. Nick and Juliette had been there to break my fall, but that was never going to happen again. I didn't take others down with me.

"Hey, Leo," Nick called out from across the other side of the club when I entered through the large heavy doors.

I sauntered over to him, skirting the boxing ring. Flashes of Jules in there a few months back made my chest swell with pride. She had been incredible, and the regret at not being able to celebrate with her afterwards still stung. That wasn't going to happen again.

"Hey, Nick," I said, stopping next to him. "Whatcha doin'?"

"Boxing for Fitness class just finished," he replied, packing away the last of the equipment. "I imagine all the mums are headed to Bea's café for their post-class caffeine hit right about now."

"I wanted to talk about your offer."

He straightened up. "Oh yeah."

"It's really generous of you, considering my dick move in Perth."

"Well, I'm a schmuck. What can I say?" He shrugged, smiling. "Are you gonna accept or not?"

"I am," I confirmed. "I want this."

Nick nodded and slapped me on the back. "We're gonna take it all the way, you and me," he said. "I'm in the middle of scheduling, so we can start next week."

"Okay, great."

"I have something else I wanted to discuss with you." He started walking in the direction of his office, gesturing with his hand for me to follow.

When we got to his office, he sat down at his desk and pulled out a folder. I took a seat opposite him and leaned forward to retrieve the folder he'd just pushed across the desk.

"What is this?" I asked, staring at the folder in my hands. It was obviously old, judging from the faded colour and dog-eared corners.

"It's everything you need to know to make your decision."

"Decision about what?"

"Buying the club."

I snapped my head up. "What?" Now I was more than surprised. I was completely shocked.

"My son isn't interested in the business at all. Think of it like a succession plan." He winked. "I'm not getting any younger."

"You're not old," I rebutted. "What are you? Fifty?"

"Fifty-two, but I feel a hundred most days."

"Shit, Nick. I've just got my head around one offer and

you hit me with this."

He nodded. "I'm offering it to you at a very fair price."

"I'm sorry, Nick, but I'm not ready for something like that."

"Come on, mate. This is a solid investment."

"I'm sorry." I shook my head and wrung my hands in my lap. "I don't have the money, and I'm not mortgaging the farmhouse." I glanced up at him, hoping I could make him understand. "I know it doesn't make sense, but that's just the way it is."

I dropped the folder back on his desk, then crossed my arms over my chest.

"You know, I've seen enough damaged fighters to know generally what makes and breaks people. You have to let what happened to your father go. Otherwise, you're a liability to yourself and to those around you."

"I'm moving forward. I lost control when I saw my mother and I should never have accepted the Perth fight, but I might never be able to move on from what happened to my father."

"Give it some thought," he grumbled. "Talk to your girl." He took the folder back and dropped it on the floor beside him. "I'll come back to you with a schedule for the young guys I want you to mentor."

"You want me to mentor them? I thought I was just helping you train them."

"You have a lot to offer, son. You'll be surprised how much the young guys will look up to you."

"Why are you doing all this for me?" I really wanted to know why a man I'd ditched more than a decade ago and then overruled in the ring was willing to help me now.

He stared straight ahead for a few moments as if contemplating his answer before turning back to face me. "I have my reasons."

When I left the club in Lilydale, I headed to the farmhouse as planned. I had to admit, the more time I spent there, the more I was starting to enjoy it.

CHAPTER 21

Juliette

WHEN I WALKED INTO MY apartment building after work, my mind was still reeling from my conversation with Charlie and the fact I was going to be unemployed in a month. Charlie had sent me several text messages throughout the afternoon, apologising for pushing too hard. I had my earbuds in, so I was startled when Leo stepped out in front of me. I pulled them out immediately and drank in the sight of him. He was wearing faded jeans that looked like they needed a wash and a dark blue, long-sleeved shirt. He was breathtaking.

"Hey," he said in a raspy voice that made my heart flutter.

"Hey." My response came out as a whisper, and I had to clear my throat.

He moved towards me, never taking his eyes off mine. I felt like a deer in headlights but without the paralysing fear because I wanted to be devoured by this man, whatever the cost. He stunned me every time, not just with his looks, but with the way the world disappeared when he looked at me like I was the only other person in it.

His arms encircled me, crushing me to his hard body. I had expected his lips to crush mine with a hunger I felt deep in my bones, but there was no crushing.

"I." A light kiss just behind my ear made me shiver. "Missed." Another feathering of kisses to my neck shot desire straight between my legs. "You." I was a goner.

He held my face and kissed me on the lips so lightly, I closed my eyes to enjoy the moment and revel in our contact. I was so in love with this man.

"I missed you, too," I managed to croak out through my lust haze.

"Let's go upstairs." He took my hand and pulled me gently towards the lift. I felt drunk and stumbled a little before snapping myself out of it.

"How was your day, beautiful?" A few fellow residents joined us in the lift, so we stood next to each other, holding hands, sexual tension filling the air.

"Tough," I replied honestly.

Leo turned to face me. "What happened?"

The reality of what I was about to tell him started to hit me. "I resigned today."

"Seriously?" he asked, staring at me with wide eyes.

The lift doors opened at my level, and we walked out. Leo dropped my hand and put his arm around my shoulders, pulling me in closer while I opened the door. I had taken the promise of hot sex and ruined it, but I really did have things to tell him.

I dumped my handbag and keys on the sideboard, then plonked myself onto the couch. Leo surprising me in the lobby had given me a much-needed boost, but I couldn't avoid telling him about Charlie. I also wanted to hear about what Nick had had to say.

Leo sat down next to me and pulled my legs over his lap and started massaging my feet. I tried to yank my feet away from his strong hands. "I know girls are supposed to love that, but I am insanely ticklish."

Laughing, he didn't release my feet, but he did stop massaging. I held my breath for a few seconds, waiting to make sure the assault didn't restart. When I was sure he wasn't going to torture me, I exhaled.

"Talk to me, Jules. Tell me all about your day, and I promise I won't tickle you."

I grimaced. "You better not." I rubbed my face with my hands. "I fell into that job. I don't hate it. That isn't fair. I just don't feel like going through the motions of gainful employment doing something I don't love." I looked at him to see if he understood. "I guess I'd like to feel a little more excited about what I do."

"Life's too short, Jules." He squeezed my feet gently, and I liked it. "You're young, and you have no financial obligations like kids or a mortgage. There's no reason you should stay there."

"That's what I figured." I took another deep breath, feeling my body relax into his gentle touch. "I just don't know what I'm going to do instead, and in a month, I'll be unemployed."

"What would you love to do if you had your choice of anything in the world?"

I scrunched my nose up. No one had ever asked me that before, and sadly, I'd never asked myself either. I pondered the question for a while, allowing my thoughts to drift to the things that I loved.

"Did something happen today specifically that triggered your resignation?" he continued, trying to prompt me. "Did your boss piss you off or something?"

"I don't think you're going to like my answer."

He raised his eyebrows. "Tell me anyway, Jules."

"I had lunch with a guy I met while I was travelling." I bit my lip. I felt his whole body tense as his gentle touch turned into a steely grip. "My dad's doing some work for him, so he's only in town for a few days." I looked into his beautiful but intense blue eyes. "And he offered me a job working for his family business in Sydney."

His nostrils flared, and what looked like a mixture of anger and fear flashed across his eyes. "What did you say?"

"I declined his job offer. I don't want to move to Sydney and I'm not interested in the job, but it made me realise I didn't want my current job either."

"Did something happen with him while you were away?" He spoke through gritted teeth, and the pressure on my feet intensified. "Is that why you didn't think I'd like your answer?"

I shouldn't have hesitated because nothing actually had happened, but there had been an undeniable chemistry between Charlie and me, and I would've been lying if I said it had never crossed my mind. I'd left behind a life of chaos and uncertainty, so the temptation to stay over there had, at times, been great.

I pulled my feet out of his hands and sat up straighter on the couch, pulling my legs underneath me. "Nothing happened between us overseas," I whispered.

Leo bristled. "What are you not telling me, Jules?"

I scrunched up my face. "He kissed me today and told me he was in love with me." I blurted it out to get it over and done with.

"What the fuck?" The murderous look on Leo's face made me regret telling him, but I was done with secrets, lies and protecting the feelings of those I cared about because, in the end, it would backfire. He stood up and stalked to the window. His chest was heaving, and his fists were clenching and unclenching. "Fuck, Juliette."

He didn't look at me.

I jumped off the couch to join him. When I placed my hand on his arm, he flinched. "I wasn't going to tell you."

"Then why did you?" he snapped.

"Because we need to be open and honest with each other," I stated firmly. "I can't begrudge you not opening up to me if I withhold potentially hurtful information." I leaned into him. "Charlie is a good man. He is smart, kind and fun."

He groaned. "Wow, Juliette. This isn't helping."

"Let me finish," I whispered. "Look at me."

Eventually, he turned to face me, but the hardness in his features remained.

"Charlie is exactly the type of man I think my mother wanted for me all along. She got it totally wrong with Richard, but her intention was to find me a respectable, safe partner to look after me and I, thinking I was doing the right thing, let her railroad me."

Leo groaned. "So your parents would approve of this Charlie guy, and he'd make your life easy."

"You're right. Being with Charlie would make my parents happy."

Leo huffed. "You told me in Perth you yearned for normal."

"I yearn for you," I shot back. "That is what stopped anything happening with Charlie overseas, and that is what brought me home to all this craziness." I moved to stand in front of him and snaked my arms around his waist. I looked into his eyes and hoped I could make him understand. "I'm done doing anything just to keep my parents happy." His shoulders visibly dropped, and I heard him exhale. "We've brought complication and heartache to each other's lives, but we're moving forward." I waved my hand between the two of us. "I will continue fighting for you, for me and for us. It's the Leo and Jules way." I gave him a goofy grin, and he attempted a small smile to let me know I was cracking through.

He ran his thumb across my lips and appeared pained. "The thought of another man..."

"I don't want anyone kissing me but you."

His lips claimed mine in a frenzy of lust and possession.

I pulled back reluctantly. "Can you ask me how my day was again, please?"

He appeared confused. "How was your day?"

"Fantastic." I smiled. "Please take me to bed."

Later, I made us spaghetti and meatballs, and we watched two episodes of *Game of Thrones* together on the couch. The contentment was bliss. When the second episode ended with more questions than it had started with, I turned the TV off and snuggled into Leo's hard chest.

I had completely forgotten about our earlier conversation, thanks to the mind-blowing sex and the drama we'd just been watching that made our lives seem boring in comparison. The only dragon I'd had to deal with was my mother, and she was fairly tame and rarely breathed fire.

I kissed the middle of his chest, then sat up and looked at him, remembering he had been to see Nick today. "Did you go to Lilydale today?"

"I did. I wanted to talk to you about it."

"Tell me."

He shifted on the couch. "I accepted his job offer to train young guys while I get serious about my own training, but he's talking about selling the club." He paused, allowing me to process. "I'll have to look for a new trainer, too, if Nick disappears on me."

"Oh, wow. That's unexpected. I thought Nick was a lifer."

"Yeah. Me too. I was totally blindsided. He asked me to buy it from him, but I declined."

"Bloody hell. Why didn't you tell me all this immediately?"

"I kinda got sidetracked when I heard another man kissed my girlfriend." He raised his eyebrows and I cringed.

"So when do you start?" I asked, keen to change the subject.

"Next week. I'm going to quit my bar job, but I'll give Adri some notice. I don't want to leave her in the lurch." He hesitated before he continued. "Nick also offered me the apartment above the fight club."

I flinched. I knew it would make more sense for him to live out there, but the idea of being that far apart made my stomach drop. "Oh."

"I said no. I don't want to live that far from you."

A mixture of relief and concern hit me. "If it weren't for me, would you move back there?"

"I don't know." He appeared pensive. "Probably, I guess, but it's a moot point."

He pulled me into a hug, and I knew whatever happened, in his arms was where I was happiest. The cogs in my brain started to turn with visions of wide open spaces.

CHAPTER 22

Juliette

"DO YOU LIKE THAI FOOD?" Leo surprised me with this random question when I got home from work on Wednesday evening. I'd given Leo a key to my apartment so he could come and go as he pleased.

"I love it, but I haven't had it in years. Richard always said all Asian food was full of MSG and refused to eat it, so I guess I just never think of it."

Leo cringed when I said my ex-boyfriend's name.

"Have I ever told you just how much I love Thai food?" he asked.

"Nope." I smiled. "You've never told me about your love of Thai food."

"Then I'm going to take you to my favourite restaurant. I'm starving."

"Well, I'd hate to see you starve." I raised my eyebrows.

~~~~~

When we arrived at the restaurant in Prahran, Leo was greeted warmly by the owner, an intimidating figure, to say the least, and I listened in rapture as they spoke in what I naturally assumed to be Thai. I heard Leo say my name and I smiled, assuming I was being introduced.

"Hello," I said, making a mental note to ask Leo to teach me a few words.

"Yin dee krap. Welcome, Juliette." He bowed and I returned the motion.

"Jules. This is my friend, Singdam, but feel free to call him Dam." They both chuckled, and I cringed at the idea of calling this scary looking guy dumb. "His chefs make the best Thai I've tasted outside Thailand," Leo informed me, eliciting a wide smile from his friend.

We were led to a table by the window of the richly-decorated room.

"Kob khun krap," Leo said when he was handed a menu, and I was determined to attempt the same.

"Kob khun krap." I repeated what I was pretty sure I'd heard Leo say.

Dam smiled and walked away.

"Kob khun ka," Leo said, leaning forward. "Men say kob khun krap and women say kob khun ka."

"Oh my god. Was I really rude? I was just trying—"

"No, no. I love that you tried. Thai is a very difficult language for Westerners to learn and speak correctly."

"I got that when you told me men and women say thank you differently." I chuckled.

"Similar-sounding words can have different meanings based on the tone they have. Like the word 'kao.' It can mean rice, nine, knee, to come in, news and a few other things."

"Seriously? How on earth did you learn it? Sounded to me like you were pretty much fluent."

"I lived in Thailand for a few years after my dad died.

When in doubt, you just say it in a flat, toneless way and hope your listener can work it out from the context. That's what I did when I was learning anyway."

"You amaze me, Leo Ashlar. You drive me crazy and often make me want to wring your neck, but you continue to amaze me."

"Ditto, Juliette Salinger."

Dam and one of his waiters arrived at our table with several plates of food we hadn't ordered.

Leo obviously noticed my surprised look. "Everything is good, so I just asked him to bring a variety for you to try."

"Kob khun ka." I spoke slowly and tentatively, hoping I got it right this time.

Dam smiled and rattled off something in Thai that made Leo laugh, and I clearly didn't understand. He seemed happy though when he walked away.

"Dam says you're far too beautiful for me."

I shook my head, thinking that was completely ridiculous. Leo was easily the hottest man I'd ever seen in real life, in magazines or at the movies. He was in a league of his own with a heart to match.

"By the way," he continued. "Dam is spelt D-A-M but pronounced Dum. I remember being terrified to call him dumb when I first met him, but he's the kindest and most generous man I've ever met. He just also happens to be one of Thailand's greatest Muay Thai fighters ever."

"Oh wow." I glanced over at Dam waiting on a table on the other side of the restaurant. "He could be called whatever you want, and no one would bother him about it."

Leo chuckled. "Very true. Nick introduced me to him after my father's funeral, and he trained me in Muay Thai. A year later, when I was still in a terrible state, he took me to Thailand to learn about his culture and train with the locals. I found some peace, thanks to him."

"Seems ironic to find peace in fighting, but I know what you mean. Do you still train with him?" I asked, riveted by this part of Leo's past I didn't know 'til now.

"On and off for five years now. He comes to my cage fights when he's not travelling back and forth from Thailand. He makes a good living from this restaurant and manages to financially support a range of youth charities in the provinces he grew up in." He glanced over at Dam, who was serving other customers. "He doesn't fight anymore, but in his day, he was a legend. Still is."

"And that's where you got the tattoos?" I remembered the first time I saw his back at the second fight night and was struck by the designs. He hadn't yet told me about them.

Leo nodded. "I got the nine-spired Gao Yord first." He reached around to instinctively rub the back of his neck.

I had studied them closely when he'd slept naked on his stomach one night. There were nine parallel spires of increasing height leading to the centre. Each spire shot out from oval shapes.

"It's a geometric design representing the nine sacred peaks of Mount Meru," he continued. "The three ovals, one above the other, is a Buddhist symbol."

"Did you practice Buddhism?"

"I wouldn't say practiced, but I studied it and have a deep respect for it."

"What does the tattoo mean?"

"It's said that the bearer of the Gao Yord is blessed with the protection from evil spirits and will have good luck."

"And the other one? The tigers?"

He sat back in his chair and crossed his arms over his chest. "The Tiger Yant. The tiger symbolises strength and power. Supposedly nothing gets in the way of the tiger because it's fearless and strong."

"So that's the meaning behind it?"

"It helps bring strength, power and fearlessness but will also drive evil spirits away."

"Evil spirits, huh?"

He just nodded.

"Well I think they're smokin' hot." I winked and was rewarded by his light chuckle.

"I'm glad you think so 'cause they're kinda permanent."

"Have you ever thought about getting any others?" I asked, intrigued.

"Not really." He leaned back on his chair and laced his fingers behind his head. "I know for a fact you don't have any." His gaze raked down my body, and a shiver ran through me. "You ever considered it?"

I leaned forward and rested my elbows on the table. "It had never appealed to me until recently."

"Oh yeah?"

"They were just far too permanent."

"Would've pissed your mum off, too, I'm guessing."

"I could've put it somewhere she'd never see, but my motives were never to piss her off." I took a sip of water and Leo did the same. "Hiding who I was and indulging my need for adrenaline with boxing, racing and fight nights was never about pissing her off."

"You are a beautiful person, Jules." His sincerity made my heart swell and my cheeks burn.

"Thanks." I scrunched my face up.

"So, I was thinking," he said, removing his hands from behind his head and reaching for mine across the table.

"Sounds dangerous."

He chuckled. "I was thinking we could head out to the farm on Saturday and spend the night out there."

Taken aback, but overjoyed, I nodded my head excitedly. "I would love that."

"I haven't forgotten what you said in that hotel bar in Perth, and I think it's time I told you what happened to my father."

I sucked in a breath as my heartbeat took off at a sprint. "Thank you," I whispered.

Dam refused payment, and we left after saying our goodbyes.

When we got outside, Leo suggested we go for a walk instead of going straight home.

Before we got too far, he piped up. "So I did have another reason for bringing you here and telling you about Thailand."

"You did?" To be honest, I didn't need him to have a point. He had started opening up to me about his past and that was massive.

"I've been thinking about your job dilemma a lot."

"And that made you think of Thai food?" I smirked.

Leo chuckled. "Most things make me think about food, but I did have a point." He chuckled and I leaned into him, eager to feel his body pressed against my side. "My point was that I thought I had everything worked out from a young age. I knew what I wanted, I studied my arse off, got into uni, changed my mind, and then it all went to shit." He huffed out a loud breath. "Life doesn't always work out the way you want it to, even when you have a tight plan and a steely determination to see it through."

He stopped and turned me to face him. "I was going

to be a doctor, and I ended up in a fight club in Thailand getting inked."

"Okay. That's a fair point."

"I know I've said this before, but life can be messy. When I thought I'd lost my way, I turned to fighting. Not because of my anger towards my mother or the grief from losing my father, but because it's what I love to do and it helped me work through my grief."

"I really appreciate you wanting to help me with my job dilemma, but all the things I love to do are hobbies."

"Start there."

"Okay. Well, then. Maybe something to do with race cars?" The joy I found in driving was never just about silently rebelling against my mother. I genuinely love it.

"Ugh." Leo's groan made me laugh. "Why couldn't your hobbies be cooking or sewing or something that wouldn't give me heart failure?"

"If you're looking for a domestic goddess, I'm afraid you're with the wrong girl."

"You don't have to come up with a solution right away, but start thinking about options. Maybe give your friend Jim a call."

We walked in silence for a few minutes, and my mind went immediately back to Leo's invitation to the farmhouse.

"Are we staying in the house?" I blurted out, not meaning to put a voice to my question.

He shook his head. "We could stay at Bea and Angus's place, but I had another idea if you're up for it."

"Tell me."

"I was thinking we could camp in the garden at the farmhouse."

I squealed. "I love camping."

"Something told me you would." He laughed at my

excitement. "I can't really see Isabel camping, so when have you done it?"

"My grandparents used to pitch a tent at their farm when I went to stay with them. They let me sleep in the garden. I loved it."

"Camping it is, then." He took my hand and started walking in the direction of my car.

"I can't wait." I could barely keep my feet from dancing on the spot.

He stopped and pulled me to him. "God, I'm so bloody lucky."

Before I had a chance to say anything, he was kissing me. It had started to rain lightly, and I felt raindrops land on my eyelashes. It was one of those beautiful moments when everything felt right in the world. Leo had started opening up and appeared comfortable doing so, and I was thinking about new careers. I smiled against his lips as the rain started to fall more heavily, and I realised we were actually getting really wet.

"Let's go home."

"Don't you two make the most adorable couple?"

We both spun around to be confronted by Gwendolyn standing on the footpath a few feet away under a large, black umbrella.

Leo's arm tightened around me. "What are you doing here?" he asked in a menacing tone.

"I just had dinner with your parents, Juliette." Her saccharine smile was really creepy. "It's so nice they are making an effort with your boyfriend's mother." She tapped the side of her nose. "I think they might still be worried he's going to be their son-in-law though."

"You have no business with Juliette's family, and you have no business with us." Leo coaxed me around so we had our backs to her.

"We need to talk, Leo."

Leo ushered me under a shop awning a few metres away to get me out of the rain. "Wait here one second," he whispered, before striding over to Gwendolyn.

I couldn't hear what was being said, but from the tension rolling off Leo and the angry hand gestures, it wasn't going well.

After several minutes, Gwendolyn left without saying goodbye to me, and Leo returned to me looking like he might explode.

"You okay?" I asked, placing my hand on his chest.

"I'm so sorry about that." He enveloped me in his arms. "I'm going to sort this out with her."

CHAPTER 23

LEO

WHEN JULES LEFT FOR WORK the next day, I headed home, then went for a long run to ease some of my tension before meeting with my mother. Having her show up out of the blue rattled me, and I needed to make sure that wasn't going to happen again. If I was going to keep moving forward with Juliette, I knew this was something I had to do, so I had agreed to meet her today.

When I arrived in Carlton where we'd agreed to meet the night before, I cursed the driver of a red Honda Civic who'd managed to selfishly take up two spots close to the café so I had to find somewhere a little farther away, then walk back along the busy street to our meeting place. I saw her immediately when I entered and grimaced when she stood up to greet me.

"Good to see you again, son."

I shuddered when she called me "son" but didn't say anything. "Have you ordered?"

"Not yet."

"What do you want?"

"Long black."

I walked up to the counter and took some deep breaths while I placed my order. I could not believe I was standing in the same room as this woman, but I had a single purpose. Then I'd be gone.

I reluctantly walked back to her and sat down. "What are you doing back in Melbourne?" I asked, trying to keep my voice calm.

"Melbourne is my home, too, Leo, and you're my only family."

"You need money, don't you?" I saw through her attempt at nostalgia immediately.

She clasped her hands in front of her on the table, and I was met with cool eyes. "I've done some research, and it turns out you received a much better deal. That farmhouse is worth a great deal more than the Sydney house."

"Are you serious?" I asked incredulously. "Everything, other than the farmhouse, went to you. You should've been set up for life." I knew it was going to be about money.

She shifted in her seat, clearly uncomfortable. "I may have made a few poor investment choices."

"So, you've blown the cash and now you've come crawling back here wanting to further benefit from my father's death?" My expression was deadpan, but my tone had bite. "Have I missed anything?"

"If you want me out of your life, you'll help me out."

I placed both hands on the table and was about to stand up. She was out of her mind if she thought I would give her one cent.

"That Juliette is quite the beauty, isn't she? Too good—"

"Stop." I cut her off. Her voice was causing bile to rise in my throat. "I don't want you to mention her name again, and after this conversation, you'll forget she exists. Do you understand?"

"Poor girl has been through so much already." Her

pout was laughable and made my blood boil.

"I can protect Juliette from you." I had to take some calming breaths to stop myself from strangling her. "You need to back off."

"She lives in Apartment 516, Highgate Building, Southbank. The concierges, whilst efficient, aren't always at the desk." She raised her eyebrows. "She does boxing training every Thursday evening from six thirty to eight with Zac, then walks home by herself." Her smile widened. "I know where she works, and her favourite café is McQuillens."

"I get your point." The bitch knew she had me over a barrel when it came to Juliette's vulnerabilities. I couldn't protect her twenty-four seven.

She held up her hand. "Wait. I have more. I met with her delightful ex-boyfriend, Richard, the other day. Despite being completely terrified of you, he is not at all happy with his fall from grace, and I know he can be bought."

"I have no proof of what you did, but we both know you could give me the closure you know I need." I knew my eyes were filled with hate, and she winced slightly when she met my gaze. "I can't believe you are here for more." I shook my head, disgusted by her. "Why didn't you just go out and find yourself a sugar daddy?"

"There's only one way to keep your little princess safe." She scoffed, and the sly grin had returned. "I want five hundred thousand dollars."

I snorted. "I don't have that kind of money."

"Sell the farmhouse," she stated, sitting back in her chair and crossing her arms over her chest. "Developers are sniffing around the area, and the value has skyrocketed."

"Never," I spat. "It was my father's house, and it has always been passed down through the generations. I'll never sell it. The farmhouse is mine." Despite the horrifying memory of that one fateful day, I loved that house and the farm because it was all him. He lived and breathed in that house, and I'd let his death overshadow that.

"Find the money, Leo." Her eyes were menacing, and my rage began to bubble. She cocked her head. "Is she worth that to you?"

I wasn't going to dignify her question. No one had a price tag, least of all Juliette. "It had been your home," I whispered. "You had the love of the best man I've ever known, and you threw it away."

"That man didn't love me," she rebuffed. "He loved that stupid house, he loved his wine cellar and he loved you."

"He worshipped the ground you walked on. I might've been a naïve teenager, but I know that was true."

She shook her head and shivered. "That's all ancient history now."

"I know you had something to do with his death." My acerbic words had no impact on her hard expression.

She smiled. "I don't know what you're talking about, son."

I was staring directly into soulless eyes, a reminder I didn't need that she was evil. That was our truth, and sometimes there was no forgiveness, no rehabilitation or acceptance. Sometimes there's just this—a forever-damaged son staring at his mother's black soul. Her cold indifference was something I'd never quite been able to block out over the years. It was the expression that had flashed through my mind every time I'd landed a punch on my opponent's face, and it was staring right at me. "If I decide to get you the money, you'll go back to Sydney or wherever the hell else you want to be as long as it's far from here and never come back." I was starting to lose my shit. "Unless you are willing to tell me what I want to know, you will stay out of my life." I stood up and leaned forward over the table to get in her face. "And you stay away from Juliette, or you and I are gonna have a serious problem." I waved my finger between us.

Though her face had visibly paled, she sat up straighter in her chair. "I was hoping you'd found someone you loved more than you hated me." She winked. "She's your weakness."

I stared at the woman I hoped to never lay eyes on again. "I'll be in contact when I've made my decision." I turned my back on her and walked towards the exit.

"Don't take too long," she called out. "Having you was the biggest mistake of my life."

I stopped and turned. "Well, I'd be happy if you pretended I didn't exist." I sounded remarkably calm. "Don't call Juliette and don't ever set foot on my property."

My body shook as I walked out of that café and away from the woman who destroyed lives.

I pulled out my phone and tapped the screen. Derek, the illegal cage fight promoter, answered on the third ring. "What's up, Leo?"

"I want in on your next fight."

"That is really great news for me," he replied. "I've had a few dropouts, so you'd actually be doing me a solid."

"I'm ready to fight. Thanks, mate."

"The next one is a couple of weeks away, so I'll text you the details as usual."

I hung up feeling a mixture of excitement and apprehension. The prize money was going to help pay my mother off quickly, but I also couldn't deny the lure of the cage. I would just have to make sure Juliette stayed away.

CHAPTER 24

Juliette

I KNEW OF A STORE that sold sexy lingerie, and not just your standard Victoria's Secret kind of sexy. From what I could tell from subtly glancing in the window, it was a whole new level of apparel designed with one thing in mind. Sweet Spot, located in Melbourne Central shopping centre, held everything I could possibly need to blow Leo's mind and take it off the confrontation with his mother. When I'd come home from work on Tuesday evening, he'd hugged me like he hadn't seen me in months. I'd asked what was wrong, and he'd told me he'd met with his mother and we wouldn't be seeing or hearing from her again. When I tried to press him for details, he'd said he would tell me everything at the farm, so I didn't push it.

Friday lunchtime, I made my way to the store with a skip in my step. Leo had spoken to Adriana the night before when he'd gone into work, and she had actually been about to tell him she was leaving, too. She was moving to Aireys Inlet with her new bank manager boyfriend, nicknamed Superman by Leo. He'd been looking for a sea change, too. Leo was worried she was moving too fast with this new guy, but she'd reassured him she was deliriously happy. Leo, bless him, couldn't argue with that.

Sweet Spot was all black, gold and expensive looking. I made the decision not to look at the price tags and was just going to be governed by my gut instinct. I'd know it when I saw it.

I knew lingerie and camping didn't necessarily go hand in hand, but as we kept realising, we didn't do anything by the book, and I was going to make him forget his own name. The thought made me smile as I entered the store.

"You look happy." The friendly sales assistant made me feel comfortable immediately, despite being surrounded by sex toys and erotic underwear. "Are you looking for something special?" She was dressed in a form-fitted white shirt tucked into a tight leopard-print skirt. Her skin-tone stockings had a black line trim down the back. Her heels were higher than I'd ever dare but completed her surprisingly classy outfit. She completely owned her look with a confidence I admired.

"I am," I replied with a small smile.

"Do you have anything in mind?"

"I... um..." I hesitated, blushing like a fool. "I'm not sure."

She chuckled. "You don't have to be embarrassed. Every girl needs sexy underwear." She glanced over at the display cabinet, hidden from the front window by well-positioned lingerie racks. "Take a closer look."

I shuffled tentatively over to the backlit cabinet and gasped when I saw a pair of leather handcuffs with a yellow-gold chain, several dildos and a variety of products in boxes. The word "lubricant" made me blush again, and I quickly looked the other way. I was no prude, but these kinds of things made me feel awkward. Thoughts of trying out a few things with Leo made me feel slightly weak at the knees though. *Perhaps I'll look online,* I thought to myself. I realised I was now grinning like a naughty school girl.

"See anything that tickles your fancy?"

She must have seen my kind of reaction a million times—not knowing whether to be embarrassed or excited by what was on offer.

"Maybe," I replied slowly, smirking uncontrollably. "I'm really just here for some lingerie."

"Okay then. Let's find you something smoking hot. What's his name?"

"Whose name?"

"The man who's going to benefit from my merchandise." She raised her eyebrows and smiled seductively.

"Leo." Even the sound of his name rolling over my tongue made my libido stand to attention. "His name is Leo, and I'm on a mission to blow his mind. Lingerie seemed like a good place to start."

"Ooh, my favourite kind of mission." She clapped her hands gleefully. "I'm Nadeira, by the way."

"Juliette." I blushed. I couldn't believe I was now on a first-name basis with the girl selling handcuffs and lubricant in downtown Melbourne.

"Nice to meet you, Juliette. Okay. Let's look around and see if anything stands out. Tell me something about hot Leo. What's he into?"

"How do you know he's hot?"

"Oh, I don't. I have Leo DiCaprio in The Great Gatsby in my head." She fanned her face. "Phew. That man is hot."

I laughed. "Well I think my Leo is much hotter than

DiCaprio." *My Leo*.

"Well, then. Sounds like I'm right, then."

"He's into lots of things. He's a fighter. He's strong. Really strong. And he's kind. He has the kindest heart I've ever known." I paused, swallowing past the lump in my throat and briefly closing my eyes. "He rides a motorbike."

"Motorbike. Yes. That's perfect. I just took delivery of a new line, and I think it might just do the trick." She pranced off towards the back of the store and I followed closely behind her, eager to see what she had in mind. "Here." She waved her hand towards the sexiest lingerie I'd ever seen.

"It's perfect."

"This is our Ezy Rider suspender set." She picked up the set on three different hangers and handed them to me.

"Is that leather?" I asked, trying to imagine the look on Leo's face when he saw me in this. Above the cup was a series of triangles with a small gold stud on every corner.

"The leatherette triangles are laser cut to mould to the breast. It's inspired by leather biker jackets." She took the underwear from me and turned it around. "See. The same detailing sits over your butt cheeks. And you have to own it. No being shy and trying to cover yourself up. Come on. Try it on."

She led me to a luxurious change room at the back of the store and gave me a quick explanation as to the easiest way to get the lingerie on. There were more straps and clasps than I was used to.

A short time later, I stood staring at myself in the mirror.

"How's it going?" Nadeira asked.

I pulled the heavy, velvet curtain back and allowed

her to see for herself.

"You flaunt that body of yours for this Leo and he won't know what hit him. Sexiness isn't about having the perfect body. Not that that's a problem for you, but I don't actually think physical appearance is the major factor. Sexiness comes from within. It's how you feel, and it's how you convey those feelings to those around you. You've gotta ride it, honey."

I burst out laughing. "I certainly hope to." A fierce blush heated my face when I realised I'd said that out loud.

"Atta girl." She winked at me. "So you don't want to look at anything else? I can show you plenty of other styles if you like."

"This is the one. I'll take it."

"Leo won't know what hit him," she said, winking.

When I'd paid, she handed me a stylish black bag with gold writing and trim. "Good luck, girlfriend. Come back and tell me how you go. Maybe bring Leo with you next time, and he can help pick out a few other sets."

I shook my head and chuckled. "With all due respect, Leo wouldn't be seen dead in here, but I will come back and let you know. Thanks for your help, Nadeira."

"You're most welcome. We're all about the happily-ever-afters in this shop, so I'm really hoping you get yours."

"Thank you," I replied sincerely. I was feeling more confident than ever about my mission, and at the very least, I'd gotten a lesson in sexiness from my new friend.

I hid my purchase under my desk when I returned to work. I had been told about the store by one of the other assistants who flirted with every man in the office. I didn't need her recognising the bag and making a big deal of it in front of my colleagues.

The afternoon passed quickly, and at five, instead of

going out for work drinks, I went home and was relieved to see I'd beaten Leo. He had been going to the farm again today and had said he'd be home around seven, so I had plenty of time. I loved that he now considered anywhere I was home. It really didn't matter where it was as long as we were together. I hid my new purchase and stripped off. It was time to relax and unwind.

I tapped on my Spotify app and hit play. P!nk was still my go-to music for most moods, but I chose Enya instead. I decided a bubble bath was in order, so I turned the taps, then went to the kitchen to pour a glass of red wine to get the party of one, soon to be two, started. As I reclined in the warm water, bubbles tickling my neck, I sipped on the wine and enjoyed the peace I felt knowing my life was really starting to come together. I'd carefully placed my Kindle next to the bath, so I switched it on and continued reading a beautiful romance novel I'd started the night before. I felt my eyes droop after about thirty minutes of reading, so I put the Kindle down and allowed my eyes to close while I enjoyed the still-warm water.

I don't know how long I dozed. Couldn't have been long, as the water was still warm when I woke up to a set of beautiful blue eyes gazing at me.

"Shit. You scared me."

"Sorry, gorgeous." He didn't look sorry as he picked up my Kindle and placed it out of harm's way on the vanity. "Mind if I join you?"

"Please do."

He had stripped naked already, so he stepped into my surprisingly large bathtub for an apartment. We manoeuvred so my back was to his front, and I lay my head back on his shoulder while he ran his hands over my soapy body.

"I could get used to coming home to this every day,"

he whispered in my ear.

I closed my eyes and enjoyed his strong, calloused hands massaging me, his erection digging into my backside. I let out a groan as he cupped my breasts and turned my head so I could kiss him. When I couldn't stand the overwhelming sensations any longer, I straddled him, not caring that a wave of water sloshed over the side of the tub and onto my bathroom floor. I smiled against his lips.

"I need to be inside you, Jules."

I didn't need any further discussion. I lined myself up and impaled myself on him. "Oh my God. That feels good." I'd never had sex in a bath before, and it wouldn't be the last time. The warm water felt like a soft blanket that moved with us as I rocked back and forth, building towards our mutual goal.

"Harder, Jules."

I lifted myself up using my knees to support my weight, then slammed back down. The impact of my body hitting his sent another wave of water over the side. At this rate, we weren't going to have any left. His warm mouth sucking my breasts sent a different kind of wave through my body. I was set to explode any second, and Leo's magic touch hovered over the detonator button.

He gripped my waist as I fought to keep my mind lucid enough to focus on the beautiful man beneath me. The hard planes of his incredible body were an intoxicating contrast to his kind heart, and the combination was breathtaking. I hugged him to me, fearful I might just float away as the explosions went off behind my eyes. Sex with Leo was never just going through the motions. It was never dull or boring. Every single time was a unique and mind-blowing experience. Perhaps that's what it's like for everyone who's found their perfect other half.

"Water's getting cold," Leo whispered in my ear some time later.

We both dried off, threw on some loose clothes, then grabbed a quick dinner at a Mexican restaurant on Southbank. Leo told me he'd set up a tent for us at the farmhouse and was going to be far better prepared than the last time we'd been there together. I couldn't wait.

CHAPTER 25

THE NEXT MORNING, WE DROVE directly to Bea's café for the best coffee in the world and for Jules to see Bea. It had been ages since they'd seen each other in person, but they had kept in touch over the phone.

"Well look what the cat dragged in," she said as the bell above the door signalled our arrival.

"Are you going to say that every time I come here?" I asked, shaking my head.

"Sure am. Got a problem with that, tough guy?"

Jules laughed at the two of us, and I just rolled my eyes. I was being ganged up on by my two favourite girls and didn't mind one bit.

When she brought our coffees over to the table by the window, she sat down with us. There were only a few customers, and they were all happy.

"So, camping, huh?" Bea scrunched up her nose. "Crazy."

"I love sleeping outside," Jules declared.

"Give me a warm bed and a hot shower any day of the week."

Jules took a sip of her coffee. "Not me. I'll take the

great outdoors, thanks."

"You really weren't cut out to be a society princess, were you?" Bea's rhetorical question made the two girls laugh, and it was music to my ears.

"Before my grandparents moved to Queensland," Juliette said, "I used to go and stay at their farm for a few nights every school holidays. I spent the whole time digging in the garden, riding horses and helping Gran with her epic vegetable patch." She stared into space for a moment before coming back to us. "I miss that. I miss them."

"When was the last time you saw them?" I asked.

"Too long. Their relationship with my mother was unbearable, and she had a meltdown whenever I visited them. They moved to Queensland and travel a lot so it became even harder. They call me on my birthday each year, and I send them a Christmas card." She patted the table with her palm. "I'm going to visit them soon. It is ridiculous I haven't in so long."

"Jules quit her job in the city," I told Bea.

"Really? That's great." She appeared uncertain. "I think it's great, at least."

I smiled. "It is great, but I haven't worked out what I'm going to do yet," Jules said.

"Would you consider moving out here?" she asked casually. My jaw dropped.

"Oh. Um..." She looked at me but quickly returned her gaze to Bea. "I don't know. Maybe?"

"Well you know Angus works for a financial planning firm in Lilydale, so I can let him know you're job hunting if you like?" Bea said, standing up and moving back to the counter where a customer was ready to order.

"Seriously?" I asked, reaching for her hand. "You'd move out here?"

She met my eyes, and her expression was warm. "I've never hidden the fact I love it out here. I love the countryside, the fresh air, the space." She inhaled as if she were smelling something she couldn't get enough of. "When I first stumbled across this area on my way to that godawful charity event, I felt drawn to it. I feel at home here, which is weird, I know, but it's true."

"Babe." I didn't know what to say.

"It's worth thinking about, right? I mean, I've resigned from my city job, and you're going to be at the fight club a lot. It makes sense, doesn't it?"

"Let's talk about it some more out at the farm. Okay?"

"I just think things are going to work out for us one way or another," she said, sincerely. "Everything feels like it's falling into place."

"I think you're right." I focused on the coffee swirling in my cup rather than meeting her gaze. I still had to tell her about what had happened five years ago and how that was probably going to negatively impact the rest of my life. The time was right, and I was going to trust her. Perhaps then she would know why I left it in the past.

"You're about to find out every last thing about your messed-up boyfriend. Do you think you're ready for that?"

She nodded and smiled, then accepted the hand I offered her. "Let's go."

"Hello, Leo." I snapped my head around to my best mate Angus's mum standing behind me. Growing up, she'd been my mother's best friend and like a second mother to me. I hadn't seen her for years. Her skin appeared grey and pasty, and the lines around her mouth made her look like a chain smoker. Similar to my mother, time hadn't been kind.

"Hello, Sandra."

It was awkward how uncomfortable she seemed

around me. She turned her attention to Jules. "I'm Beatrix's mother-in-law, Sandra. You must be Juliette." She held out her hand, and Jules shook it warmly.

"It's really nice to meet you," Jules said. She had no idea about the connection to my mother or the problem she had with me.

Sandra returned her gaze to me, rubbing both sides of her head with two fingers as if she were itching to say something. We stared at each other in silence for what felt like an awkwardly long time.

"I saw your mother yesterday," she said with bitterness dripping from every syllable.

"We were just leaving. It was lovely to see you again, Sandra," I lied, ushering Juliette towards the door ahead of me.

"Bye, Bea," Jules called out over her shoulder.

Sandra grabbed my arm. "You're a bastard, you know that, Leo." She narrowed her eyes. "It's bad enough you cut her out of your life, but she's finally come home and you're forcing her to move away again."

Juliette stopped in her tracks, then turned around, wide-eyed.

"Sandra!" Bea exclaimed. She'd obviously heard the bastard comment. "You can't say that to him."

"It's true." She addressed Bea. "You know as well as I do that it's true. His sweet mother doesn't deserve the way he treats her."

She crossed her arms. "Leo is my best friend, and I won't have you talking to him like that in here."

Huffing, Sandra strode to the counter.

"Sorry about that," Bea said. "She rarely stops by, so it's an unfortunate coincidence you were here." She turned to Juliette. "Ignore my mother-in-law. She's not usually like that."

"Okay," Juliette said, drawing out the first syllable.

I shrugged. "I don't give a shit what Sandra thinks." I took the basket and cooler Bea had packed for us. It was no doubt filled with enough food to feed an army. She also handed me a bunch of flowers. "Thanks, Bea," I whispered.

When we were outside, Juliette scrunched up her nose. "Sandra was... intense."

"She and my mother were best friends. Still are I guess."

She reached across and touched my arm. "You okay?"

"I'm fine." Sandra's outburst had had very little impact on me, I was happy to acknowledge. "Do you mind if we take another quick detour on the way?" I asked when we were back in my Jeep.

"Of course not." Jules smiled and my heart clenched. She was so incredibly beautiful. Ever since she'd quit her job and I'd suggested coming out here, she seemed happier. Her navy eyes appeared bright and full of life.

The Anglican church I grew up near had stood the test of time. Despite it being built back in the early 1900s, it was extremely well-maintained by the community. My mother was a fierce atheist, but my father had had a quiet faith. Whilst my father had regularly attended the Sunday church service, my mother had flat out refused.

When I pulled up in front of the church, Jules peered out the window then back at me. "You brought me to church?"

"Come on." I reached over to the back seat and grabbed the flowers, then placed my hand on the door handle. "I want to share something with you."

We walked down the narrow dirt pathway that ran along the church boundary and turned into the cemetery behind. It was approaching midday, and the sun felt warm on my back when I knelt down in front of my father's grave. Juliette knelt down beside me, and I felt her comforting hand on my shoulder.

"Five fucking years today, Dad." I paused, shaking my head as I carefully placed the flowers on the ground in front of me. "Five fucking years."

"Today?" Jules asked in a whispered voice.

I nodded.

"Wow," she whispered. "Thank you for bringing me here."

I looked at her angelic face and knew she was meant to be there with me. I sat back on my heels and stared at the inscription.

Jules leaned forward and traced her finger over his name. *William James Ashlar.*

"I should've personalised it more, but at the time, I didn't know which way was up."

"I don't know what to say."

"Perhaps I'll make him a new headstone one day."

"I think that would be an amazing thing to do."

"How did he die, Leo?" Jules asked after a few minutes silence.

"Stab wounds to the chest." He took a deep breath, then exhaled slowly. "He bled out."

"Oh my God." She gasped. "That is horrible."

I nodded. "I can't enjoy the sunrise because that's *when* I found him. Until you, I couldn't be in that house because that's *where* he died." I paused to take a breath and compose myself before continuing. "Most of all, I hate being so full of rage because I have no closure." I looked her in the eye and saw nothing but compassion. "It's exhausting, Jules."

"You don't know who did it?"

I shook my head. "Unsolved murder."

"So the caged Muay Thai and Buddhism helped you

channel your grief and your rage."

She understood. "The cage fighting was such an incredible outlet, but I want more now." I gave her my hand and helped her to her feet. "I want more for us."

She stood on her tiptoes and kissed me lightly. "I just want us." She whispered against my lips, then rested her forehead on mine.

I was irrevocably in love with this girl.

Both our gazes returned to the headstone, and we stood in silence for a few minutes before Jules asked the question that had most likely been running through her mind.

"What does your mother have to do with it?" I'd been wondering how to answer this question since she found out. "I mean, you lost your father, but she lost her husband. Why is she dead to you?"

"I'd like to explain it to you when we're at the house if that's okay?"

"Of course." She looked at me and smiled. "I'm just so happy you're finally telling me." She squeezed my hand. "It means a lot."

She leaned into my side as we walked back to the car hand in hand. I had never taken anyone to his grave despite Bea's annual request. She gave up asking a few years ago. It's always just been something I wanted to do alone.

CHAPTER 26

Juliette

A RED HONDA PULLED OUT from next to the Jeep when we rounded the corner of the Church. I only took note because the driver spun the tyres on the loose gravel and then fishtailed. *Ease off the throttle,* I thought to myself then mentally chastised myself for thinking about it at all after what Leo had just shared with me.

I sat sideways on the seat with my back to the door so I could give my full attention to Leo. "Thank you." I just felt compelled to let him know again how grateful I was that he had shared such a big thing with me on today of all days. I'd had no idea it was the anniversary of his father's death.

He glanced sideways at me and smiled before watching the road again. "You're welcome. I'm glad you were there." He reached his hand over and took hold of mine. "It was easier with you there."

"I'm glad." I picked up his hand and kissed it before letting our joined hands rest in my lap.

I was so happy to see the farmhouse come into sight a short time later. It had been winter the last time I was there, and it looked so different in the spring. Ivy covered most of the house in green, and wildflowers bloomed everywhere.

"Wow. It's even more beautiful than I remembered," I gushed as we rumbled down the cobbled driveway. I was eager to get out of the car. "It was freezing last time we were here."

"I'd rather not think too hard about the last time we were here, to be honest." I glanced back at him and could see his jaw clenching.

When he pulled up, I jumped out and headed straight for the back garden. The gazebo was no longer visible. Thick wisteria covered it in a purple blanket, and the smell of jasmine filled my nostrils. It was glorious, and I just stood there taking deep breaths.

"I have a surprise for you," Leo said, appearing at my side.

"What?"

"Come on." He took my hand and led me through the back gate and across the field towards the neighbour's fence. We climbed over the style and dropped down onto their side.

"What's going on, Leo?" I asked, intrigued.

"This is why I suggested you wear jeans this morning."

I glanced down at my jeans and white Converse sneakers. I'd just thought he was going to put me to work around the farm.

"Can you give me a clue?"

"I know you'll love it." His cheeky grin made me smile. "That's your clue."

I looked around. All I could see was the back of his neighbour's house and a stable block. Then it hit me. I'd told him I loved horses.

"We're going riding?" I could barely contain my excitement waiting for his confirmation, which came in the form of a nod and a smile.

I threw my arms around his neck and kissed him. "I'm so excited." I might've squealed a little. "You are amazing."

"I just want to see that smile all the time."

"Oh my God." I was a swooning puddle of jelly.

He took my hand, and we walked the rest of the way to the stables. An older lady came out of the stables, trailed by a couple of dogs.

She smiled warmly. "Leo. Hi."

"Hi, Wendy," Leo said, giving her a kiss on the cheek. "This is my girlfriend, Juliette."

I shook her hand. "Lovely to meet you, Wendy. Thank you so much for this."

"Anytime. Seriously. I'm always looking for extra help exercising my horses."

My face nearly split from the grin I couldn't contain. It was like a dream come true.

"Come on." She beckoned us with a wave as she headed back into the stable block.

Nostalgia hit me square in the nostrils when I inhaled the combined smell of hay and horse manure. It reminded me of the good times spent with my grandparents and how much I had loved my time at the farm. I counted four horses in the stalls, plus the two already saddled up.

"These are your mounts." She pointed to the smaller of the two, a chestnut. "This is Tony." She then pointed to the larger black horse. "And this is Thunder."

She showed us to the mounting block, and before we knew it, we were clip-clopping our way down the stone path leading us back to the field.

"Follow the trail at the end of my field," Wendy called out. "It's beautiful this time of year."

"Thanks, Wendy," we both called out over our shoulders.

Wendy had been right. We were surrounded by nature exploding in all its glory. There were a few clouds gathering to the south, but other than that, it was a perfect spring day. I knew I could be happy with Leo anywhere, but this was as close to a perfect scenario as I could imagine.

"Are you okay there?" I asked, watching Leo's white-knuckle grip on the front of the saddle.

He looked over and relaxed his tense expression. "Absolutely. My balls aren't enjoying it much though."

I threw my head back and laughed. "I guess they wouldn't."

We'd been following the path for about an hour when we reached a clearing surrounded by pine trees. We dismounted and tied the horses up.

"Oh my God." Leo groaned.

"We haven't even been riding that long," I said, laughing.

He rubbed the inside of his thighs. "I'm going to be walking like a chicken for days."

"It definitely uses muscles you don't normally use, but a big, tough fighter like you should be able to handle it." I smirked but was grabbed around the waist and tickled as highly effective payback.

We sat on the blanket roll Wendy had attached behind my saddle, ate sandwiches Bea had made for us, and I wondered if life got any better than that. After lunch, we both flopped down onto our backs, holding hands. We stared up at the sky and watched the clouds drift lazily by.

We lay there in silence for a while, enjoying the peaceful sounds of nature.

"I love it here." I said, tilting my head to the side so I could admire his side profile.

"Me too." He turned his head to face me. "This can be our place."

"Do you ever think you could live in the farmhouse again?" I asked.

His gaze returned to the clouds. "I never sold the damn thing, so that's gotta mean something."

"So how did you end up with the house and not your mum?" I knew it was a risk asking these questions, but Leo had promised to tell me everything, so I was going to give him a gentle nudge. "The place is named after her."

He met my gaze. "Everything else went to her. The farm has been in my father's family for generations, passed down to the eldest child." His hand felt sweaty in mine. "My father renamed it as a wedding gift to her." He laughed without humour. "What a joke. "Come on." Leo stood up and offered me his hand. "Let's head back."

I wanted to hear more, but it was a start, and the horses were getting restless.

CHAPTER 27

Juliette

LEO HAD PITCHED A TENT about halfway between the house and the stone wall separating us from the field. Excitement bubbled in my stomach. "I love that we're camping here."

"I'm glad, babe." Pushing a few of the loosened tent pegs farther into the ground, he smiled. "I know Bea really wanted us to stay with them, but this was my preferred option." He winked. "I get you all to myself."

"I'll be back in a sec." I remembered I'd left my phone in my car. I was annoyed I hadn't had it with me to take photos when we went out on the horses.

I jogged up the garden and around the side of the house. The farmhouse was on a quiet road, so the sound of a car passing caught my attention and I glanced up towards the front gate. It was another red Honda, and it appeared to have slowed down as it passed. I thought it was a little strange and that I might mention it to Leo. I was probably being completely paranoid, but after all we'd been through, I wasn't going to just shrug it off.

Leo appeared next to me. "I'll grab our bags." I smiled

thinking about the raunchy lingerie I had hidden in mine.

"Hey, babe," I said casually. "I just saw what looked like the same car as the one at the cemetery slow down as it passed."

Leo appeared amused. "Tourists drive around these parts all the time." He gave me a cheeky grin. "I seem to recall a certain nosey blonde doing more than slow down in front of this house."

I grimaced, remembering how Leo had caught me trespassing in the farmhouse. It had caught my eye when I'd become lost on the way to my mother's charity event all those months ago. "You're right." I dropped my shoulders, allowing the tension to flow out of me. "Ever since I found out you were held up at gunpoint thanks to my mother, I guess I'm a little edgy."

He pulled me to him and held me against his strong body. I felt so safe in his arms. "I won't let anything happen to you, Jules." He kissed the top of my head. "Promise."

"I'm not worried about me," I whispered.

"Time for a proper tour." He pulled back and took hold of my hand. Slinging our bags over his shoulder, he walked me towards the front door.

"The name plaque is gone." I noticed the clean, rectangular section of stone next to the door where it had once been.

Leo nodded but said nothing as he held the door open for me.

"Don't you ever lock the door?" I asked.

His shoulders tensed. "If someone wants in, they can just smash one of the many windows. There isn't a whole lot to take now anyway. I gave a lot of the valuable items to charity shops."

We walked down the hallway, and Leo dropped our

bags outside the bathroom door. "We might be camping, but I thought you might like a few creature comforts."

"I don't mind roughing it, but if there's a hot shower, I'm not going to say no."

He flicked the light on. "I've had plumbers and electricians in, so everything is in working order."

"That's great." I smiled. "Thank you."

"Come on." He took my hand and led me back to the bottom of the staircase. I thought we were going to go up, but instead, he led me into a room just to the left. It was the front corner of the house.

The first thing I saw was books. Hundreds and hundreds of them. I perused built-in bookshelves covering two of the walls. My eyes were drawn upward to the intricate decorative ceiling. The enormous sash windows allowed natural light to fill the room, as well as highlight the dust.

"This is the library, as you might've guessed." He wandered over to one of the bookshelves and let his finger run along the spines. "I know how much you love books, so I thought I'd start the tour here. I couldn't bring myself to give them away."

"Maybe you knew your future girlfriend would be a bookworm," I suggested, wandering into the cosy room."

He chuckled. "Maybe that was it."

"My father never came in here." He shrugged. "He had other interests."

I joined him at the bookshelf and leaned in to read some of the titles. "So these are all your mum's books?" I asked, recognising Homer's *The Iliad* immediately.

"Yes, but most of the ones on the other wall are mine."

I immediately headed to the other bookshelf, and I wasn't surprised to find countless titles on astronomy and anatomy. What caught my eye, though, was a collection of books by Oscar Wilde, my favourite playwright, novelist, essayist and poet. I picked up a beautiful hardback copy of *The Picture of Dorian Gray* and clutched it to my chest. "God, I love Oscar Wilde," I gushed.

He nodded. "I know. I saw you had a few of his titles on your bookshelf next to your extensive romance section." He winked at me and I chuckled.

"My mother was a strong believer in education. She always told me knowledge is power." He shook his head and mumbled. "The irony of it."

"Do you agree?" I asked, noting how he spoke of her in the past tense. "That knowledge is power."

"Sometimes ignorance can be bliss, but when your father is murdered and no one pays for the crime, knowing might give me the closure I seek." He walked over to the window that overlooked the front garden. "The unknown can drive you insane with what ifs, burning questions and a mind overtaken with rage without warning."

I joined him by the window. "Talk to me, Leo." I placed my hand on his arm. "What happened to make you speak about your very much alive mother in the past tense?"

He nodded, took a deep breath and exhaled slowly, whistling quietly as the air left his body. "I moved out while I was at university."

I nodded as I sunk my teeth into my bottom lip.

"Halfway through my degree, I had started having second thoughts about medicine." He stared out the window.

"What had made you change your mind about being a doctor?'

"It just never felt like my path when I was actually on it. I'd worked so hard to get there, and it was pretty devastating to realise it just wasn't me at all. I liked the idea of helping people, and Nick was always banging on about me having magic hands."

"I wouldn't disagree." I chuckled hesitantly, unsure if that was highly inappropriate given the seriousness of our discussion.

"Mind out of the gutter, Ms Salinger." He winked at me. God, he was sexy.

"*We are all in the gutter, but some of us are looking at the stars.*" I quoted one of my favourite Oscar Wilde quotes.

"You are getting me off track."

"Sorry." I smiled sheepishly. "Did your father want you to be a doctor?"

"He wanted me to work with him in the family business. He was disappointed but one hundred percent supportive of my choice." Sadness flashed across his eyes. "He was such a good man, Jules. Whatever that woman said, it's all lies." His chest heaved as he drew in a breath.

"She didn't mention him, but I gave her almost no rope." Sensing he could use a break, I decided I would change the subject. Moving forward so my nose was nearly touching the window, I peered out through the dirty panes. "I could do so much with this garden." The flowerbeds were all overgrown, and whilst Leo had obviously mown the lawns, there was so much scope for improvement.

He put his arm around my shoulder, and I rested my head against him. "I was going to pay a landscaper to come in to do it, but if you want to, I'd love it."

I turned to face him and snaked my arms around his waist. "Would you pay me in sexual favours?" I met his gaze and raised my eyebrows.

"Absolutely." He kissed me as if he had no choice.

Eventually, I pulled back. "I have a surprise for you later."

"You do?" he asked, obviously intrigued.

"You'll have to wait though." I yanked on his hand to pull him towards the door. "We're in the middle of a tour."

Leo groaned as he followed me back into the entry foyer. "Okay." He pointed to the door opposite us. "That's a spare bedroom." He then pointed to the next door along. "You know that's the bathroom, and then the next room is the main lounge room. The door at the end leads down to the basement and wine cellar."

"Coffee, wine and chocolate make the world go 'round."

He smiled. "When dad wasn't outside, he was down there with his wine. I remember playing hide and seek with him, and I decided it would be the perfect hiding place. I locked myself down there, and it took him ages to find me." He chuckled to himself.

"I remember the beautiful room with the fireplace," I said, glancing down the hallway.

"Well there's a fireplace in most rooms, but yes. You've been in that one before."

I ran my hand along the bannister as we climbed the stairs. "So much work went into this house. I love it."

Leo glanced around as we reached the top. "It is a beautiful house, but it was far too big for the three of us."

"Did you parents ever say why they didn't have more children?"

"Dad told me once he would've liked ten kids."

"Good God." I scoffed. "No one has ten kids these days.

"I guess Mum didn't want anymore." He shrugged. "I never asked her and she never told me."

"So all these rooms are bedrooms except that one." He pointed to the door second from the end. "It's a bathroom."

We walked past several closed doors before stopping in front of the one I already knew. "I was so mortified when you found me in this room." I grimaced.

"It was a pretty big shock finding you here." He pushed the door open and waited for me to go first.

I cringed. "I don't know what I was thinking coming in here uninvited."

He grazed the back of his hand along my cheekbone. "Well I'm bloody glad you did."

"This was your bedroom, right?" I asked, a little breathless.

He nodded and blew out a long breath. "I was home for term break during my third year at uni and had told them about my change of heart." His jaw clenched. "Mum was pissed and stormed off to bed early. I stayed up for a while with Dad, and we were able to have a rational conversation. He was a night owl, and I knew he'd be up for hours yet. I'd said goodnight around eleven and gone to bed."

"What happened?" I found myself holding my breath waiting for him to continue.

"We need to go back downstairs for me to finish the story." He grabbed my hand and dragged me out.

"It was unusually quiet in the house when I came down the stairs the next morning," he said as we descended. "But I assumed someone was up, as I could smell the coffee wafting through the house. For years, I had come down for breakfast each morning to the sound of the seventies music."

I held my breath, and butterflies flapped wildly in my stomach. We moved down the hallway towards the kitchen, where I knew something awful had happened based on his reaction last time I had been in there with him. I wasn't going to interrupt him with any questions.

Standing in the kitchen, Leo continued his story, the story I'd been waiting to hear since I'd stumbled across this farmhouse and walked in uninvited.

"When I reached the kitchen door ready to surprise them, I was confronted with a sight I'll have to live with for the rest of my life. I found my father lying on the floor in a pool of blood and my mother standing over him smiling."

I gasped, and my hands flew to cover my mouth. "Are you serious?" I spoke through my fingers. I stared at the floor, then back at Leo, then back at the floor. "You found him like that and she was smiling?"

He nodded and closed his eyes. I could see pain all over his body from his tense shoulders to his furrowed brow to his clenched fists. "When she saw me, her face dropped and the colour drained from her face. She looked so guilty, and in that moment, my world simply stopped."

"What did you do?" I asked in a whispered voice.

"I rushed forward, dropped to my knees and tried desperately to find a pulse. 'Please don't be dead,' I begged repeatedly, but I already knew he was gone. I tried to tell my mother to call the police, but nothing came out. My mind and body were shutting down."

"Jesus, Leo."

He snapped his head to me. "I've never told anyone this story, other than the police, for what good that did."

"Did your Mum...?" I asked. "Did she...?"

He shook his head.

I snaked my arms around his waist and hugged him. "Are you sure she was smiling? I don't think anyone could be blamed for reacting irrationally in that situation." I tipped my head back so I could look him in the eye.

Leo pulled away from me and leaned against the kitchen bench. I was about to suggest we go outside to give him a break when he continued. "She was happy. I walked into the kitchen and found her smiling while she looked down at her dead husband. She was happy, and not the *rainbows and butterflies* happy." He narrowed his eyes. "More like the *devil who'd just taken ownership of your soul* happy."

"Holy shit, Leo."

"Once the police arrived, she transformed into the distressed wife, but she'd already shown me her cards." The anger that flashed across his eyes made me shudder. "And so began the murder investigation."

"So there was an intruder?" I asked, trying to get my head around what he was telling me.

"Mum said she came down and found Dad shortly before I did. All evidence at the scene proved we were both in the clear. They never bothered locking the doors, so there was no forced entry and there was no murder weapon. He had no enemies, and they had no leads." He rubbed his face with his palms. "It felt like it was a cold case before I'd even started to process what happened."

"And you cut your mother off because of how she reacted to what most would agree was an all-round shocking scenario?"

"Partly," he stated.

Oh, I mouthed.

He started pacing and my eyes tracked him. "My instincts told me she knew who did it."

"Instincts?"

"Somewhere deep in my gut, I knew she had something to do with my father's murder. Clearly she didn't drive the knife in, but she knew something. I'd bet my life on it."

"Did you tell the police that?"

He shook his head. "As I said at the cemetery, I barely knew which way was up. It was agonising knowing I was in the house at the time completely oblivious. I didn't cope."

"Did you confront your mother about it?'

He nodded. "She was pissed. And not just slightly pissed. More like she went fucking ballistic, and I saw a level of crazy I had never seen before." He slammed his hand down on the benchtop, and I jolted backward. "She's a fucking manipulative, lying bitch." He exhaled a long, loud breath. "Fuck. I'm sorry."

"It's okay, babe. Do you want to keep talking about this or leave it for another time?"

He ran both his hands through his hair and stared out the window. "I'm okay. I just haven't let myself think about this in a while, and being in here..." He shuddered. "It's hard." He met my gaze, and I saw nothing but pain in his eyes. "Honestly, Jules. Her reaction had cemented her guilt in my mind. She was far too defensive."

"We don't have to keep talking about this." I ran my hand down his arm, then gripped his hand. "Why don't we go back outside?"

Leo let me lead him out the back door and into the garden.

He ran his free hand through his hair and stared back at the house. "I'm okay. It's hard, but it feels good to talk about it."

We started walking down towards the gazebo. "So what does she want from you now?" I asked.

"Money." He shrugged. "Greed is an ugly, ugly beast." He shook his head and clenched his fists. "My father was gentle, kind and good. He deserved more." He glanced back around the garden. "He loved this place and he loved me. His big downfall was loving her."

"This is a lot to take in. Surely if she was just after the money, she could've divorced him and taken half?"

"I've asked myself the same question and I don't know the answer. I might never know who killed my father and if my mother was involved."

My mouth opened and closed while my brain attempted to form words. There were no words. I was rendered mute by the complete clusterfuck of emotions I was feeling about a situation too horrendous to believe. I was completely floored by what he'd told me, and I had a whole new understanding for what he'd gone through the past five years.

"Your reaction pretty much sums it up."

"God, Leo," I managed to whisper. "I'm not sure I would've been able to handle that at all."

"I didn't handle it. I turned to alcohol and easy women. Pretty cliché, huh?"

"There is absolutely nothing clichéd about this situation. I don't even know what to say, but I wish you'd told me before."

"Why? Dredging it all up just forces me to relive the darkest days of my life, where I didn't know how to even begin to cope with any of it. For a long time, I drowned myself in alcohol, but Nick introduced me to Dam, who introduced me to Muay Thai cage fighting to unleash the rage inside me, and best of all, I found you."

I reached for his hand and squeezed gently, running my thumb across the ridge of his knuckles. "No wonder you hate being in that kitchen."

I had come up with so many scenarios since the first time I'd been to that house and watched Leo freak out. This was not something my brain could've conjured up.

"I'm so sorry you had to go through all that. I know it's ridiculous, but I wish I could've been there for you."

"Bea and Angus were there, but I found it hard to lean

on anyone."

We continued walking around the boundary of the garden. I let my hand rise and fall with the newly repaired dry stonewall. "Are you going to give her any money?"

"She knows I have an Achilles' heel, and she's going in for the kill."

"Achilles' heel?"

"You." He cupped my face. "She knows I'd do anything to protect you." He exhaled a long, loud breath. "She saw you as a way to get to me, and it worked."

"Shit."

"I told her I'd think about it, but I want her gone" he said. "She gets the money and the fuck out of our lives."

"So that's what Sandra was talking about in the café earlier?"

He nodded.

"Do you think you'll ever be able to move past your anger?"

He locked his jaw. "You might've been able to forgive your mother for what she did to you, but I think you'll agree mine is on a whole other level. I'll give her what she wants, but I can't ever forget what happened in there." He pointed to the house.

"You've been trying to forget all these years, but I don't think that's possible until you find a way to forgive." I stood on my tiptoes and kissed him lightly on the lips.

"Why don't you tell me what you'd do with this garden?" He took on a lighter tone, and I, too, was glad of the happier subject matter.

I clapped my hands and started walking backward away from him. "Big plans, Leo." I held my arms wide. "Big plans."

He shook his head and laughed. "Tell me everything."

CHAPTER 28

LEO

THE SUN HAD ALMOST MET the horizon when I finally interrupted Jules. I'd never seen her speak with such passion about anything other than how she felt about me—about us. Being there with her made my heart swell with love instead of clench with fear. All the garden beds would be, in her words, explosions of colour. The hedges would be returned to their former glory, and she had visions of a garden swing hanging from one of the large trees around the back. This girl was having an incredible impact on my life, and I could no longer imagine my future without her in it.

"Vines," she exclaimed as I took her by the hand and led her back to the house so we could organise some dinner. "I'm going to look into it." She could barely contain her excitement as she danced on the spot. "How amazing would it be to have your own grapevines?"

I smiled at her enthusiasm. My father had always talked about planting a vineyard, but Mum had said he spent enough of his time thinking about wine as it was.

"It's up to you, babe. Whatever you want to do, just do it." I put my arm around her shoulders. "I'm behind you one hundred percent."

"Mind if I take a shower before dinner?" she asked, holding up her dirty hands. She hadn't hesitated to get down on her hands and knees to check out the soil.

"Course." I waved her off. "There are towels in the bathroom."

"This is glamping, you know."

"Glamping?" I asked, confused.

"We're camping but hardly roughing it." She smiled. "Glamorous camping."

"You're the one who asked for a shower, princess."

I could hear her laughing as she disappeared down the hallway.

Given my limited skills in the kitchen, we were having soup for dinner. Stirring the red liquid, I found myself staring out the window, down the garden to the fields beyond and wondering how on earth this had happened. Exactly five years ago, my life as I knew it had ended abruptly. Now, with the sound of Juliette's laughter fresh in my ears, I was stirring soup and considering the possibility of living here again. I'd be lying if I said I was completely at ease or that I could ever be okay with what happened, but I bloody loved this house and I bloody loved being here with Juliette.

~~~~~

"Penny for your thoughts." Juliette's sultry voice snapped me out of my startling thoughts. Freshly showered and gorgeous, she leaned against the doorframe, wearing black leggings. A long cardigan was wrapped around her body, and her hair was pulled up on top of her head. She was simply stunning.

"How was the shower, princess?" I asked when I managed to stop ogling.

She closed the distance between us and wrapped her

arms around me from behind, resting her cheek on my back. Still stirring the soup, I placed one hand over hers. "It was amazing." I heard her inhale. "Is that tomato soup you're making me?"

"Making is a stretch, but yes, I'm heating up tomato soup for you."

"How did you know it was my favourite?" she asked, clearly chuffed.

"Well, the countless cans in your kitchen cupboards were a bit of a giveaway." I laughed. "Hope you weren't just stockpiling for a potential holocaust."

Her infectious laughter rumbled through me, and I knew I'd gotten something right.

I'd set up a pair of deckchairs in front of the tent so we could enjoy the sunset while we ate.

"This is the good life," she said, sighing as she scraped her spoon across the bottom of her bowl. "You were lucky growing up here."

I met her pensive gaze. "I spent a lot of time thinking about life beyond this place, to be honest."

"I spent all my time looking sideways." She broke eye contact and fixated her gaze on the ball of orange melting into the horizon.

"What do you mean?" I asked.

"My mother, in one way or another, stood directly in front of me, dictating my every move. Instead of upsetting her, I looked sideways and found little pieces of myself in the dark."

"You did what felt right to you, and I shouldn't have judged you for that."

She looked at me with watery eyes. "Thank you."

I reached out and took her hand. "You're my Venus, Jules."

"Are you saying I'm the goddess of love?" she asked

with a cheeky grin.

"Absolutely, but I'm trying to make a romantic analogy here, so hear me out."

She giggled before clamping her other hand over her mouth. "Sorry."

I pointed to the sky. "Can you see it there?"

She followed my arm up and nodded. "I see it."

"It gets referred to as the morning and evening star. Venus is brightest before the sun rises and just after sunset, but it doesn't need the darkness to be seen." Juliette stood up and climbed onto my lap, wrapping her arms around my neck. "Your light shines from within, Jules. It shines in the dark and it shines in the midday sky."

"You are very romantic, you know?" She kissed me lightly on the lips.

One of her hands made its way under the hem of my t-shirt. "Your hands are freezing." I yelped when it made contact with my stomach.

She pulled it back. "Sorry." She wrapped her arms around herself. "I'm getting a bit chilly."

I hugged her to me and rubbed my hands up and down her arms. "Come on." I gently pushed her off me. "I've been wanting to get you in bed all day."

"I'll just use the bathroom first."

"Do you want me to come with you?" I asked. "It's dark." We hadn't left any lights on in the house.

"I'm a big girl." She winked. "And anyway, I'm Venus, the brightest object in the whole solar system."

"Not quite true, but I like your thinking." I kissed her, then gave her backside a slap before she trotted back up the garden. I was glad to see a few lights come on in the house. Reconnecting the electricity had felt like a big step.

She returned a short time later, a little out of breath, and even in the dim light, she appeared pale.

"You okay?" I asked.

"I just had a really strange feeling I was being watched."

I glanced up to the house. "Did you see anyone?"

She shook her head. "It was just an uneasy feeling. I'm sure it's nothing though. It's probably just paranoia."

"Last time I discounted your fear, I was threatened at gunpoint. I'm gonna check it out."

"Well you're not leaving me here," she insisted.

She gripped my hand with both of hers, and we walked the perimeter by torchlight. A bird cry made her jump, and the grip on my hand was cutting off circulation.

"There's nothing to worry about, Jules." I eased my hand from hers and put my arm around her shoulders. I didn't want her to be afraid, but I loved being able to protect her.

"I guess I'm just not used to it." Her body relaxed into mine. "I'm too citified."

"Well that'll change if you decide you can live out here with me, you know."

Her body froze and my head darted around, looking for the reason why. "What is it?" I whispered.

"You just asked me to live with you?"

"I did, didn't I?" I turned her to face me. We were standing in the front garden, which was flooded by moonlight. "Well if we decide to move out here, we won't be getting separate places."

"I guess not. But here?" Her gaze darted around the garden and up at the house.

"The more time I spend here, the more I realise I can never part with it." He glanced up at the large sandstone farmhouse, a little eerie in the moonlight, and sighed. "I feel connected to my father here. How can I ever give that up?"

A grin split across her beautiful face. "I love it here, too."

"What's your middle name?" I asked when I realised I didn't know it.

"Random question, Leo."

"Just tell me what your middle name is."

"Elizabeth."

"Pretty name."

"It's my grandmother's name," she whispered.

"Okay. Juliette Elizabeth Salinger. I love you, and whether we stay in the city or move out here, will you move in with me?"

I couldn't resist kissing her because I could never resist kissing my girl. When I pulled away, she was still grinning.

"I love you, too, and yes, I'll live with you, Leo..."

"William. After my dad and grandfather."

She nodded. "Leo William Ashlar. I want to go to bed with you every night and wake up with you every morning. I want you to heat up tomato soup for me, and I want to cook you dinner using the vegetables from our very own vegetable garden." She looked at me with glistening eyes. "I want it all with you."

I closed the distance between us and kissed her hard on the mouth. The night sky darkened as we lost ourselves in that kiss because we had both said the words that had been like an elephant in the room since she'd returned from overseas. I needed her like I'd never needed anyone before. I wanted to bury myself so far inside her, I'd never find my way out. My heart and soul had belonged to her from the beginning. It was my mind that had needed to catch up.

When we came up for air, she took a step back and unwrapped her cardigan. She pulled her top down, revealing the top of a very sexy-looking bra. She pulled it back up quickly and rewrapped herself in the damn cardigan.

"I told you I had a surprise for you." She winked and nearly killed me with a seductive smile.

Without thinking, I scooped her up and threw her over my shoulder. Slamming my hand on the doorhandle, I opened the front door and stormed into the entry foyer with one thing on my mind and one thing only. I went for the closest door, the spare bedroom in the front right-hand corner of the house. I'd only ever been in that room a handful of times, but I knew there was a large bed in there covered in a cotton tarp.

"Let me down, you caveman." She squealed, batting my back while she made her demands.

I flung her on the bed, and she yelped as she landed softly on the mattress, a plume of dust rising up around her. "Well this is just like camping." She giggled, coughing a little.

Standing at the side of the bed and admiring her, I was too driven by the lust that her little sneak peek had sparked to worry about a little dust. "I need you naked, princess."

"We're going to do this here?" She glanced around the room.

I nodded, holding on to my senses with a tiny thread of will. Thankfully she started to pull at her clothes as I kicked off my boots. The curtains over both the windows were open, and the soft moonlight made her glow. My beautiful girl was spectacular.

Lust was overtaking me, and I needed to have her immediately. I would take my time with her later, but she'd just said she loved me for the first time since returning home from overseas and formally agreed to live with me. Flashing her sexy bra tipped me right over the edge, and I was on borrowed time. I reached behind my neck and grabbed the collar of my shirt, pulling it over my head in one quick movement. She had removed her cardigan and had pulled her hair tie out so her long hair hung loosely over her shoulders. She was a fucking vision, and she still had most of her clothes on.

I popped the button on my jeans and unzipped, eager to be completely rid of anything that would get between my skin and hers. My jeans pooled on the floor, and I bent over to help wrench them the rest of the way off. When they caught up on one of my feet, I was irritated, extremely horny and in no way prepared for what I was about to see.

I stood up, ready to help her finish stripping, but when my eyes landed on her, my mouth went dry and my heart felt like a jack hammer hard at work against my chest. I had to place my hand over it to make sure it didn't burst through. Juliette was sexy in track pants and a t-shirt, she was sexy sitting on the couch reading her Kindle and chewing on her thumb. She was sexy behind the wheel of her car, pushing it to the limit with her mad driving skills, and she was sure as shit sexy in a boxing ring, glistening with sweat and determination. However, lying on the bed in front of me was a vision I would find hard to surpass in my wildest fantasies. Her eyes danced with excitement, and her knowing grin ended me.

Propped up on her elbows, she had laid herself out for me in some kind of leather lingerie with one leg bent. She was the sexiest fucking thing I'd seen in my life.

"I was told it was inspired by a biker's leather jacket." She glanced down at herself encased in black leather triangles I couldn't even begin to get my head around. "I thought you'd like it."

"Like it?" I croaked and had to swallow for a little lubrication on my dry throat. My gaze roamed further down her body, and my wet dream was officially complete. "Did you think there was any chance I would want to resist you?" I asked with one knee on the bed. "You would be irresistible in a hessian sack, but this...." I prowled my way up the bed to get closer to my prize. When I reached her, I enjoyed a closer look at the lingerie designed to give men heart attacks. "This is the sexiest damn sight, Jules." I grazed my fingers up her legs, then lazily explored the rest of her incredible body.

"I wanted to blow your mind."

"Mission accomplished." I couldn't take any more talking when what I wanted to do was rip the leather from her body and devour her.

So, that's what I did, except that getting her out of the leather contraption wasn't as easy as I'd hoped. After far too long pulling, yanking, unclipping, I sat back and threw my hands in the air. "Well, fuck." I huffed. "You'd have to be Houdini to get out of this."

She threw her head back against the canvas and laughed. I was unamused, and my balls were turning bluer by the second. "I'm sorry," she spluttered, propping herself up on her elbows and casting her gaze down her body, which was now trussed up like a Christmas ham. She was still chuckling, but thankfully started deftly slipping her body from the lingerie.

"This didn't go quite as planned," she said when she was finally naked. "Maybe I'll go for something a little simpler next time. The lady at the shop—"

I thrust into her and she gasped, ceasing whatever she had been about to say.

"No more talking, baby." I was officially ready to take her and claim her as mine.

When our bodies were sated and our breathing returned to normal, it dawned on me that it was fucking freezing. "Jules," I whispered, holding her close to my body.

"Yeah," she whispered back, nuzzling her nose into my neck.

"I think we should resume this position in the tent."

She nodded, pulling herself up and redressing. I did the same, noticing the leather contraption was left on the bed. I picked it up and twirled it on my finger. "Nice surprise, babe."

Her smug smile made me laugh as we headed back outside. When I closed the front door, I remembered why we'd been out there in the first place rather than heading straight to the tent.

Possibly having the same thought, she glanced around the front garden and up to the deserted road. "It's so quiet." For some reason, she whispered.

"It's just you and me, Jules."

She looked into my eyes, lit up by her beautiful smile. "Always."

I woke the next morning with Jules safely cocooned into the crook of my arm. I didn't think I'd ever slept so soundly in my whole life.

Out of the blue, I felt Jules's body shaking against mine. I was pretty sure she was trying not to laugh. "What's so funny?" I asked, tightening my arm around her.

She propped herself up on my chest. "Nothing." She smiled and kissed me.

I pushed her back gently. "Tell me what was so funny."

She scrunched up her nose. "I already told you that

sometimes I get an uncontrollable urge to laugh when I'm either really happy or really scared."

"You really laugh when you're scared?"

I nodded. "Yep. It's weird and often quite inappropriate."

"So were you happy or scared just now?"

Her blue eyes brightened. "I've never been so happy in my whole life. I guess there's still a little fear associated with it, but I'm really starting to believe in our happy ever after."

"Believe it, baby." I kissed her, pushed her on her back and quickly made her forget what we had just been talking about.

When we emerged from the tent a while later, Jules stretched her arms above her head and yawned. "God, I love it here."

"So you're not having doubts about moving out here with me, then?" I asked.

"I can't wait," she said, wrapping her arms around my waist. "What's our plan?"

Still holding her close to me, I glanced around the garden, across the fields and up to the house. I felt an overwhelming sense of calm that I had shared my tightly-guarded memories with Jules. "You have to see out your notice at work, so I'm thinking we make the permanent move after that. What will you do with your apartment?"

"I've already talked to my father about giving it back to him. I know it's in my name and I can do with it as I please, but it symbolises who I was, not who I am or who I want to be." She pulled back a little and met my gaze.

"What did he say?" I asked.

"He appreciated the rationale behind my offer but said it would make him happy if I kept it as a nest egg for my future." She cocked her head. "I am going to be an unemployed bum in a few weeks, so I guess I shouldn't be too self-righteous."

"You'll work out what you want to do, and I'll back you up one hundred percent." I kissed her nose. "Come on. I'll make you a coffee."

We spent the day pottering around the farm discussing what we needed to get done before we moved in.

"Are you ready to head back to the city?" I asked as the light started to fade.

She scrunched up her nose. "Not really, but I guess we should."

"Do you miss the cage?" she asked, seemingly out of the blue when we were packing up the Jeep.

I stopped what I was doing and turned to face her. "Where did that come from?"

She shrugged her shoulders. "I've been thinking about it a bit lately."

"Why?" I asked, hesitantly. I really needed to tell her about the fight I'd agreed to.

"I'm just concerned you gave it up for the wrong reasons."

"Look, Jules." I took a step towards her. "Before you start telling me I'm some big martyr, you should know I've agreed to go back into the cage at the next fight night." I studied her face for any negative reaction. "They are short a few fighters."

"You don't want me to come, do you?" She shook her head, appearing resigned.

I closed my hand around her forearms. "I really don't."

She stared into my eyes and gave me a beautiful smile. I wondered why I'd been so nervous about telling her when she was being so understanding until she spoke. "I'll think about it and get back to you." She pulled her arms from me and patted my cheek with the palm of her hand. The little smart arse winked at me.

"You're not coming, Jules."

"Zip it, caveman." She raised her eyebrows and smirked. "I'm a big girl with my own avenues for getting a ticket, and I love watching you in the cage."

Fuck! "Babe. Please. The last time you went, you were attacked, and I won't be able to concentrate if you're in the crowd."

"I get it, but you have to relax. The guy who attacked me wasn't just a random guy, and all that stuff with my mother is over."

"I will never stop wanting to protect you, babe." I cupped her face in my hands. "I know you are independent and strong, but you're mine and we've been through a lot. I'm not going to apologise for being overprotective."

She sighed. "Fine." She then rolled her eyes so I knew she wasn't thrilled about her concession.

On the drive home, I called my mother on the hands-free and informed her I'd give her the money in a couple of weeks. I had some investments I could sell but would also need a win at fight night.

CHAPTER 29

Juliette

THE NEXT FEW WEEKS FLEW by, and before I knew it, my last day at Donoghue's working for Heath had arrived. Knowing I was leaving a safe and secure job without a solid plan, on top of Leo going back into the cage tonight, had sent my anxiety levels through the roof. I wasn't in a great mood when I arrived at work but had to put on a happy face for my well-wishing colleagues. I'd had my replacement sitting with me for last week—an arrogant yet mildly amusing British backpacker. I knew I wasn't leaving Heath in safe hands, but I'd done the best I could.

After market closed for the day, everyone assembled around my desk. I hated being the centre of attention and could feel my cheeks heating when Heath cleared his throat. I really hadn't been expecting speeches, and I desperately hoped I wouldn't be expected to say anything.

"What can I say about the best desk assistant I've ever had?" I looked up at him and smiled. He never complimented my work, but I knew I was good at my job and he never complained, which was probably as good as a compliment for someone like Heath. He went on for a good five minutes about my work ethic and attention to detail, and I was burning up by the end. "You have big boots to fill," he said, looking at my replacement. Poor Mark had no idea what he was in for come Monday when I wasn't there to put out his fires. "Thank you, Juliette. It's been a pleasure working with you, and I'll miss you." After a round of applause, Heath piped up again and shocked everyone. "First round of drinks at the Z Bar are on me."

I was taken aback by his speech. Leaving was absolutely the right thing for me, but I would miss this place. I might've fallen into the job, but I'd picked myself up, worked hard and earned the respect of a man who didn't dish it out lightly.

"Drinks time," Nicole said, linking arms with me. "I'm totally gutted you're leaving."

"Thanks, but I'm really happy." I bumped shoulders with her. "Feels like the fresh start I really need."

"Come on, ladies," Evan said, ushering us towards the lifts. "Let's send Juliette off in style."

As we left the building, we were laughing at the punchline of Evan's last joke. Nicole was right in front of me and I wasn't prepared for her to stop dead in her tracks, so I bumped into her back and nearly lost my footing. I was about to ask why she'd stopped when I glanced up and saw Leo moving towards me with a concerned look on his face.

"Are you okay, babe?" he asked as I pushed my foot back into my heel and smoothed down my skirt. Leo kissed me lightly on the lips and put his arm around my shoulders.

"Holy hotness," Nicole whispered.

"This is my boyfriend, Leo." I waved my hand

between them. "Leo, meet Nicole and Evan."

Leo shook hands with both of them, and Nicole looked at me and mouthed the word 'wow.'

I chuckled, completely understanding her reaction to my man. "I didn't know you were coming," I said, smiling. "I thought you'd be getting ready for the fight."

"We'll see you guys there," Nicole said, waving. "Really nice to meet you, Leo." She glanced at me and winked.

"You too," Leo replied. "I won't be able to come in, but I'll drop Jules there soon."

He turned his attention back to me when Nicole and Evan left. "I wanted to see you before I headed out. How are you feeling now you're a free agent?"

I considered his question for a moment before answering honestly. "I'm actually really, genuinely happy."

Leo dropped another kiss on my lips. "That's awesome, Jules. I wish I didn't have to leave you now, but I really should get going. I'm meeting Dam out there." He pulled me in for a hug, and I wrapped my arms around him.

I pulled back and met his gaze. "It's okay. Thank you for coming into the city to see me."

He held the Jeep's passenger side door open for me, and I climbed in. I watched him jog around the front and climb into the driver's seat. Before he turned on the ignition, he sat back against his seat and turned to face me, chewing his bottom lip. "My mother called me this afternoon and asked if I'd meet her out at the farmhouse tonight. I told her I couldn't because I have a fight, but I'd meet her there tomorrow afternoon."

"What does she want now?" I asked, confused. Leo had managed to come up with the money she wanted without needing the fight prize money by selling his investments. He'd arranged a bank transfer earlier this week. We'd thought that was the end of Gwendolyn, but clearly not.

"It's the other reason I wanted to see you. I think she's going to tell me who killed my father."

"Seriously?" I propped my leg up on the seat and leaned my back against the door so I could give him my full attention. "What did she say?"

"She said she'd received the money and was prepared to give me what I wanted in return. She knew what I wanted was closure."

I leaned forward. "Do you trust her?"

"No, but I'll hear her out." He shrugged. "What have I got to lose? She could've just disappeared with the money."

"Why the farmhouse?"

"I asked her the same thing, and she simply said she wanted a little closure herself."

Something didn't feel right to me, and I could tell Leo was feeling the same. "Do you want me to come with you?"

He shook his head. "This is something I want to do alone. I'll talk to you about it again in the morning though."

I shook my head. "Shit, Leo."

He leaned over the centre console and kissed me. "It's all going to be okay, Jules."

Leo dropped me off at the bar and promised he'd be home as soon as he could and in one piece. I stood on the footpath outside the Z bar and watched his Jeep disappear around the corner, hoping tomorrow would bring us a big step closer to our happy ever after.

True to his word, Heath shouted a couple of rounds at the bar, and I even managed to relax. Little did I know, within twenty-four hours, I would be faced with the possibility I'd lost Leo forever.

CHAPTER 30

LEO

I HADN'T BEEN TO FIGHT night for months and had actually missed the buzz of driving to a secret location. Tonight's fight was to be held at a warehouse west of the city in a deserted industrial estate.

"Leo Ashlar." Reaper greeted me in the passageway just before I entered my change room. "I was hoping you'd be here tonight. I'm ready to show you some manners."

"Pretty sure I showed *you* some manners last time." I had no interest in goading him, but I couldn't resist a little jab.

"I'm looking forward to a little retribution tonight."

"Good luck with that," I said casually.

"Not just for me," he spat. "For my mate."

I had no idea, nor did I care, who his mate was, so I just shrugged. Everyone who came to the cage consented to the consequences. No one was holding a gun to their head. "So?"

His nostrils flared. "So I'm gonna enjoy a little payback. He was just doing a job when you rearranged his face, all over your little blonde slut."

The penny dropped. His mate was the hooded dickhead who had attacked Jules at fight night, then shown up at the farm with a gun and a message. I saw red, slamming him up against the breeze block wall. "First of all, don't ever refer to my girlfriend as a slut. And secondly, if your mate is that hooded motherfucker who attacked a woman and put a gun in my face, then I'll be the one enjoying the retribution."

He laughed. "See you in the final." He spat in my face, and it was all I could do to stop myself from headbutting him. I did not want to get thrown out before I had a chance to smear his body parts across the canvas.

I stepped back from him and swiped the back of my arm across my face. "Looking forward to it."

Moving into my room, I slammed the door and dropped my bag on one of the benches.

"Mate." Adam, the Ginger Ninja, poked his head around the door. Still reeling from my encounter with Reaper, I let out a breath and crossed the room to shake his hand. "You're back?"

"I'm back."

He chuckled. "The girls in the crowd will be happy."

I shook my head at his ridiculous comment. There was only one girl I cared about, and I was really happy she wasn't going to be in the crowd. "Glad to be here."

"Okay, boys." Derek came in holding a clipboard. He pulled a pencil from its resting place above his ear and scribbled something down before looking up again. "Here's the line-up." He glanced at me. "You're up first, Leo."

He rattled off the fighter names, and I realised I didn't recognise many of them. There'd obviously been some turnover in the past few months, which wasn't uncommon given the fact many left in an ambulance.

"Nick Matthews," Derek said. "Long time no see."

I was shocked to see him. "What are you doing here, Nick?"

Derek took Nick in a headlock and scruffed his head good-naturedly. "This pussy could've taken down the mighty Leo Ashlar once upon a time." He released him, and Nick gave him an equally good-natured shove.

"Doubt that." I chuckled. "Nick likes the gentleman's sport these days."

"Watch yourself, pretty boy," Nick said light-heartedly. "Caged Muay Thai is no longer my bag, but it's a part of my past. I'm here to support you."

"See you later, mate," Derek said as he disappeared out the door.

I returned to my bag and grabbed a bottle of water. Dropping to the bench, I took a swig.

"Stay focused and use that brain of yours." He tapped the side of his head.

"Hey, Nick. You know how you're always telling me to leave the past in the past?"

He nodded.

"Well, I got a call from my mother earlier, and I'm meeting her out at the farmhouse tomorrow afternoon." I paused, still finding it hard to wrap my head around the enormity of what I was about to say. "I think she's going to give me some closure on my father's death."

His eyes widened. "You think she knows who killed him?"

I nodded. "I do. Always have. It's been a long five years." I stared at my hands. "I just need to know."

He took a step closer and patted me on the shoulder. "Good luck, Leo. I'll see you at the end."

Before he left the room, he turned back. "Jules out there tonight?"

"Nope. I asked her not to come."

"And she agreed?" He chuckled. "Bit surprised, I have to say."

A feeling of dread churned in the pit of my stomach. I bloody hoped she kept to her word. "She did." I focused on wrapping my hands to try to distract my thoughts.

"I'll keep an eye out, so you just focus on your opponent. Okay?" He winked, then disappeared out the door.

Ten minutes later, Derek poked his head around the door and glanced around the room. "Nick was one scary motherfucker in his day."

"I've known him since I was a kid," I stated. "He's an incredible boxing coach."

"You're up soon," he said. "Dam just arrived."

After going through my usual warm-up routine with Dam, who had kindly agreed to come in for the night, I was escorted into the warehouse. Even though I'd distanced myself from this scene, it still made my heart pump faster, sending blood and adrenaline streaming through me at an addictive rate. The music thumped against my chest, making me jog up and down on the spot, expelling the overflow of energy threatening to explode out of me.

As always, the cage was set up in the centre, surrounded by the crowd buzzing with the unique level of excitement this taboo sport could muster. Both cage fighting and boxing were brutal. No doubt about it. The late Mohammed Ali's quote sprang to mind. "Float like a butterfly, sting like a bee." He was referring to the boxing ring and his imminent fight with George Foreman. There would be no references to butterflies or even bees in the cage. Maybe hornets and wasps, but no butterflies, not even bees. There would be no speaking of beauty or grace. I moved better than my opponents, outsmarting them until victory was mine, but oblivion was the real winner and I'd let it claim me willingly.

Dam wasn't into pep talks. He had a quiet strength I admired greatly, and it rolled off him in waves. "Sacrifice, dedication, honour and respect." It was all he needed to say.

I sized up my opponent from the moment I saw him enter the cage. He was introduced as Mr X. He was medium height and build, and his bald head was so shiny, the light from the massive spotters appeared to bounce off it. A large, angry, crescent-shaped scar ran over the top. I didn't know if the X stood for anything, but I immediately figured he was a tosser based on his name alone. I wouldn't make the mistake of underestimating him though, as average-height fighters often had a combination of power and speed. The short guys often had the power, and the tall, skinny guys had the speed. Nick told me I was a rare combination of size, speed and power, making me almost unbeatable. *Almost* thanks to the Perth disaster, but I couldn't think about that.

Mr X was sidestepping around the cage, working the crowd and himself into a frenzy. I jogged on the spot, keeping my muscles warm, but had no intention of wasting any of my energy before the fight started. That's when I'd give them the real show. Eventually, the bell sounded and we tapped fists. I looked him in the eye and recognised fear flashing through them. It was as if he hadn't noticed me until that point, and cranking his neck back to look me in the eye was a shock to him. *Dimwit.*

We both moved back a few paces, and Mr X let out a guttural roar as he beat his fists against his chest. *Whatever works, pal,* I thought to myself. *Not gonna help you though.* As expected, speed was his best asset, and he used it to the best of his ability. Unfortunately, what he had in speed, he lacked in skill, and I was able to easily use it against him. The faster you're travelling, the greater the impact when you slam into a wall. Mr X managed to knock himself unconscious by barrelling into my fist at full speed. All I had to do was plant my feet and time my hit perfectly. It would've been almost comical for the crowd, and even I couldn't constrain a small smile. I left the cage without a mark on me, and I hoped for a bigger challenge on the next round.

I headed back to my room out back but was kept informed of the goings-on. A guy called Buck won the next round. His opponent was apparently a bloody mess and was sent to the hospital.

Adam poked his head around my door. "I'm up next." His bloodthirsty excitement was hard to miss. "I'm gonna take out that Reaper fucker." The guy lived for this, and a large part of me understood why. "Earl just won his fight."

"Good luck, mate." I slapped him on the back. "Cut him a new butthole in case I don't get the chance."

"Consider it done."

In a shockingly short period of time, Adam returned to the change rooms with what looked like a broken nose and his arms slung around the shoulders of two officials. His wife was following close behind, dangling her car keys. She glanced at me as she passed my room. "Hospital." It was all she said, but the resigned look on her face spoke of worry and fear. Unfortunately, Reaper had proved too good for him, and he was clearly gutted. You'd think he'd just been told he had a terminal disease and had months to live. I felt bad for the guy.

He spat out some blood on the ground in front of me and swiped the back of his hand across his mouth. "If he's in the final against you, can you do me a favour and throw the final punch for me?"

"Sure, mate," I agreed. "It'll be my pleasure."

My next opponent was the winner of round two. He looked like a henchman from mafia movies. He was massive and had my number in height and weight with a huge, square head and thick, black eyebrows. This was more like it. Assuming he had any level of skill, I would need to bring my A-game.

The MC introduced him, but I missed his name. It sounded Russian. In my mind, his name was Lurch. He ignored the crowd completely and focused on me. I had a fight on my hands, and I felt the adrenaline start working its magic through my veins. This moment. This exact moment was my bliss. The hairs on my arms raised, and I shook out my body, releasing some of my excited energy.

My eyes zeroed in on his left leg, and I immediately knew I'd spotted his weakness. He wasn't limping, but he was definitely favouring his right leg and that was all I needed. We moved to the centre and tapped fists before retreating a few steps. Lurch moved slowly around me in a lame attempt to make me his prey, but I was having none of it. *I don't think so, pal.* I went on the attack, and Lurch didn't even get a chance to raise his fists. When his weight was on his vulnerable leg, I moved my upper body in a quick bend, dropped my left knee and catapulted my left fist forward. I then doubled up with another feint combination, raising my right arm and executing a straight cross with blinding speed. Lurch would've had no idea what happened as his body dropped to the canvas, out for the count. Too fucking easy.

Just before I entered the cage again, Dam spoke to me in Thai, and I felt transported back to Thailand, where he had taught me his craft. "Why is Muay Thai referred to as 'The Art of Eight Limbs'?"

I cast my mind back. "Muay Thai fighters use eight

points of contact on the body to mimic weapons of war."

"That's right," he confirmed with an intensity I'd only ever known from this man. "Now, tell me what they are."

"One and two." I looked at my hands. "My hands are the sword and dagger."

Dam nodded.

I shifted from one foot to the other. "Three. Forearms and four, shins. They act as armour. Five and six." I bent my arms. "Elbows are a heavy mace or hammer."

"And?" Dam whispered, surprisingly audible over the chanting crowd.

"Seven and eight. Legs and knees. They are the axe and staff." My Thai felt rusty, but I was pretty confident with what I'd said.

Dam nodded, clearly pleased. He meshed his fingers together and held them up in front of me. "Eight points of contact working together for maximum efficiency, looking for weakness to go in for the kill." He straightened his fingers emphasising his point. "Go in for the kill, Leo."

I was pumped when I entered the cage. Motherfucking Reaper was already in there dancing on the spot. He held a grudge and was obviously thrilled to have a chance to exact his revenge. The bell rung, signalling the first beat of the last dance. I knew without a shadow of a doubt I was physically fit, in the zone and I was going to win. Memories of the Perth fight flashed through my mind, and instead of regretful, I felt energised. I had needed that blow to hit rock bottom, and it was from that solid base that I was clawing my way back up. I narrowed my eyes on Reaper as he did on me. We were the two kings of the cage, but there was only room for one tonight. I wasn't being arrogant or blowing hot air up my own arse. It was fact. Reaper was about to be dethroned.

It wasn't lion versus zebra. It was predator versus predator, and I was going to relish every second of taking him down. We both had the same idea at the same time, and we moved quickly, engaging in a perfectly synchronised combination of jabs, hooks, uppercuts and straights. Reaper was a first-class arsehole, but he was also a first-class fighter. He met me head-on and, despite taking a few blows to the head, I fucking loved it. This was the challenge I had craved.

I knew I could win easily if my opponent was more interested in entertaining the crowd or if they were clearly inferior in skill. Reaper was focused solely on me, and his skillset was impressive. My edge would have to come by anticipating his moves and capitalising with killer blows. Reaper was a worthy player and, if he wasn't such a douche outside the cage, I would've actually had some respect for him.

It was time to lift my game, be smarter, fight harder and take this motherfucker down. The bastard had referred to Jules as a slut and spat in my face, and his mate had stuck a gun in my face. We'd been going at it long enough for me to start seeing a pattern in his movement, and he was no doubt seeing a pattern in mine. It was time to change it up and mess with the fucker's mind. I needed Reaper unconscious.

The crowd was deafening, and the energy was electric as we both jogged on the spot, waiting for the moment to end this one way or the other. I knew he felt it, too. One of us was about to go down, and I was determined it wasn't going to be me. I saw his eyes flash with excitement. Then we both exploded in a frenzy of kicks and punches. His head tilted back in such a small movement, I could've easily missed it, but my instincts anticipated a head butt was coming my way. In a split second, I raised my elbow like a hammer and smashed him in the face. I'd taken him by surprise, but I wasn't done with Reaper yet. My final move required flexibility, technique and training as well as the perfect set up. I had all those bases covered.

When Reaper locked his eyes on mine, I broke his gaze and looked down at his feet, giving him the impression I was going for a low leg kick. His eyes naturally followed mine, but by the time he realised his mistake, it was too late. I executed a killer high kick, pivoting on my standing leg while my shin and ankle did the work of knocking Reaper off his feet. His eyes rolled into the back of his head, and his whole body appeared to freeze before crumpling to the canvas.

≈≈≈

"Congrats, Leo." Nick appeared at the door of my change room after Dam had left. "You were incredible."

"Thanks, mate." I rubbed my head. "He landed a few good ones in, but I reckon he'll have a headache tomorrow."

Nick laughed. "I reckon you might, too."

I shrugged. "Probably."

"You heading home now?"

I nodded, standing up and grabbing my bag. "Sure am. I have a beautiful girl waiting for me in bed. Why would I stick around here?"

We walked out to the carpark and parted ways. "See you 'round, Leo."

I waved and turned towards my Jeep, parked at the far end of the lot. The lighting was terrible, and I had to allow my eyes to adjust to the darkness. As I reached in my bag to grab my car keys, I felt a jab in my upper arm and then a heavy blow to the back of my head before everything went black as my knees gave way.

CHAPTER 31

Juliette

WHEN I WOKE UP, MY room was light and I was alone. I sat up and rubbed my eyes, looking at the empty place on what had become Leo's side of my bed. My stomach turned with worry. This wasn't like him. I reached for my phone and saw a message from Nick. He'd sent it just after midnight.

Leo's with me.

I released the breath I was holding and tears pricked my eyes. I had been terrified for his safety, and the relief was overwhelming.

Everything okay? I replied.

His reply came back. *He took a nasty blow to the head. I wanted to keep an eye on him.*

I sent Nick a text back, thanking him for letting me know and then I sent one to Leo asking him to call me when he could. I let him know the time I'd be training with Zac.

I cleaned my apartment like a woman possessed. When I was worried about something, I became borderline obsessive compulsive. At eight thirty, I changed into my gym gear, put my headphones in and let P!nk once again meet my mood head-on as I jogged through the city to the gym. I was glad I could unleash on Zac the worry that had built up in my system.

"What's going on, Jules?" Zac asked when he stumbled backward, having held the pads up for me to punch in my warm-up.

"Nothing." I slammed my gloved fist into the mat, gritting my teeth.

"Come on. I know you pretty well by now. What's going on?"

I stopped and bent over, resting my lower arms on my knees. I'd already exerted too much energy, but it had felt really good. When I stood back up, I looked into my friend's concerned face. "Leo went to fight night last night, and he wouldn't let me go with him, and then I woke up alone. It wasn't a good feeling, even when I found out he was okay."

Zac scrunched his face up. "Have you spoken to him today?"

"No. I guess he's still asleep."

Zac chuckled. "He's protective of you, Jules."

"I'm not made of glass."

"Well I know that. In fact, I've signed you up for another amateur fight night."

"Oh. Really?" I didn't want to take it any further, but as a hobby, I really enjoyed it. Between my training with Zac, the occasional competitive fight and the monthly car racing supersprints, I was one very happy adrenaline junkie.

"Come on. Let's get back to it, and I'll buy you a coffee afterwards to tell you more about it. I know Juni would love to see you, too. She's meeting me down the road after this."

"That would be awesome. I've really missed her and Sia."

I had skyped with Sia a few times. She was enjoying London, and things were going well with Matt. I was so happy for her, but I missed her desperately.

When I returned to my locker, thoroughly spent after an awesome session, my phone was ringing. I grabbed it, hoping to see Leo's number on the screen, but was disappointed.

My parents' home number was flashing. I hit the green circle and held the phone to my ear while I slung my backpack over my shoulder and headed out.

"Hey, Dad."

"Hi, Juliette. Are you busy for lunch today?"

"I'm not sure yet. Why?"

"Your mother and I have something very important to discuss with you, and we hoped you would come by the house today."

I cringed. "That sounds ominous."

"We have some news, and it impacts you. I really don't want to talk to you about it over the phone."

"Okay. Sure." I figured Leo would go straight to the farmhouse from Nick's, so I might not see him until much later anyway. "I'll be there in a few hours."

"Thanks, sweetheart."

After a quick shower, I changed into my favourite long, flowing dress cinched in at the waist with a belt. Sitting on the change room bench, I pulled on my gorgeous, long-heeled, brown leather boots, then headed out to meet Zac.

"Where is this fight you've signed me up for?" I asked, pulling on my short, denim jacket as we started in the direction of the café.

"Footscray. Is that okay? It's local."

"Absolutely." I smiled, knowing I no longer feared my mother's reaction.

"It'll be very much like the Lilydale fight, but you'll be matched up with a more experienced fighter given your win last time."

"Do you think I'm up for it?"

"Absolutely, Jules." He slung his arm around my shoulders. "You're the ballsiest girl I've ever come across."

I chuckled at his comment. "Thanks. I think."

"It's a compliment. Hold your head high and accept your awesomeness."

I smiled, grateful for his friendship.

When we entered the café, Juni stood up and waved from a table by the front window. When I reached her, she hugged me, and I found myself clinging to her. "It's so good to see you."

She held me at arm's length. "You too, Jules. How are you?"

"I'm great." I was feeling so much better after my training session, but I really hoped Leo would've called by now.

Zac went to the counter to order our coffees while Juni and I made ourselves comfortable on the cushioned window seat.

"I spoke to Sia early this morning."

"God, I miss her," I said, sighing. "How is she?"

"I told her she was going to be an aunt." She rubbed her flat stomach and winked.

Elated, I glanced at her hand. "That is so fantastic. Congratulations." My face felt like it might split from the grin stretching across it.

"It's made Sia want to come home though. She says she is craving sister time and doesn't want to miss my pregnancy or the birth." Zac arrived with the coffees and sat down opposite us. Juni leaned down to her bag on the floor and pulled out a packet of choc banana Tim Tams and placed it on the table. Without skipping a beat, she continued. "I just don't want her to give up her chance of happiness with the wonderful-sounding guy she met."

"Matt divides his time between Europe and Australia, so I doubt it'll be a problem, and what's with the Tim Tams?"

"Cravings." She winked. "I'm blaming the cravings."

"Perfect. Choc banana though? Ugh." I made a face and stuck my tongue out. "You can't mess with the original."

"I agree, but I've become obsessed with them. Anyway, Sia said Matt's brother, Charlie, is already here."

I cringed. "He is. I saw him earlier this week."

"Sia didn't elaborate at all, but she might've hinted Charlie was pretty eager to chase you back to Australia."

I grimaced. "I'm with Leo. Charlie and I are just friends. Nothing more."

We spent the next hour chatting about their honeymoon and plans to move to a bigger place before the baby was born. It was wonderful to be around a couple so completely in love and making a future together. I wasn't jealous. I was inspired. Leo and I would get there in the end. I was sure of it.

"I better get back to the gym," Zac said regretfully, tapping his watch.

"I better go, too," I said. "I'm having lunch at my parents,' which is always good fun." I was sure they hadn't missed my sarcasm.

In the time we'd been sitting inside the cafe, the weather had deteriorated dramatically. Dark clouds had moved in, and the temperature had dropped from fresh to straight-up cold. I pulled a cream scarf from my bag and double looped it around my neck. I was very glad of the denim jacket I'd shoved in my bag at the last minute, but I still shivered as I said my goodbyes to Zac and Juni, promising to catch up with them again soon.

Rather than bothering to go home for my car, I got a cab straight to my parents' house. It wasn't too far, and I was intrigued by their big news. I just hoped it was something positive. I didn't think I could cope with any more drama and yearned for some quiet time. I turned my phone back on and called Leo to see how he was doing. It went straight to voicemail, so I just popped it back in my bag, figuring I'd speak to him after lunch.

Dad opened the door for me, and I was a little taken aback by his borderline slovenly attire. My dad was always dressed smartly and would never be seen dead in track pants. It was a strange sight. He laughed. "I know. I know. They are actually really comfortable."

I chuckled. "Yes, they are."

Feeling something wrap itself around my legs, I screeched when I glanced down to see what I assumed was a cat.

"What the hell is that?" I asked, frozen to the spot while the creature began prancing around me. It looked like a hairless cat but was behaving like a dog.

Dad bent over and scooped it up, patting it affectionately. "This is Cleopatra. She's a Sphynx cat."

"Cute," I said with a tight grimace. She really wasn't cute, but on closer inspection, there was something strangely regal about her with her large, oval-shaped eyes and prominent cheekbones.

Dad laughed. "She was your mother's choice. They are renowned for showing great affection towards their owners."

I patted Cleopatra's head tentatively at first but with more confidence as I ran my hand over the chamois-like texture of her body. "Good luck, Cleopatra," I whispered.

"Your mother is in the kitchen making tea."

I wandered through the house and was equally surprised to find her in what looked like yoga pants and an oversized t-shirt.

"What's going on?" I could hear the fear in my voice. I'd had a feeling something was off all day, and my parents' weirdness wasn't helping.

She kissed my cheek, then went back to pouring tea into their expensive china cups. The whole scene was giving me whiplash. "Nothing bad, Juliette. Calm down."

Dad appeared behind me. "Let's go sit in the lounge room."

They certainly both seemed far more relaxed with each other than they had the last time I had been there.

When we were all seated, I looked at them both expectantly.

"We're moving to Sydney," Dad announced with no build-up.

"What?" Mum had mentioned moving when I saw her at Dartmoor, but I hadn't thought she was serious. "Why?"

"It's time for a change, and there's an opportunity for me to open another office in Sydney, so we're going to take it."

"When?" I asked, a little surprised that my overwhelming feeling was relief.

"You might've pretended to be a little sad," Dad said. "We were hoping you would come, too. Charlie told me he'd offered you a job at his company, so you already have a job lined up in Sydney. We could all start afresh."

I shook my head adamantly. "I'm not moving to

Sydney. No chance. No way."

My phone ringing from the kitchen was the perfect excuse to cut this conversation short. I wished Dad had just told me this news over the phone to save me the trip. I stood up and left the room.

"Juliette." Gwendolyn's voice sounded frantic. "You need to come out to the farmhouse."

"What's wrong?" I asked, standing at the French doors overlooking the courtyard.

"Leo was acting really weird. He was slurring his words and was calling out for you just before he collapsed."

My body froze. My brain didn't know what to do with those shocking words. My parents appeared next to me, looking curious. Nick had told me he'd taken a nasty blow at the fight. A lump in my throat made it hard to speak without losing my mind.

"I'm coming." I sounded like a robot, and I felt my whole body start to shake with fear. I didn't even have a fucking car. "I'll call you on the way."

Tears started running down my face when I hung up.

"What wrong?" Dad asked, placing his hands on my shoulders.

"It's Leo," I choked out. "There's something wrong with Leo."

"What happened?" My mother's concerned voice sounded like fingernails being dragged down a chalkboard. I knew she would never approve of him.

"Not that you'd care, but it sounds like he has a concussion and has passed out."

"Thug," my mother mumbled under her breath.

"I need a car. I don't have my car." I ignored my mother's spiteful words. It wasn't worth the energy when Leo needed me.

"Take my car." Dad grabbed the keys to his beloved and barely-used Porsche from the bench. "Go."

"Thanks, Dad." I took the keys, grabbed my phone, stuffed it in my bag and bolted for the back door. The black, pristine-condition Porsche 997 GT3 was waiting for me in their garage. It was a few years old but had barely seen the light of day. Such a waste. This car was made for speed, and that's exactly what I needed today. This beautiful piece of German engineering was going to take me to Leo in record time.

Dad was behind me as I entered the garage. "Go easy on the clutch, Juliette. It's a lot heavier than you're used to, and it's easy to miss a gear." I smiled sweetly but gritted my teeth, eager to get going. "And the Pirelli P-Zero tyres might not be as grippy as they used to be, so please be careful."

I tried not to roll my eyes. He had no idea about my driving experience. If he did, he possibly wouldn't have offered me his baby. "Don't worry, Dad. I promise I'll bring it back in one piece."

Jumping in the driver seat, I waved to my pale and mildly frazzled-looking dad. I started the ignition and heard the engine roar to life. If I hadn't been so desperate to get out of there, I might've sat back and enjoyed one of my favourite sounds. Instead, I ensured there was no slack in the lap sash seatbelt, opened the garage door with the buzzer in the centre console and eased it out in first gear. I rumbled down the back alley, sure that Dad was still watching my exit. However, the second I turned the corner, I changed up a gear and gave it a bit more throttle. When I was sure the engine was warm enough, my foot went to the floor. The car responded to my need for speed instantly, as I knew it would. My back pressed into the seat as I surged forward, assessing the pattern of the cars ahead to make the best lane selections. The city was quickly behind me, and the highway opened up ahead.

I hit Gwendolyn's number on my phone and waited as the Bluetooth picked up the ringing. There was no answer. No need to panic. I refused to panic. I called again, and officially panicked when it went to voicemail. I tried Leo's number, hoping Gwendolyn might pick up, but it went straight to voicemail, too. Telling myself she was probably on the phone to a doctor, I sucked in some much-needed oxygen. Oh God, how was he? I was desperate to know.

Even for experienced drivers, there's a limit you don't exceed on public roads, and I knew I was dancing precariously close to it. Every time a car in front of me slowed, I'd edge out, and with any kind of a gap to the oncoming traffic, surge past in a flash. This car could outrun any highway patrol car, and I was more than willing to risk a speeding ticket and even my license to get to Leo faster.

When I turned off the highway and onto the quieter streets leading me to the farmhouse, I really opened up the throttle. This car was a die-hard car enthusiast's wet dream. I dropped down to third gear to take a tightening corner a touch faster than I should've, controlled the oversteer with a quick touch of opposite lock and a gentle squeeze on the throttle, and rocketed out the other side. I said a quick danke schön to the Porsche engineers when the farmhouse came into view much sooner than it would've in my Mini.

Rather than bump down the cobbled driveway, I screeched to a stop near the front gate, leapt out and dashed down the path to the front door. I didn't stop to wonder why I couldn't see Leo's Jeep; however I stopped in my tracks when I saw a red Honda Civic parked in the driveway. It had to have been Gwendolyn at the church and slowing down in front of the farmhouse weeks ago. Why had she been spying on us? With no time to deliberate further, I knocked on the door. When no one answered in the two seconds I was prepared to wait, I turned the handle and was relieved to find it unlocked.

CHAPTER 32

LEO

I HAD NO IDEA WHAT time it was when I felt the first moments of consciousness. As my sluggish brain kicked into gear, I realised something was stuck across my mouth and I couldn't move my arms or legs. Panicking, I opened my eyes and tried to make sense of my surroundings. I was in my Jeep, lying face down across the backseat. Zip ties bound my legs at the ankles and arms behind my back at the wrists. I figured I had duct tape over my mouth, every muscle in my body was screaming at me and my head was pounding.

What the fuck?

I struggled fruitlessly against the ties, but all that did was make them cut into my skin. When I almost pulled my shoulder from its socket, I knew I needed to stop. My heart was hammering in my chest, and I sucked in some air through my nose. *Do not panic.*

I tried to sit up, but all my limbs felt like jelly. I was sure I'd been drugged, and the pain in my arm brought back memories of a sharp jab shortly before I had blacked out. In all my years of fighting, there had never been any retribution outside of fight night. It was fighter's code to leave retribution for the cage. I didn't even think Reaper was capable of this, and he was a raving lunatic.

I strained my neck back so I could look out the window. It was overcast, and there wasn't a soul in sight. From what I could tell, I would guess it was late afternoon. Had I really been out for over twelve hours or maybe longer? It was the weekend, there were no other cars in the lot that I could see and I had no way of alerting anyone I was there. There was a chance no one would be around until Monday. I tried again to sit up and managed to get enough momentum to be successful this time. Everything swayed, so I closed my eyes and took in some more air. Once I felt my equilibrium return, I opened my eyes again.

Think. Think. Think. Who would've done this and why? My greatest fear was that Juliette was in danger, but if I thought too hard about that, I would drive myself insane. Every scenario I could come up with made no sense. I decided the only good use of my energy was getting free.

CHAPTER 33

Juliette

As I burst through the front door of the farmhouse, I yelled out for Leo, but I was greeted with silence. As I moved into the house, something felt really off. It was eerily quiet. Perhaps it was my fear for Leo's safety, but I could almost feel the tension pulsing through the walls. The bricks were cracking in places where the mortar was crumbling with time and lack of maintenance. The wooden balustrade I'd once glided my hand down to admire the woodwork was missing some posts and actually looked to be rotten in places. I tried desperately to think clearly.

Feeling panicky, I walked quickly down the hall towards the back of the house, calling out as I went. My nerves were on tenterhooks, and paranoia was taking hold of my brain.

"Gwendolyn? Leo?" I called out, trying not to scream the house down. I should've asked her for more details. Where had he been when he'd passed out?

I ran up the stairs, taking three steps at a time, and checked all the rooms, calling out as I went. When my search was fruitless, I stopped at the top of the stairs, realising I wasn't thinking straight at all. Gwendolyn would've called an ambulance and had forgotten to call me in the drama of it all. I exhaled a loud breath, realising I'd been holding it for too long, and descended the stairs two at a time. I had no idea which hospital they might go to, but I was sure Google could locate the closest one for me.

At the bottom of the stairs, I stopped when I thought I heard a sound in the kitchen. I turned left and rushed back down the hall. As I turned the corner, a visceral tension hit me full force. Nick Matthews was pushing Gwendolyn roughly into the kitchen through the back door. *What the hell is going on and where is Leo?*

Nick appeared shocked to see me and grabbed hold of Gwendolyn to stop her going any further. "What are you doing here?" Nick asked in a tone that sent fear shooting through me like a shot of adrenaline. Gwendolyn had a sly grin on her face, and I knew I'd been played.

My stomach dropped as my eyes zeroed in on the gun Nick was holding and the fact it was being pushed up against the side of Gwendolyn's neck. He had a freaking gun! My eyes met hers and all I saw were dark pools, devoid of light and warmth. I wondered if she was drunk, high, both or just plain crazy. My heart felt painfully restricted as it jackhammered against its bony confines, and I could feel a light sweat break out on my forehead. *Is this really happening?* Standing in the very place where Leo's father had been murdered, I was terrified. I took a deep breath and swallowed the lump in my throat but couldn't yet find my voice.

"What are you doing here, Juliette?" Nick repeated his question.

"I... um..." I stuttered. "Gwendolyn called me and said Leo was unconscious." I took a deep breath. "Is Leo here?"

Gwendolyn yelped as Nick pushed the gun into the side of her neck. "Planning on telling her, too, were you?" When she didn't answer immediately, he pressed the gun harder against her neck.

She tried to tilt her head away from the gun as she pointed to me. "My bastard of a son thought he could get away with giving me a paltry sum, while he keeps the crown jewel. I needed her here as leverage." Despite being held at gunpoint, her eyes darkened with excitement. "I'd give him the closure he so desperately wants in exchange for the house. I knew the only way he'd agree was if his precious Juliette was in the equation."

I was incredulous. "You are insane."

"I prefer opportunistic."

"Stupid bitch," Nick spat, pushing her away from him. She stumbled towards me and turned so we were standing next to each other. "Leo would've skinned you alive if you'd hurt her."

"Are you going to let me go?" I croaked, trying to swallow the laughter I knew was inappropriate and wildly dangerous but difficult to stifle.

"What? So you can run straight to the police? I don't think so." He held out his hand. "Give me your phone."

I reached into my pocket and reluctantly took a few steps forward, handing him my phone. He dropped it to the hard travertine and crushed it with the heel of his boot.

"I won't go to the police," I promised, knowing full well he wouldn't take my word for it. It was then I felt a cold dread work its way up my spine. I looked towards the back door as a possible escape route. I'd never actually seen a gun in real life before, and my knowledge of disarming an attacker was purely theoretical. The reality was not the exciting adrenaline rush I had imagined. It was paralysing and terrifying. *Breathe, Juliette. Breathe, god damnit.*

Nick smirked. "Don't bother with any of your fancy moves. I'll shoot you without a second thought."

"I don't understand what's going on here," I whimpered, trying not to lose the plot completely.

"Shut up, Juliette," Nick scolded. "This is between Gwendolyn and me. She shouldn't have brought you into it, and I made sure Leo is having a nice, long sleep far from here." He sounded so cool and calm. "I actually give a shit about the kid, you know?"

I was so relieved to hear Leo was safe, my knees almost gave way and I reached for the bench to steady myself.

"Ask him what he did for me," Gwendolyn piped up. "Ask him what he did for me in this very spot."

"Shut up, Gwendolyn," Nick spat, cocking the gun.

"You're going to kill us both, so you might as well confess your sins." She laughed manically like a hyena on crack, then stopped abruptly when she locked eyes with Nick, who had raised the gun higher so it was now level with her head.

Holy shit! Holy shit! Holy. Shit. I was sweating. I was freezing. I was outraged. I was terrified. I felt everything and nothing.

"My sins?" Nick asked incredulously. "I killed him for you. I killed him for us."

I just stared at Nick, and I was pretty sure I had stopped breathing. His revelation was not only completely shocking; it also sealed my fate. He had just confessed to murder in front of me, and he had a loaded gun.

"I never directly asked you to kill him, Nick," Gwendolyn snickered. "And I certainly never told you there was any chance we would be together if you did."

Nick had moved right in front of her now, and I could see the skin on the back of his neck turning red. "I left my wife for you." His hand covered his forehead. "All these years I've carried the burden of what I did, and you were about to throw me to the wolves."

I held my breath watching the train wreck unfold.

"You were merely a pawn." She was clearly resigned to her fate and was determined to drive the knife in. "You were never part of the end game."

Nick's eyes flashed with rage as her words sunk in.

She glanced at me. "I wish Leo had died that day, too."

"He's your son." I was horrified, and the tears I'd been trying desperately to control slipped down my cheeks at the thought of my life without Leo. I would never have known he existed, and neither of us would've ever known a love like ours. Was it going to end here? Was I going to die in this farmhouse like Leo's father?

"My husband and son, the freaking superheroes," she continued. Her whole body shuddered as if the very thought of them was unpleasant.

I struggled to find a word to adequately describe their heinous pre-meditation. Clenching my fists, I could feel my blood pressure rising.

"I left my wife to be with you." I snapped my head to Nick, who was about to blow a gasket. "You let me kill for you, and I think it's fitting you meet the same fate right here."

While they were locked in a standoff, I knew I had to use the opportunity. I was as good as dead anyway with these two maniacs. I glanced around, wondering if I could bolt for it. I had no idea how good Nick's aim was, but it was better to assume he was a crack shot than take my chances. Then I remembered Leo telling me about the wine cellar where William spent a lot of time. The door was right next to the kitchen, so only a few feet away from where I was standing. Leo had said he'd locked himself down there playing hide and seek, so I just had to make it through the door before he could take his shot. My veins were loaded with the biggest shot of adrenaline they'd ever experienced. *You can do this, Juliette,* I told myself.

Just as I was about to make a dash for it, Gwendolyn spoke. "You won't kill me," she spat. "You've been in love with me for years."

I clamped my hands over my ears when a loud shot rang out. My eyes bugged out of my head, and I stumbled backwards. Gwendolyn dropped to her knees, then slumped forward onto the pale travertine floor. I stared at the middle of her back and watched blood ooze through her shirt.

"Oh my God." Nick stared at her lifeless body. The gun slipped out of his hand and made a horrible thud when it hit the floor.

Knowing I had seconds to escape, I didn't hesitate. I bolted for the basement door, ripped it open, threw myself through and slammed it shut. I was beyond relieved to see an impressive-looking deadbolt. It was a little rusty, and I had to put all my strength behind it to slide it across. I let out the breath I was holding but didn't stick around to enjoy my relief.

I turned around and was faced with steep stone steps leading down into darkness. I really didn't want to go down there, but I had no choice. I had a lunatic with a gun on the other side of the door and no phone to call for help. I was up the proverbial creek without a paddle. When I heard Nick calling my name and saw the door shake, I took off.

As I descended the stone steps, I shivered when I felt the temperature drop. I reached the bottom of the stairs and it was almost pitch black, so I had to go by feel to find a light switch. Instead, I found a fine rope hanging from the ceiling. A metal bauble hung to the bottom and banged me in the forehead. When I pulled on it, one lonely bulb illuminated, casting a soft glow on my surrounds. It was a far larger area than I had expected, and I felt vaguely relieved that I wasn't trapped in a tiny space. I wasn't necessarily claustrophobic, but I'd defy anyone to not feel nervous down there, particularly under those circumstances.

Wine racks lined both walls. I shuffled past them, not having a clue whether I was headed for safety or my grave. I couldn't hear anything from the house above, but I'd take my chances down here rather than face a certain death. I had no idea how long I would wait it out. Would he wait for me to come back out or would he flee the scene of his crimes? For the time being, at least, I felt far safer down in the cool, protected basement where William Ashlar, a man I'd never know, had spent much of his time.

I snapped my head towards the steps when I heard a strange crackling sound coming from above. I jogged back up the stairs and was horrified when the smell of smoke filled my nostrils. *Oh shit!* Was Nick trying to flush me out or was he going to burn the whole house down and simply disappear? He now had another body on his hands, and this time, I was a witness. Smoke was puffing through the cracks around the door. I knew I couldn't open that door, so my only option was to head back to the basement.

I jogged quickly back down the stairs and past the wine racks. The sandstone wall I'd been edging along came to an end, and I stepped cautiously around a corner, grazing my shoulder on the rough surface. I felt around for another piece of rope but couldn't find anything. I was cold, I was terrified and I was alone. I leaned against the rough wall and sunk to the ground, torn between trying to escape and staying where I was, where I felt relatively safe surrounded by stone. I decided on the latter.

The little butterflies that had been fluttering around in my belly erupted in a nausea-inducing swarm. *Is Leo okay? Is Nick out there waiting for me?* I was pretty sure shock was about to hit me full force, so I rested my elbows on my bent legs, placed my face in my hands and made a wish. *Please let Leo be okay.*

CHAPTER 34

LEO

I SCANNED THE BACK SEAT and foot well for anything sharp that I might be able to use to cut the zip ties, but there was nothing. Then I realised my brain was still not functioning properly. What exactly was I going to do with it? My hands were tied behind my back. The light was fading, and I needed to take a piss badly.

Strength and brains had always been my greatest assets. *Think!*

The zip ties were plastic. They might be super strong, tight and holding me in an awkward position, but I needed to break them. I was lying flat on my stomach with my legs bent to accommodate my size in the back seat. Taking a deep breath in, I raised my arms as far above my back as I could manage. I closed my eyes and repeated a Buddhist quote that had resonated with me in Thailand.

Do not dwell in the past, do not dream of the future, concentrate the mind on the present moment.

With everything blocked out, I focused all my energy into my raised arms, then slammed them down on my backside in one killer blow. The distinctive snapping sound was music to my ears as my arms flew apart and fell to my sides. The relief was extreme when I sat up, groaning with pleasure as I worked the strained muscles of my arms and shoulders. After I'd ripped the duct tape from my mouth, I looked around again for something sharp to cut the ties around my ankles.

It suddenly occurred to me that my tool kit was in the boot. I turned onto my knees and leant over the backseat and rummaged under the canvases to find my stonemason tools. I knew exactly what I needed and found it quickly amongst the trowels, pointers, chisels and hammers. The cock's comb, with its serrated blades, was used on limestone, and I knew it would make light work of the zip tie around my ankles.

The second I was freed from the tie, I flung myself over to the driver's seat and opened the door, almost falling out onto the bitumen. I relieved my bladder on the lonely, half-dead tree in front of the car and once again groaned with pleasure. Back in the car, I was surprised to see my bag was in the passenger seat foot well. Grabbing it, I ripped the zip open and searched desperately for my phone. I quickly discovered I'd been left with no wallet, no keys and no phone. If they'd only been interested in the cash, they wouldn't have bothered tying me up.

I had no choice but to leave the Jeep and find another way to get back to the city and to Juliette. I might've been considered a thug by some, but I did not know how to hotwire a car. I still felt wobbly, but I broke into a jog as I made my way through the industrial estate and out onto the road. I stuck my thumb out and didn't have to wait long before a car stopped for me.

"Where you headed, son?" the driver of the brown sedan asked when I climbed in. He got a better look at me when I turned to face him. "Dear Lord. What happened to you?"

"I'm headed for St Kilda. If you can get me closer to the city, I'd appreciate it." I ignored his question about what had happened to me.

"This must be your lucky day," he said. "I'm heading home to Brighton. I'll drop you off."

I'd woken up in the back of my car, tied up and drugged. I was one hundred percent certain it was *not* my lucky day, but it sure was a break that this guy had stopped for me.

"Appreciated. Any chance I could borrow your phone?"

"Sorry, son." He shrugged. "Those things will fry your brains."

Shit.

"You sure you don't want me to take you to the hospital?" he asked when we'd been driving for around fifteen minutes.

I must've really looked like shit. "No. I'm good, thanks." I shot him a friendly smile, then returned my gaze to the road ahead.

Thankfully, he nodded, then cranked up the radio and proceeded to sing along enthusiastically to Kenny Rogers' "The Gambler."

When he dropped me home, I thanked him profusely before dashing down the side of my apartment building. Despite it being a terrible security risk, the window around the back didn't lock, so I could slide it up with a bit of brute force. Climbing through the window, I winced. The past twenty-four hours had taken a terrible toll on my body, but I couldn't dwell on that. I grabbed the keys to the Ducati and my helmet and headed into the hallway to knock on my neighbour's door.

"Hey, Leo," Susie from 1C purred, propping herself up against the door jamb. Clearly her boyfriend wasn't around.

"Susie." I tried not to sound impatient. "Can I borrow your phone, please?"

"You sure can, honey." She swished back into her apartment, glancing over her shoulder and batting her eyelashes.

Fuck. Just hurry up! I thought to myself, throwing her a reluctant smile.

She returned with her diamante-covered pink iPhone and handed it to me. Thanking her, I pulled up Google and ran a quick search for Juliette's apartment building. Joel rang through to her apartment, but there was no answer. He said he hadn't seen her all day. Next, I called her gym. The only thing I knew she was doing today was training with Zac.

When the guy at reception tracked him down, he told me they'd had coffee together this morning and she'd left to go to her parents' house for lunch. Knowing lawyers' home numbers were never listed, I handed the phone back to Susie, thanked her, then bolted out the door.

The Ducati roared to life, and I fishtailed on the loose gravel near the side of the road and took off for Toorak.

Screeching to a halt outside the plush townhouse, I threw my leg over and dashed up the path. I simultaneously rang the doorbell and banged on the door.

Isabel opened the door and looked a little shocked to see me. "I thought you had a concussion?"

"I'm looking for Juliette," I stated, looking past her into the house.

"She's not here anymore." She took a step closer to me. "She flew out of here in a mad panic hours ago."

"What are you talking about?" I asked, shouting now. I'd managed to stay relatively calm, but now I knew something was really up.

"Juliette got a call from your mother telling her you had a concussion and had passed out. She wanted her to go to the farmhouse. John gave her the keys to the Porsche."

"Oh, shit!" I exclaimed. "I need a phone." I was willing to get down on my knees and beg at that point. "Can you lend me a phone?"

"What's going on?" Juliette's dad appeared in the doorway.

"Give him your phone," Isabel demanded.

I scrolled through his contacts and called Juliette. No answer. *Fuck!*

Panicking, I called the Lilydale Police Station. Detective Joe Peters was the lead investigator on my father's case and had always kept me up to date. He was almost as gutted as I was that the killer had never been apprehended.

"Leo. Thank God. I've been trying to get hold of you." That was not what I wanted to hear, and a cold dread was threatening to swallow me whole.

"What's going on, Joe?" I asked.

"The fire department was called to your farmhouse and is still there trying to get it under control."

"What the hell? Is anyone in there?"

"I don't have those details yet," he replied. "Can you get out here?"

"Please, Joe. Gwendolyn is behind this. My girlfriend was heading out to the house, and I can't get hold of her."

"I have men at the house diverting traffic, but I was just on my way there."

"Thanks, Joe. I'll meet you there."

"I'll let my men know to let you through."

I hung up. "Can I keep this phone?" I asked with full intention of taking it regardless.

"Of course," John replied. "What's going on, Leo?"

"I don't know," I said, already heading down the path. "But I'll let you know when I do."

CHAPTER 35

LEO

THE DUCATI'S ENGINE WAS PUSHED to the limits of its capacity as I flew towards God only knew what. Ducking and weaving through the traffic then flooring it along the open road would've been enjoyable in different circumstances. As it was, I couldn't seem to go fast enough, and I cursed every single kilometre.

The police had set up a detour at the last turnoff before my house, but they waved me through. I just had to pray Juliette was okay and not in the burning house. The worst was too horrible to contemplate.

The closer I got, the more intense the smell of smoke became. When the house came into view, I skidded to a halt. The farmhouse, my childhood home, engulfed in flames was something out of nightmares, but the fear that struck my entire body like a tornado was like nothing I'd ever experienced before. *Please don't let Juliette be in there.* I begged, prayed, chanted and pleaded to any god who'd listen.

Fire engines were parked on the grassy verge, as well as down the driveway. There was also an ambulance, which just made me want to throw up. Huge torrents of water were flooding the house at multiple places. A loud bang sent shockwaves through my body, and I watched as the roof collapsed. I pulled out the borrowed phone and hit Juliette's number. It went straight to voicemail without ringing. "Please don't let Juliette be in there." I repeated my desperate plea out loud as I rode closer to the house. I left the bike on the side of the road and started down the driveway.

"Hold it right there, pal." A fireman stopped me at the front gate.

"This is my house." I tried to dodge him but was stopped by one of his colleagues, who appeared from behind the closest truck. He held up both his hands to stop me. "I need to get in there."

"It isn't safe. The roof has collapsed, and I've had to pull my men out."

"My mother and girlfriend might be in there." I pointed to the house, shocked by the tears glazing my vision. "Have you found anyone in there yet?"

He nodded, and I felt my world begin to fall apart. "I'm so sorry, son, but one female body has been recovered. Before it got too dangerous, my men were in there looking for other casualties."

My hand covered my mouth. Either way, I was about to find out this house was the scene of both my parents' deaths or Juliette's.

"Can you tell me anything about the woman you pulled out?"

"I didn't see her." He looked at the other man. "Did you?"

"The burns were pretty bad." His sad eyes gave away the strain of a job not everyone could do. As with all the first response services, they must see some hideous sights along with the reward of saving lives.

"Do you know if she was brunette or blonde?" I

pressed.

I held my breath, waiting for the reply, knowing this was the obvious distinguishing feature. *Please don't say blonde.*

Detective Peters materialised next to me, placing his hand on my shoulder. "It was Gwendolyn, Leo."

The combination of relief that it wasn't Juliette and devastation that she might still be in there was overwhelming. I stood frozen in place, frozen in time and dying just a little bit more with every passing second.

A loud bang roared, snapping me out of my stupor. The glass from the upstairs windows shattered and flames licked the eaves.

"You can't just leave her in there." I rushed forward but was restrained by two strong sets of arms. "What about Juliette?" I screamed. "You're going to let her die in there. Please let me go and get her." *I can't live without her.*

"I'm really sorry, but I can't let you do that. We'll keep working on the fire, and when it's safe, we'll go back in."

Joe pulled me back, but I shrugged him off. I started pacing, all the while willing it to be just one big nightmare I could wake up from. In my mind, I was formulating a plan to get around the firefighters and into the house, which I knew rationally was insane, but I was far from rational at that point. I couldn't just stand there watching the inferno.

Joe rushed over to me holding his phone up. "We just got an anonymous tip."

My head snapped up. "Tell me," I demanded.

"The basement."

"What?"

"The tip was to check the basement, and that's all the

information given."

Without any further thought, I made a bolt for it. My whole body went into fight mode, and I dodged anyone crazy enough to get in my path. I was headed for the northeast corner of the house, where I knew there was an external access point into the basement. Dad used it for his wine and home brew supplies.

Every second felt like an hour as I closed the distance to my destination. If she was in there, it was because of me. I simply couldn't lose her. Not again. Not ever.

I was horrified to find the sloping door set and the ventilation points were covered by fallen stones and timber. I immediately started heaving them off.

"Are you insane?" A voice called out from behind me, but I didn't stop.

"Help me or leave me the hell alone," I shouted, glancing back to see a group of angry firemen fully kitted up.

To my relief, they all joined me in clearing the debris, and minutes later, the job was done. One of the firemen stepped forward with bolt cutters and made light work of the heavy, rusted padlock. A split second later, I ripped the steel door open.

"Jules," I shouted. "Are you down there?"

I thought I heard a voice, but the sounds of the burning house and the thick torrents of water trying to contain it made it hard to hear. Before the firemen could stop me, I scrambled down the ladder into the darkness, calling out to Jules with increased urgency.

"Leo?" I could hear her faint voice, and my heart skipped a beat. She was alive. Jules was alive.

When I found her, she was lying on the floor in the foetal position but was trying to raise her head. I thought I might die of relief and happiness. I crouched down next to her, and the tears started to pour down her face. My heart broke for whatever she'd just gone through.

"Baby." It was all I could utter as I picked her up and cradled her against me. Her arms wrapped around my neck. "You're alive," I whispered into her smoky hair. She coughed into my chest.

"We need to get her out of here," urged one of the firemen who'd followed me down into the basement. "She needs medical attention."

I followed them back the way we'd come, gripping Jules to me with a wild possessiveness.

"She's one lucky lady," the fireman said when we were at a safe distance from the house. "The basement was built like a stone fortress. She would've been fine down there until the ventilation was compromised."

I looked up to the sky. "Thank you, Dad."

"I was so scared I'd never see you again," she sobbed. "I didn't know if I should stay down there or try to get out."

"Shh." I kissed her head. "It's over now, angel."

"I'm alive." She clung to me and spoke against my chest.

"I don't know what I would've done," I managed to croak out. She looked up at me and I kissed her, tasting her tears. "I was so scared."

"I'm okay." Her voice was shaky. In fact, her whole body was shaking. "Everything's going to be okay," she whispered.

The ambulance officers wanted to examine her, but there was no way I was letting her go anywhere without me. The first thing they did was place an oxygen mask over her face and check her for wounds.

"I just went to Hell and back thinking you were dead."

She lifted her mask. "I would've called you, but my phone got smashed." Her voice broke. "Your mum...

Your dad…" She placed her hands on either side of her head and rubbed at her temples. "I need to speak to the police."

"Don't talk now, baby." I stroked her hair. "It can wait."

"I have more to tell you though. I know—"

"Please keep the mask on, miss," the ambulance officer insisted.

"I agree." I felt guilty and stepped back to let them do their job properly.

Unsurprisingly, the overall experience was taking its toll on her, and she looked to be on the verge of collapse. I wished I could've taken her place. I had no idea what impact this terrible experience had had on us individually, but we were alive and we were together. We could get through this. I could hear the raging inferno and the occasional crash as my family home continued to burn, despite the untiring efforts of the firefighters.

I had no idea yet what she had gone through, but I wouldn't be leaving her side for a really long time. The hours of not knowing where she was and then if she were dead were something I never wanted to go through again. She was half my heart, half my soul and my whole life. I couldn't and wouldn't live without her.

When she was given the all-clear, I helped her out of the ambulance and put my arm protectively around her. "Are you okay?"

"I have to tell you someth—"

She was interrupted by the appearance of Detective Peters. "I know you're probably anxious to get out of here, but I'd like a word with you first, Ms Salinger."

"Nick," she blurted out, tears running freely down her cheeks. "Nick Matthews is the killer."

I snapped my head to the side. "What? What are you talking about?"

"He did it for your mum, but she just wanted the money. He got away with it all these years until Gwendolyn came back for more and he thought she was going to tell you what he did so he came out here to stop her."

She was rambling, and I couldn't process what she was saying. It couldn't be true. It just couldn't be. I shook my head as my whole childhood flashed before my eyes. Nick had been my boxing coach, mentor and my friend. I had respected him like a father figure. Was that all a lie?

I stood there in complete and utter shock as Juliette gave further details of what happened today, but it was all a blur. I felt my legs give way, and everything started to sway.

"Sit down, Leo." Jules and Joe ushered me to the police car, and I collapsed into the seat. I leaned forward and tried to get oxygen into my lungs.

I was vaguely aware of Joe making a call as he walked away from us, but a million moments I'd shared with Nick Matthews continued to rage violently in my head. It wasn't possible. "It can't be true," I spoke my thoughts out loud.

Within half an hour, Joe returned with a grave expression on his face.

"What happened?" I vaguely heard Jules asking. She was so strong when I was unable to string a few words together.

"His number plate was picked up by highway patrol. He was pulled over heading north up the Hume." Joe paused. "He pulled a gun on the police officers, who had no option but to defend themselves, and he died at the scene."

Silence was our only response. What could either of us say?

"I'll drive you home," Joe said. "I'll get one of the guys to look after your bike."

"We are home," I mumbled.

Juliette crouched down next to me and took hold of my hands. "Leo. My home is wherever you are. I don't care if that's here, an apartment in the city, an igloo or on the freaking moon." She smiled. "It's been a rough day. We'll stay with Bea and Angus tonight, then work out what to do from there. Okay?"

I nodded but felt completely numb.

Before we took off, I stared out the window at what was left of the farmhouse. In front of my eyes, it had been reduced to a pile of stone and rubble. It was gone. My father's family home that had been passed down through the generations was gone. It was hard to believe that yesterday, I had been a cage fighting champion and the king of the underground. Today, I felt so damn weak, crushed by the truth and the weight of a deception that had been right under my nose.

We sat in the back of Joe's police car and drove away. Juliette gripped my hand. She had been through far worse than me today, but my girl was strong and she was trying to give me the resolve I needed.

CHAPTER 36

LEO

WE STAYED WITH BEA AND Angus for the next couple of months. They had plenty of room and were both thrilled to have us there, despite the fact I was pretty much a dysfunctional human being. When my lease ended, Jules organised for the furniture from my apartment in St Kilda to be moved into storage. She rented her Southbank apartment out fully furnished, reaping an incredible weekly amount. Angus secured her a job at his financial planning office almost immediately. I wanted to talk to her about finding her dream job, but I couldn't muster the energy.

Unlike Jules, who was just getting on with it, some days I struggled to even get out of bed. I felt so weighed down by all that had happened on top of having to deal with my mother's funeral and subsequent estate issues. On those days, Juliette lay quietly with me in the darkness, knowing that her presence helped.

Other days, I felt like a huge weight had been lifted from my shoulders, and I wanted to join her in the light.

Today was one of the good ones.

"Merry Christmas, baby," Juliette whispered against my lips.

I pulled her closer. "Merry Christmas, angel. Do you want to get up?" I asked, nuzzling her neck.

"You stay here," she said, surprising me. I'd been sure I was about to have Christmas sex.

She pulled the sheet back and leapt out of bed, rushing from the room. She returned holding a long cylinder and I sat up in bed, immediately intrigued.

"What's in there?" I asked.

"Just a little something I've been working on for the past few months."

Now I was really intrigued. "I'm dying here, Jules."

She smiled. "This present is really for both of us. I wanted to show you this in private without Bea and Angus." She scrunched up her nose. "I didn't want to put you on the spot in front of our friends."

"Open the bloody cylinder, Juliette," I demanded, laughing.

"Okay," she said, pulling the plastic disc from one end. "So bossy."

I watched her as she pulled a roll of paper out and laid it across the bed in front of me. They looked like architectural drawings. That much I could work out. I just had no idea what they were for.

"One of the financial planning clients I've been working with is a local architect. When I was dropping off some forms for her to sign, I ended up chatting to her for ages about local buildings and, well, it got me thinking."

"Oh yeah?" I looked at the drawings again and zeroed in on a few details. I still had no idea what it was for. I leaned down to take a closer look. "Is this a gym?"

She nodded. "I asked Jennifer to design an all-purpose gym for you with a focus on Muay Thai training." She bit her bottom lip. "I may have paid Dam a visit to get his input. I know you've been trying to move away from the cage and back into the boxing ring, but I think Muay Thai and martial arts is a passion for you. I don't want to see you give that up, especially if it's for me."

"Why haven't you told me about any of this before now?"

"You've had so much on your plate, and I wanted to surprise you." The colour drained from her face, and I realised I wasn't giving her the reaction she'd probably hoped for.

I held out my hand, and she moved around the bed next to me. I pulled her onto my lap and pushed the hair away from her face. "You are amazing." I kissed her lightly on the lips, and she relaxed a little. "I am so sorry I've been a downer the last few months. This is just a bit out of the blue."

"Leo. You haven't been a downer. You lost your mother and a man you trusted the same day you lost your family home." She looked at me as if I were crazy. "I would've been more worried if you'd carried on as if nothing had happened." She turned to look at the drawings. "This is just an idea for the farm."

"This is designed to be built at the farm?"

She nodded. "Where the big old shed currently is, I thought." She repositioned herself so she was straddling me. "Before everything blew up in our faces, we'd planned on living at the farm, but the rest of the details of what we would do out here were all a bit sketchy."

"That's true. I guess I've just been focused on getting through each day rather than what comes next."

"And there's no hurry, but we can't bunk in with Bea and Angus forever."

"We can't live in a gym though, Jules."

She laughed. "I thought we could design a new home together, too." The excitement dancing in her eyes was infectious. "We can recycle the stones from the original farmhouse and build something even more beautiful." She placed one hand on my cheek. "If this is too much too soon though, it's totally fine."

I covered her hand with my own. "I think it's the most perfect idea I've ever heard in my life."

Her eyes lit up again. "You do?' She climbed off me and sat down on her side of the bed, pulling the drawings towards her.

"I do."

"That is great news, 'cause I have more to tell you."

"Oh God, Jules," I said, laughing.

"You know Nick's son sold the Lilydale fight club to a developer, right?"

I nodded. Nick's son had no interest in the fight game, and as I would never set foot anywhere near that place again, he had sold it to a developer who was going to demolish it and put up townhouses.

"So, apparently the young guys you had started training and mentoring have been commuting into the city gyms but have been asking around about whether you're coming back."

"Really?" I'd been so lost in my bubble of misery, I hadn't even thought about the guys I'd been letting down.

"If you want to start your own gym, you already have a base to start from. Plus I'd like to keep up my boxing training, so I could use the gym, too. Zac has said he would come out here once a week, and he and Juni are even looking at property out this way. They want more space for when the baby comes along."

"Wow, Jules. You have this all worked out."

"I've given it a lot of thought." She winked.

"What about you though? Working at Angus's financial planning firm is hardly your dream job. Where are you on that?"

"I was never going to be the big career girl, and despite being devastated for you with what you're dealing with, I'm happy here." She beamed, and I think I fell even more in love with her. "I like working in the smaller office, and I'm meeting really interesting people who value me. I'm boxing with Zac, and you're going to be my navigator in the upcoming Targa High Country rally."

"I am?"

"You'll love it. Trust me."

"I've been in a car with you, and I'm still willing to do this. That's love for you, baby."

"You know, more than what job I do or what hobbies I have, I have you." She picked up my hand and kissed my palm before placing it on her face and leaning against it. "Loving and being loved by you is like having a dream I never dared dream come true. The rest is just an exciting adventure that I'm open to completely."

"Best Christmas ever and it's barely started." I pulled her into my arms and claimed her mouth, pulling the thin straps off her shoulders.

"Leo. Jules," Bea called out to us and knocked on our door. "Get up. We want to open presents."

I groaned, and Jules fell onto her back, laughing. "Come on. We'll have to save that present for later."

We headed out of our room hand in hand. "This way, babe." Instead of going into the lounge, I guided her towards the front door.

"Where are we going?"

"It's been a rough couple of months, Jules, but it didn't stop me from getting you something for Christmas, and I'm even more confident about it than I was before you showed me your ideas."

I opened the front door and ushered her out ahead of

me. Parked in front of the house was my Jeep attached to my Christmas gift for Jules.

"A caravan?" She squealed so loudly I had to cover my ears until she was far enough ahead of me I could risk dropping my hands.

"Well I know how much you love camping, and you said you wanted to visit your grandparents in Queensland, so I thought we could make it a road trip."

"Then we could live at the farm in it while we build our home and the gym?" She bounced on the spot, barely able to contain her excitement.

I cocked my head to the side. "That part just fell into place perfectly this morning."

"Does this mean you're moving out?" Bea and Angus appeared behind us.

"Looks that way," I replied. "You've been amazing having us so long."

"You could've stayed as long as you wanted," Angus said, slapping me on the back.

"I don't want you to go," Bea said, linking arms with Jules. They had become as close as sisters over the past few months. Her best friend, Sia, had returned from overseas, but I couldn't remember whether she was sticking around or not. It was like I'd been floating round in a bubble for the past few months.

"We won't be far away," I said.

Five years ago, my world had changed from colour to black and white when my father had been ripped from my life. Despite the horrors I'd faced culminating in the deaths of my mother and Nick, two people I had once loved, I'd been given closure. With that closure came hope, and with hope came the colour, brighter than ever.

EPILOGUE

Eighteen months later

"DID YOU KNOW THAT MYTHOLOGY influenced the naming of many objects in the night sky?" I asked. I knew how to turn my crazy girl on.

She smiled. "No. I did not know that."

"The planets all have names from Roman mythology."

We'd thrown a massive bonfire party, and the last of our friends had just left. It was a cold night, but that never bothered Jules. She was wrapped up in her warm jacket, and she was cocooned in my arms.

"Tell me more." She turned and leaned her back against me, looking skyward. I heard her sigh contentedly.

"Mercury is named after the speedy messenger god because it revolves fastest around the sun, and you already know that Venus, the goddess of love and beauty, shines the brightest."

"I love that." She sighed again.

"I can keep going if you like?"

"Of course. You can keep going all night if you like."

I chuckled and tightened my arms around her. "Mars is named for the god of war because it appears blood red, and Jupiter is the single most important god, so his name was given to the largest planet in our solar system."

"I am fascinated by all of this, you know?"

"I have gotten that impression." She elbowed me gently, and I kissed her neck.

"Less well known are the names of the Galilean moons of Jupiter. The four largest are named after mythological women: Io, Europa, Ganymede and Callisto. They were all desired and subsequently taken by force by Jupiter. Unsurprisingly, they revolve around him."

She turned her head and scrunched up her nose. "Ugh. That's not fair, is it?"

"Life isn't always fair, Jules, especially in the myths."

"Look." She squealed, pointing to the sky, startling me with her sudden outburst.

"What?" I asked, my eyes following the line of her arm up to the clear night sky.

She gave me a nudge. "A shooting star. You have to make a wish." Her navy eyes sparkled in the moonlight.

"I don't need any wishes." I kissed the top of her head. "I have everything I need right here."

"You're a sweet talker, Leo Ashlar." She whispered, turning in my arms to face me. "You still have to wish on a shooting star. It's the law."

I chuckled. "Hate to break it to you, Jules, but it's not even a star."

"Do tell." She used her husky voice and raised her eyebrows.

I swivelled her around, and holding her firmly against me with my left arm, I pointed my free arm to the sky.

"They get called 'falling stars' or 'shooting stars,' but they actually have nothing to do with stars." I feathered kisses along the back of her neck and was now more than ready to call it a night and whisk her off to bed.

"Well what are they, then?" she asked breathlessly.

Not wanting to let my girl down, I answered. "The visible streaks of light like you just saw are meteors. They're interplanetary bodies that burn up as they enter the Earth's atmosphere at extremely high velocities. The air friction vaporizes them into the white-hot streaks of light."

"I love it when you talk dirty." She ground her backside into my crotch, and I was just about done for.

"You are insatiable. Lucky I have an endless supply of astronomy trivia to keep you happy."

She turned, wrapping her arms around my neck. "I am happy. You know that, right?" She placed her gloved hand over my heart. "I'm happy when we're together. It doesn't matter where we are or what we're doing. We belong together, Leo."

Her words resonated with my soul. "It's the only thing that matters to me, Jules." I pushed a strand of her hair that had fallen across her face behind her ear. "You are the most important person in the world. You are my everything."

With eyes brimming with tears, she whispered, "I love you, Leo."

"I love you more." My mouth crashed down on hers, devouring her body and her soul through our joined lips. I belonged to her and she belonged to me. Nothing would ever change that. We were connected on a level no one could touch. We were soulmates.

"Let's go inside." I kissed her forehead and took her hand, leading her back towards our house—the house we'd built from the ashes.

We didn't speak as I led her through the back door. We kicked off our boots and removed our coats, placing them on the hooks in the utility room before walking quickly down the hallway. The sexual tension heightened with every step. I was concerned I might spontaneously combust at any second. Our bedroom just seemed too far away, and I chuckled when she stripped her clothes, dropping them one by one along the hallway. She was reduced to underwear by the time we reached our bedroom door at the front left corner of the house where the spare room used to be in the original farmhouse.

"Slow down, princess." I chuckled as I scooped her up and carried her towards our bed, kissing her neck and loving the sound of her whimpering groans.

"I need you naked five minutes ago." She groaned again as I sucked a little harder on her neck.

"I'm going to enjoy torturing you for a while yet I think," I said against her lips, then took the opportunity to deepen the kiss.

She ran her hands through my hair and held my head as she opened her mouth for my insistent tongue. I lowered her to the bed and came down on top of her.

"You're a bit feisty tonight, babe." I hovered above her, pinning her hands above her head. "I'm a sure thing, so just relax and enjoy it. Okay?"

Her cheeks reddened, but her body relaxed and I released her hands.

"Close your eyes, Jules," I demanded firmly.

She did as she was told, and I stopped a moment to admire the incredible beauty lying on the bed before me, blonde hair splayed out around her like a halo. My angel. I was so hopelessly in love with this girl, and I would be forever grateful that she was a permanent fixture in my life. I kissed the swell of her breasts, one then the other as her nipples screamed for attention. Snapping the front clasp of her bra, I tugged the lacy material from her body and flung it across the room. She opened her eyes briefly, and I gave her a stern look.

"Sorry," she muttered, closing them quickly.

I rewarded her with my mouth on her left breast, flicking the nipple with my tongue, a delicious torture I knew sent her right to the edge of sanity.

"I want you," she panted out, her back arching to push her breast further into my mouth.

I cupped her other breast with my right hand and massaged it as I continued my sensual assault. When my mouth replaced my hand, she let out a loud groan and tried to wrap her legs around my backside to pull me closer to where I knew she needed me most. She was falling apart at the seams, and I knew she didn't want to be put back together.

My mouth started blazing a trail south. When I hooked my fingers in the lace underwear, she lifted her hips to make their removal swift. She was now lying on our bed completely naked and wanting.

"Open your eyes, Jules." She complied immediately, and I was met by a frenzy of navy-coloured lust. I could never get enough of those incredible blue eyes, and I was momentarily spellbound.

"What are you waiting for?" she asked, propping herself up on her elbows.

"I'm just appreciating the view before I take what's mine."

"Can you at least get your clothes off so I can appreciate the view, too?" She winked at me, and I had to laugh as I reached behind and pulled my t-shirt over my head.

Her eyes perused my chest as if I were a tasty dish, but she was welcome to the whole damn menu. "There is no part of your body that isn't absolute perfection." She glanced at my jeans, then back up to my eyes, raising her eyebrows to indicate her desire for me to hurry up and lose the jeans.

"Your wish is my command, angel."

"I love it when you call me angel," she whispered.

"You were sent to me from somewhere. I have no idea where, but I'm grateful every day."

"Fewer beautiful words," she panted. "Fewer clothes."

I shook my head and chuckled but pushed my jeans and boxers down, letting them pool at my feet. I leant down and pulled my socks off as I stepped out of my jeans. She groaned, knowing I was doing it slowly just to torture her. When I stood up, as always, she went into full-ogle mode. Her eyes were drawn down to my straining erection.

"Babe, that looks uncomfortable."

"Are you done ogling your poor boyfriend yet?" I asked when she dragged her gaze away from my crotch and met my eyes.

"I will never be done ogling my smokin' hot boyfriend, but I'd rather do it from close up."

Without hesitation and done with my torture, I knelt on the bed at her feet and gently pushed her legs apart, kissing my way up her inner thighs. She gripped the bed covers as my mouth got closer to its final destination. I picked up her legs from under my thighs and placed them over my shoulders before giving her what she needed, exactly where she needed it. What felt like hours of foreplay erupted almost instantaneously as her thighs clenched around me and my name was said as two extra-long syllables.

Before she came down from her high, I moved up her body and thrust into her. I don't think she even realised I'd changed position until she opened her eyes and found me staring at her, smiling triumphantly.

"You are so fucking beautiful when you come apart like that for me." I pulled out and then quickly thrust back inside her harder this time. "I need to see that again, but this time I'll be right there with you."

She opened her legs wider, allowing me to deepen the penetration.

"Yes." She groaned, and it was the sweetest sound coming from my gorgeous girl.

My thrusts got harder, and my mouth found its way back to her swollen breasts that I knew were aching for my attention.

"Don't stop, Leo," she begged. "Please don't stop." She wrapped her legs tighter around my waist and dug her heels into my butt, willing me to go faster, willing me to launch us both into glorious oblivion.

"I'll never stop, babe." I said, pressing a kiss into the dip between my breasts. "Never."

I lifted my gaze to hers, and our lust-filled eyes burned only for each other.

"I love you."

"I love you, too, Leo."

My mouth crashed down on hers, devouring her while I resumed my thrusts, building to a frenzy within moments. "Come for me, baby." My demand was spoken against her lips, and she obeyed with reckless abandon.

"Leo," she said, over and over again, her chant pushing me over the edge, and I released into her in one final thrust.

We remained joined, unwilling to break the beautiful connection. Eventually, I rolled off her and lay on my back, still holding her hand. I turned my head to the side so I could watch her chest rise and fall, still out of breath. She was magnificent, and she was all mine.

"You are amazing," she whispered, her eyes glazed in a post-orgasmic haze.

My smile widened. "Ditto." I leaned forward and kissed her lightly before promptly falling asleep on my back.

~~~~

Hours later, I woke up desperate to take her again.

When I moved on top of her, she opened her eyes. "I need you again," I whispered.

"Take me," she whispered.

We made love, revelling in our closeness and absolute devotion to each other. When she kissed me, her whole body spoke a language meant just for me. When we climaxed together, it was to the beat of our joined hearts. There was nothing more beautiful, more sensual or more perfect than our bodies coming together.

I kissed her gently before pulling out and replacing the covers over us. "Sorry to wake you up."

"Never apologise for waking me up for that." Her eyelids were heavy, and she was already back to sleep before she finished her sentence. Before I closed my eyes, I stared at her, knowing she was the most precious thing on Earth. We'd gone to Hell and back to get to this point, but we were here and we were here to stay.

~~~~

I got up well before I knew Juliette would wake and headed for the kitchen to put part one of my plan into action—breakfast in bed. When I was done making an incredible mess in the kitchen, I returned to our bedroom, tray in hand.

"Morning, sunshine," I said when I came through the door and found her sitting up in bed, yawning. "Breakfast in bed."

"Seriously?" She grabbed the European pillow from

the floor and propped it up behind her. "How did I get so lucky?"

"Luck has nothing to do with it, Jules." I winked. "You put out twice last night."

"Cheeky." She couldn't help chuckling, and her cheeks reddened. It blew my mind I could still make her blush.

I placed the tray on her lap and picked up the coffee mug while she balanced it properly. I gave her a kiss to say good morning properly. "All set?"

She took the coffee from me and inhaled the fumes, then looked up at me and smiled. "Thank you, babe. This is amazing. I feel very spoilt."

"I want to spoil you. I love that I can spoil you whenever I want."

"I love that you can spoil me whenever you want, too," she said, her grin only partly hidden by her coffee mug.

She replaced the mug on the bedside table, then surveyed the other items I'd put on the tray. I was proud as punch and couldn't wait for her reaction. A plate stacked with pancakes sat on one side of the tray with a small jug of maple syrup next to it. A bunch of freshly-picked wildflowers lay above the plate. "Nice touch."

"Thanks."

"I think I burnt the pancakes slightly," I said, still irritated.

She smiled. "Better than undercooked. Uncooked pancake batter is gross."

"That's true." I walked around the bed and climbed in next to her. "I've turned the heating on, so the house should warm up soon, but until then, we're staying right here."

"Fine by me." She picked up one of the forks and handed the other to me. Two white napkins were folded, and I was mentally willing her to pick them up. She did, and when she looked back at the tray, she noticed a narrow black box.

"What's that?" she asked, intrigued.

I felt suddenly hesitant at my gift. "Just something I had made for you." I picked it up and handed it to her. "Open it."

She lifted the hinged lid, and when she peeked inside, she gasped.

A few tears slipped down her cheeks, and I knew I'd done well. "Venus," she whispered without breaking her gaze from it. Carefully, she picked up the white gold, star-shaped pendant and draped the fine silver chain over her hand. Smiling, she raised her eyes to mine. "I love it so much."

"It's to remind you that you're the brightest star in my world, baby."

She leaned forward and kissed me. "Thank you." She undid the clasp and handed it to me. She held her hair while I attached it. Her hand gravitated straight to the pendant now lying against her neck. "I will treasure it always."

Part one was a success.

We stayed in bed for another couple of hours after polishing off the pancakes and coffee. She kept telling me how much she loved her necklace and that she'd never take it off. I'd been planning this day for a long time and, so far, it was going perfectly.

"Come on, lazybones," I said, pulling the covers back. "Time to get up." I felt an odd mixture of excitement and shitting myself. "I have something to show you."

"Can't we stay in bed?" she groaned. "It's Sunday, and we have nowhere to be."

"Nope." I was out of bed and around to her side before she finished her complaint. "Out of bed now or I'll tickle you."

She groaned again. "Fine. I'm getting up." It was the ultimate Achilles' heel being ticklish. I could get her to do just about anything to avoid being tickled.

"Put on something warm," I instructed. "We're going outside."

I noted the change in her demeanour, and I knew she was now intrigued. "Okay, Mr Bossy."

Taking her by the hand, I led her out of our bedroom, down the hall and into the utility room, where I pointed to her red jacket. "Where are you taking me?" she asked, pulling it off the hook together with her black scarf and beanie.

"Patience, Jules."

"Not my strongest virtue," she said, looking at me with raised eyebrows. "You know this."

"I do know, babe, but it'll be worth the wait." I pulled her to me by her scarf and planted a scorching kiss on her lips before pulling back so I could look her in the eye. "I promise."

I pulled on my black coat and charcoal-grey beanie.

"God, my boyfriend is hot," she said, shamelessly ogling me again.

I chuckled at her as I held the back door open for her. She shivered when she stepped outside, but she closed her eyes while she inhaled the cold, wintery air deeply. While I knew she was admiring the frost-covered grass, the bare trees and the perfect, cloudless blue sky, I sent our next door neighbour, Wendy, a quick text as planned.

"Our home is paradise in all seasons, but winter is my favourite," she stated, taking another deep breath, smiling. Her irritation at being dragged out of bed and forced patience had evaporated like I knew it would.

"This way," I said, seizing her hand in mine and gently tugging her down the garden. I pushed open the gate leading to the field and ushered her through. Halfway across the field, I stopped and turned her to face me.

"You are so beautiful." I held her face, and the rest of the world didn't exist.

"Thank you." She looked me in the eye. "You're not so bad yourself, but did you drag me out of bed to tell me that?"

I closed the gap between us, wrapped my arms around her and kissed her. We never just kissed though. The impact of our lips meeting was incomparable.

I pulled back and had to laugh when she gripped my jacket and tried to pull me back to her. "I have something to show you." I took hold of her shoulders and turned her so she was facing the direction of Wendy's farm. I could see Wendy removing the head collar from and releasing my present for Juliette into our field. We waved to each other before she returned to her farm. The horse whinnied, then trotted towards us. I looked at Jules and could see confusion written on her face.

"Did Wendy get a new horse?" she asked, meeting my gaze.

"Nope." I shook my head.

"Surely not," she whispered more to herself than to me.

We walked in silence towards the horse that was now grazing. He lifted his head from the grass when we got closer. His ears were forward, and he appeared very interested in us.

"What's going on, Leo?"

We were standing right in front of him now, and she reached up to stroke the white star between his eyes. He dropped his head slightly, enjoying the attention it seemed.

"This is Cardinal, and he belongs to you now," I informed her.

She snapped her head up and studied my face, probably deciding how serious I was. I smiled, making sure she knew I wasn't pulling her leg.

She covered her mouth. "Are you serious?" She was speaking through her fingers.

"Are you happy?" I asked.

"I'm always happy with you."

"Good, because I'm deadly serious."

She threw her arms around my neck. "You are something else, Leo Ashlar. You know that?"

"Do you remember when we came here the first time and I asked you to tell me the top five things you loved?"

She smiled at the memory. "Horses were on the list." She nodded. "I remember."

"Cold weather." I held up my hand and splayed my fingers. "Your number five. Today is a beautiful winter's day—your favourite time of year." He pointed at Cardinal. "Horses were your number four." He patted his sleek neck. "A few months ago, I asked Wendy if she could keep an eye out for a good horse I could buy for you. I've seen a few since, but somehow I knew Cardinal was meant for you."

She looked back at her horse. "My horse." She shook her head as if overwhelmed by the idea.

I held up three fingers. "Getting dirty in the garden was your number three." I snickered. "I seem to recall being incredibly turned on when you told me you loved being on your hands and knees."

She chuckled. "I think I called you a pervert."

"I think you did, too. But look what you've accomplished." I pointed back towards the house.

"*We've* accomplished," she insisted.

We had spent the last eighteen months working on our garden. It was now the garden of her dreams, and as she'd hoped, she regularly made us dinner using vegetables from her sacred vegetable garden. I pushed a loose strand of hair behind her ear that had blown across her face and kissed her. Eventually, my brain kicked back in and I pulled back.

"Kissing me was your number two."

"You're the only man I'll ever want to kiss, my love."

"That's a good thing," I said, knowing I would kill any man who tried. "A very good thing."

As I approached the end of our trip down memory lane, I could feel a light sheen of sweat break out on my forehead despite the frosty temperature. I was nervous.

"What's wrong?" she asked, suspicious.

I pushed her back to arm's length and then took a step back. I held up my hand, indicating she should wait. "Nothing is wrong in the world, Jules. Trust me."

She cocked her head and bit her bottom lip. "You are being very cryptic," she said as her gaze dropped to my hand, which was pulling a small black box from my pocket. She then gasped when I dropped down onto one knee.

"Oh. My. God," she gasped, her hands flying back over her mouth and her eyes immediately filling with tears. A few slipped down her rosy cheeks.

Once I knew she was listening and over her initial shock, I spoke the words I hoped she'd remember for the rest of her life.

"Juliette Elizabeth Salinger. Cold weather, horses, the garden and kissing me. That just leaves your number one."

"You," she whispered, more tears breaking free.

I nodded, placing my left hand over my heart. "I have

always been and will always be yours. We had to fight to get here. We had to fight for this life, but falling in love with you was the easiest thing in the world. I want you to be my wife, and I want to have babies with you who will always know how much their parents love each other and them." I held up a ring, but she didn't break eye contact. "You are, and will always be, my number one, Juliette. Will you marry me?"

She let out a sob. "Yes. Yes. Of course." She was still nodding furiously as I stood up, pulled off her glove and gently placed the ring on her wedding finger. I then wrapped in her in my arms and kissed the love of my life.

She pulled back, wide eyed. "In the space of half an hour, I've been given a horse and a fiancé. I think I might be dreaming." She stared at Cardinal, then back at me. "How long have you been planning to propose?"

I answered her immediately. "Since the moment our lives collided, I knew you were it for me. The impact was a once in a lifetime event."

"Like a comet?" she asked, and I think she was mentally patting herself on the back for the astronomy reference.

"Actually, no." I scrunched my nose and chuckled. "Nothing like a comet, my gorgeous fiancée."

Then it was her turn to scrunch up her nose. "That's a weird word."

"Well, then. We'll just have to make sure I can use the word wife sooner rather than later."

"Wife." She pondered that for a second. "I like the sound of that." She smiled and looked down at her ring for the first time. Her eyes widened as she brought her hand up for closer inspection. She appeared mesmerised by the dark red ruby and pavé-set diamonds on a fine platinum band.

"Everything I read about rubies made it the perfect

choice," I stated.

She lowered her hand and took a step closer to me. "Tell me everything," she murmured, seductively.

I smiled, grazing the back of my hand down her cheek. "The Greeks called rubies the mother of all gemstones, the Romans said it was the flower among stones and it's a sacred stone for Buddhists. The clincher for me was that rubies are associated with rising Kundalini energy and are said to help you follow your bliss." She sighed, glancing down at her wedding finger again. "Around the world, in different religions and different cultures, the ruby is considered precious, sacred and beautiful." I looked into the eyes of my future wife. "You, my love, are all these things to me."

She placed her hands flat against my chest and gazed up into my eyes. "You, Leo Ashlar, are something else."

"So you like it then?" I asked. "Bea came with me to look, but I knew this one was special the second I laid eyes on it." I winked. "Bit like the first time I saw you."

"Like it?" she asked incredulously. "I love it for all those things, but mainly I love it because it symbolises my future with you." She picked up my hand and kissed my palm without losing eye contact. "It's a perfect winter's day, I have a horse, I love being in the garden and of course I love kissing you." She placed my hand over her heart and held it there with both her hands. "You have my heart, Leo. You have all of me and I want all of you—mind, body and soul."

"You have it all, Jules. You have all of me."

She gave Cardinal another pat and told him how she already loved him because the most wonderful man in the world had given him to her. He just sniffed her pockets to see if she had anything tasty to offer him. She told him she'd come back with carrots.

I held out my hand and she took it immediately,

snuggling into my side. When she shivered, I let her hand go and wrapped my arm around her shoulders, pulling her in closer. "Let's go inside, beautiful."

"I love you."

I squeezed her tighter and pulled her impossibly closer to me, wanting to give her my warmth. "I love you, too, Jules. So damn much."

When we made it back into the garden, we stopped and looked up at our home. The farmhouse I'd grown up in and Juliette had been drawn to before she knew me was unrecognisable, even though we'd used a lot of the original stones. I had done a lot of the work myself but had employed the best tradesmen in the state for everything else. Our home was a comparatively modest single-story farmhouse with a verandah that wrapped all the way around it, a slate roof and plantation shutters on every window. I loved our forever home, but it was primarily because of the woman I shared it with.

"I don't ever want to live anywhere else," she said as if reading my mind.

"Me either. This is where I belong and you belong with me."

"I do." She glanced at me, and I gazed at her reverently. "This farm led me to you. There was a reason I was drawn to it, and it wasn't the bricks and mortar. It was you. I was drawn to you in the cage, and I was drawn to this farm. Both places have the good, the bad and the ugly, but they brought us together. Neither of us can escape the ugliness in our pasts, but we faced it together and now we make our own memories." Her eyes were so full of intense love and conviction. "We overcame our pasts here, and we came out stronger. We both tried running, but the road led us back here."

I leaned down and whispered in her ear. "God, I can't wait to make you my wife."

"And just like that our crazy, mixed up boy-meets-girl love story got its happily ever after."

I kissed her head. "Just like that."

I no longer fought with rage, using it as a Band-Aid to shield my wound. I fought with something far more powerful. I fought with pride, I fought with love, but most of all, I fought for our life. Juliette's and my life. We'd both faced our own individual battles, but they ended the moment our souls recognised their mate and became the Leo and Jules way. That was a fight we'd won.

ALSO BY
KATE STERRITT

The Fight for Life Duet *(Romantic Suspense)*

Collision (Book 1)
Impact (Book 2)

Standalone Novels

The Holly Project *(Contemporary romance)*
Love My Way *(Contemporary Romance/ Women's Fiction)*
*Releasing in 2019—*In My Own Time *(Contemporary Romance/ Women's Fiction)*

FROM THE AUTHOR

Thank you so much for your support. I hope you enjoyed the story as much as I enjoyed writing it and will consider leaving a review. If you'd like to get in touch with me there are plenty of ways and I'd love to hear from you!

Facebook.com/authorkatesterritt

Twitter.com/KASterritt

Instagram.com/katesterritt

www.katesterritt.com

Email me at kate@katesterritt.com

You can also chat to me in my Facebook readers group
Kate Sterritt's Hummingbirds

If you'd like to subscribe to my email newsletter, here is the signup form www.eepurl.com/bxylHH

ACKNOWLEDGEMENTS

This book has been an epic journey and the final result exceeded my own expectations. I couldn't have done it without the love and support of an ever growing group of people.

First and foremost, I want to thank my husband. Regardless of how many hours I spent at my desk, how many times I left him with the kids to go to the library or how many cricket games I missed, he was nothing but supportive. He never questioned why I do this or if it's worth it. He is proud of me and knows I'm following my dream. I love that he will read my romance novels even though it's not something he would ever pick up otherwise. I can write about soul mates because I'm married to mine.

Eli Peters. A massive thank you for all your help. When I got lost in the fog, I found my way out because of you.

To my beta and proof readers—Eli Peters, Tesrin Afzal, Brittainy McCane, Tara Hanrahan, my sisters and dad. Thank you so much for your time, attention to detail and positive feedback, especially when it came down to crunch time. You helped me make Impact the best it could be.

Adriana, you continue to be the greatest book bestie I could ever ask for and I forge on with you.

When I wrote the acknowledgements for Collision, I listed the founding members of my newly formed readers group, Kate Sterritt's Hummingbirds. The number of members has grown so much and continues to be a source of great happiness and motivation for me.

I would like to thank every member of the group for being there and I hope I've done you proud with this book. A special shout out to Pam Lilley who set up the group, is one of the greatest promoters of my books and is a valued friend.

Kell Donaldson. I'm so glad you read and loved Collision because it brought you into my life. I believe we were meant to be friends. Thank you from the bottom of my heart for all the incredible support you give me, but more importantly, for your friendship. Kell's Bookmark Clique rocks and so do you!

Eli Carter, my northern hemisphere twin. I'm thankful every day for you. I've got your back always and I know you have mine. What a blessing!

To all the bloggers and friends who have supported me and helped promote my work, please know that it is appreciated and admired. The book world is full of loving and generous spirits and I'm grateful to be a part of it. I'd like to make a special mention to my friend, Darlene. She is truly one of the kindest, sweetest and most generous people I've ever known. As an avid reader and diehard book lover myself, her group, Darlene and Dexter's Book Nook is one of my favourite places on Facebook.

Another big thank you to Nick Lundh, founder of the Lightning Fight Centres in Victoria and former World Professional Middle Weight Kickboxing Champion, Professional Boxer and Muay Thai Fighter. He continued to help me ensure the Impact fight scenes were as authentic as possible. I admire, and am inspired by what he does.

And finally, to my sisters and best friend—Zoe, Susie and Jen. I'm so proud of you and the amazing women you are. Thank you for always supporting me and my books.